Women of Straw

Carole Llewellyn's mother-in-law hailed from Luton in Bedfordshire and worked as a milliner making the famous Luton Straw Boaters.

Women of Straw

Carole Llewellyn

ROBERT HALE

First published in 2016 by Robert Hale, an imprint of
The Crowood Press Ltd, Ramsbury, Marlborough
Wiltshire SN8 2HR

www. crowood.com

www.halebooks.com

British Library Cataloguing-in-Publication Data
A catalogue record for this book is available from the
British Library.

ISBN 978 0 7198 1922 3

*In memory of my dear mother-in-law
Kathleen Carlton Llewellyn*

Typeset by Catherine Williams, Knebworth

Printed and bound in India by Replika Press Pvt Ltd

CHAPTER ONE

LUTON, BEDFORDSHIRE, JUNE 1865

'COME ON, SIS, I'll race you to the crossroads,' Liam Devlin challenged as they left their house at 10 Plaiters Way.

'I'll only race you,' Kate said, 'if you promise not to cheat and wait until we get to old Larry there, before you start racing.' She pointed to Larry Gates, the lamplighter with his long hand-held pole, igniting the gas lamp at the end of the street.

'I promise.' Liam grinned.

But they were still a few yards from the lamplighter when he broke into a run and sped ahead.

'Liam Devlin, you are such a cheat,' Kate called out, as she hitched up her skirt and chased after him.

Minutes later and out of breath on this breezeless summer night, she arrived at the crossroads to find Liam leaning against a dry stone wall. There could be no denying they were siblings. The same shape face, brown eyes and unruly hair, except that her brother's was kept short, regularly cut by Ma. After all, Pa said, 'Long curls are for girls.'

'What kept you?' he teased.

'You promised,' she chided, as she raised her hand in the pretence of cuffing him behind the ear. His timely shift in position made her miss her target, and they both burst into laughter.

'Haven't you heard? Promises don't count if you keep your fingers crossed,' he said, waving his crossed fingers in front of her face.

'And I was daft enough to believe you. It's a good job you're due back to work at Groves' Farm or I'd be dragging you home to let Pa deal with you. And it would serve you right if he gave you a good leathering – you know how he feels about cheats and fibbers.' Kate tried to sound angry, when in truth she loved the way her brother always attempted to get one over on her.

Liam gave a heavy sigh. 'Part of me wishes Pa was well enough to leather me. Only we both know that, even if he was, he would never lift a hand to any one of us. Sis, each week when I come home he's worse.'

Kate nodded. 'It's heartbreaking. Despite all of Ma's efforts to feed him up, he's naught but skin and bone – and at night his coughing fair rattles the windows.'

'I feel so helpless,' Liam said.

'I know. Farmer's lung is such a curse. I'm afraid it'll just run its course and there's nothing any of us can do about it.' Kate hugged her brother. 'Now get yourself back to the farm and I'll see you next Sunday.'

Liam worked and lodged at the Groves' wheat farm, not far from the small picturesque village of Lilley, one of several such farms surrounding the agricultural market town of Luton. Most of the wheat harvested locally was sold for plaiting to supply the straw-hat manufacturers in the town.

As she watched her brother head off, she became aware of an approaching cabriolet gig being pulled by a chestnut mare. Her heart missed a beat.... Luke Stratton was about to ride past her. He was the eldest son of old Mr George Stratton who owned the Stratton Hat Company. A handsome man who had the pick of any girl in town, he probably wouldn't look twice at her.

But as he drove past, he slowed and courteously touched the brim of his bowler hat, giving her a lazy smile. 'Good evening, Miss Devlin.' And then, before she could respond, he was gone.

Kate watched his gig kick up dust behind its wheels and she took her time returning home. She loved this time alone with her thoughts and dreams. She forced herself to nudge the elegant Luke Stratton out of her mind and concentrate instead on her ambition to become the best hat-maker in the county. It was growing dark and as she gazed up at the clear summer night's sky, studded with the first of the glittering stars, it fair took her breath away. She wasn't sure how long the walk took her but, as she headed up Plaiters Way toward her family's end of terrace, three up, two down, rented cottage, she saw Mrs Sawyer enter the front door to number 10. Kate felt a sick feeling in the pit of her stomach and was overcome with guilt for not rushing home earlier. Mrs Sawyer was only called upon to lay out the dead.

As Luke Stratton headed for home, he felt annoyed with himself. It wasn't often he came across Kate Devlin unaccompanied. She was usually surrounded by that close-knit family of hers. He snapped the reins across his horse and wanted to kick himself for not having stopped the gig to talk to her. He had admired her striking appearance and the way she had of looking you straight in the eye as if determined to find out what was inside your head. The truth of it was, when he saw her standing there on the side of the road, it took him completely by surprise. He'd wanted to invite her to step up into his gig but knew she would reject such an offer, however innocently meant. He'd only had enough time to tip his hat and smile – a smile she didn't return.

Kate heard voices around her. The quiet murmur of friends and neighbours – all at the graveside to pay their respects to her father who lay cold and indifferent in the dark hole at Kate's feet. Their attendance greatly touched her. It went to show how well thought of her father, Michael Devlin, had been. She felt tears threaten but she refused to shed them in front of all these people. She stared across at the old oak tree towering over the entrance to the graveyard, the sunlight shimmering through its high branches; she felt the soft summer breeze touch her cheek and had the sudden urge to run ... to get away. But she stayed put. It was her duty.

For a while, her dark brown eyes stayed focused on the oak tree and on the realization that her father would never see it again. It was then that she noticed the stranger loitering behind the tree's thick trunk; a tall, middle-aged man, dressed in a long black coat and wearing a bowler hat. Kate moved closer to her mother. Since her father's death her mother seemed to have grown smaller. Never robust, Rose Devlin now looked older and frailer than her forty-two years, her grey eyes restless, and her small face pale and gaunt.

'Ma, that man standing behind the tree, do you know him?' Kate spoke quietly.

Her mother looked across the graveyard. 'Yes, child, and although I haven't seen him for a long while, I do believe it to be Joseph Devlin, your father's elder brother and your uncle.'

'Did you think to see him here today?'

Her mother shrugged her thin shoulders. 'No, in fact, he's the last person I expected to see.'

As the oldest, at seventeen, Kate knew that her father, William Devlin, was the son of Irish immigrants, and that his parents had moved to Britain to escape Ireland during the devastation of the potato famine in the early 1840s to work as labourers in the wheat fields of Luton. She was also aware of some sort of family feud – she was never given details, but had always thought it might have had something to do with the fact that her mother, a Luton girl, was neither Irish nor Catholic, which her father's family had been. Whatever the reason, it was common knowledge in the village that the brothers hadn't spoken for years.

Out of the corner of her eye, Kate saw the minister approaching the grave with a Bible in hand. It was time for the committal service. She slipped an arm around her mother, aware of her struggle to hold in her grief, while on the far side of her, Kate's sister, Annie, and brother, Liam, were standing white-faced and silent.

Kate stared down at her hands. If she stared at her hands she didn't have to look at the dark hole in front of her. Her hands were cracked and red-raw, the result of bleaching the straw. She remembered her father's nightly ritual, of tenderly rubbing them with a few drops of lavender oil to ease the soreness – she hoped these thoughts would help take her mind off the proceedings about to unfold. But it was not enough – nowhere near enough to dislodge the pain that had taken root in her chest. Kate tightened her grip on her mother's arm, and at the same time, watched her pull Annie and Liam closer to her.

After the short committal service – a service so painful to endure that Kate chose to block it from her mind – the mourners began to file past to offer their condolences. One of the first was the tall figure of Luke Stratton, his expression sombre, his dark hair ruffled by the summer breeze as he stood with his hat respectfully in his hand. In his late twenties, he was already the manager and head dealer of his family's hat-making company here in Luton, a regular customer of the straw-plait produced by the Devlins' plait school.

'Mrs Devlin, may I offer my sincere condolences to you and your family for your loss?' Luke Stratton offered. 'If there's anything I can do, then please ask.'

His words were polite but there was something stiff in the way he stood and the way he spoke. And the brief moment when his intense gaze flicked to her made Kate uneasy.

'Mr Stratton, thank you. It's so good of you to come,' her mother said quietly.

Kate found it hard to know why he, of all people, had chosen to attend the funeral. And then it came to her.

'Mr Stratton,' she spoke more abruptly than she intended, 'just in case you're wondering, we'll be back at work in the morning. The plait you ordered will be on time, I promise.' Kate felt it had to be said – clearly that's what he had come to check up on. With her father's wage gone, the straw-plaiting school had to succeed to keep bread on the table and money in the rent box at the end of each week. Now more than ever, they had to keep their main customer happy.

His dark eyes fixed on her. 'That's not why I came. Your school's record speaks for itself. You've never let us down. And I meant what I said ... if there's anything I can do, just ask.'

'Thank you, but I'm sure we'll manage,' Kate assured him.

With a reluctant nod, Luke Stratton replaced his fashionable straw hat on his head and moved away to make room for others.

For a long moment, Kate's eyes stayed firmly fixed on the back of his hat, a Luton straw boater, worn in the summer by men and women alike and a trademark of the Stratton Hat Company. Even in the midst of her grief, it pleased her to think that the straw-plait used to make the boater Luke Stratton was wearing could well have been woven by her own skilful fingers.

Next to offer his condolences was Daniel Groves. At twenty-one he was almost four years Kate's senior, a well-built young man with a mop of blond hair, sun-bleached from working in the fields of his family's farm in north Hitchin, where Kate's brother had worked for the past eighteen months.

'Mrs Devlin,' he said, nervously twisting his soft cap in his hands, 'I … and my family are so deeply sorry for your loss.'

'Thank you, Daniel. Like yourself, my William loved working the land … and now it's to be his final resting place.'

'I think it fit and proper. He was a good, hard-working man,' Daniel said before turning to Liam. 'Look, lad, I don't want to tear you away from your family. As I said earlier, it's all right with me if you want to take the rest of the day off work. But if you're planning on returning to the farm, I've left the horse and trap tied up in the lane in case you want a lift back.'

Liam Devlin had chosen to follow in his father's footsteps and work the land. He had applied to work at the Groves' farm – not all farmers contracted farmer's lung, his father had been one of the unlucky ones.

The lad looked to his mother. 'What do you think, Ma?'

'I think you should take young Daniel here up on his kind offer.'

It always warmed Kate when her mother called him 'young Daniel'. The lad was past twenty, but he understood it was meant as a term of affection.

'Anyways, it'll save you the four mile walk later,' Rose Devlin added.

'Only if you're sure you'll be all right, Ma. I really don't mind the walk back.'

'Get away with you. It's not as if I'm on my own, now is it? Why, haven't I got Kate and Annie for company?' His mother forced a smile.

'Well, if you're sure.' He reached over and brushed her cheek with a kiss. 'Now you take care, Ma. I'll see you Sunday.'

'And will we be seeing you this coming Sunday, Daniel?' Rose Devlin asked.

Daniel Groves had an open invitation to join them any time he was passing, an offer he only took up when the weather was really bad, providing Liam with a lift to and from his mother's house. He looked to Kate, knowing that *she* could read him like a book. 'I'm not sure if I can make Sunday, it'll depend on my work up at the farm. But you never know.' He turned to Liam. 'Come on, lad, we'd best be on our way,' he said, replacing his soft cap, removed as a mark of respect.

Kate had long since decided that she liked Daniel Groves. He was a thoughtful, kind and hard-working young man, who had taken her brother Liam under his wing. And for this she would be eternally grateful.

Next to pay their respects were Maude Proctor, her husband, Jake, and their four children. Dilly, the eldest, attended the Devlins' plait school – the red sores around her lips were the result of working with bleached straw. The Proctors lived next door to Kate and her family and were good neighbours, always there to lend a hand if needed.

'Rose, ducks, if there's anything me and mine can do, you only have to ask,' Maude assured her. 'Look, me and the other neighbours have put on a small spread ... nowt fancy, just a brew of tea, bread and cheese and some oatcakes. Make sure you call in on us before you go back home, eh, ducks.'

'Oh dear, *I* should have thought to put some food on for the mourners. What must they think of me? Maude, you must let me give you some money.'

'Don't be daft. I'm sure you'd do the same for us.'

Kate was overwhelmed by this generosity, and felt so lucky to be living in such a close-knit community where folk were so caring of each other. One by one the mourners filed passed, each stopping for a few kind words with her mother. Everyone except Kate's Uncle Joseph – the man in black was nowhere to be seen. Kate was sure she saw a look of relief on her mother's face. They left the graveyard and, with Annie walking on ahead, made for the Proctors' house.

*

Luke Stratton stood in his office situated high above the noisy factory floor. The room around him was cluttered with files, ledgers and various samples of plait. He stared with pride down at his workforce: twenty female hat-makers of varying age from seventeen to thirty-five, their nimble fingers flying back and forth. There was a knock on the door.

'Come in,' he called, expecting it to be his clerk with more damned paperwork for him to sign.

But it was Ruby Cooper who entered carrying a tea tray. Although only twenty-one, she was one of his most gifted workers.

''Scuse me for int'rupting, but I seen you come back from the funeral and thought you might feel in need of a cup of cha.' She smiled and pushed back her dark auburn hair.

'Thank you, Ruby, just set the tray on my desk,' he said, as he tried not to look at her. There was something about this girl that got right under his skin. While not being what most would call a beauty, she was tall and willowy and her face was covered in freckles. What had attracted him to her was the striking colour of her hair and her piercing green eyes ... they still did ... and she damn well knew it.

'Is there *anything* else I might do for you?' Ruby asked, slanting a coquettish look at him beneath her long eyelashes.

'No, thank you, Ruby. You just get back to your work.'

As the girl turned to leave, she shrugged her shoulders. 'My, how things have changed,' she murmured softly and, with a suggestive wiggle of her hips, left the room, closing the door behind her.

Not for the first time Luke regretted the dalliance he'd had with Ruby Cooper. It had been fun while it lasted, that was until his father got wind of it and laid the law down....

'If you must sow your wild oats, I'll thank you to look further afield than our employees. In my experience, it can and will ultimately lead to unrest and petty jealousy among the workforce. There will be accusations of favouritism,' his father had admonished. 'Have you no sense in that clever head of yours?'

Luke knew he spoke the truth — it was never wise to shit on your own doorstep, so he instantly finished with Ruby. To his surprise, she had accepted without a fuss but she continued to flirt openly with him at every opportunity in an attempt to weaken his resolve.

It was late evening when Kate and the family, after an emotional gathering at the Proctors, returned to their home. As they entered the yard, they were hit by the pungent smell of bleach; a mixture of charcoal, brimstone and sulphur, used to preserve straw and produce a whiter plait. The process took several hours of soaking in wash tubs and was followed by a long drying out process.

They made directly for the kitchen, the only furnished room downstairs – the parlour was used as a stock room. Kate looked around the kitchen, the long table covered in a green tablecloth, lovingly hand-stitched by her mother from a remnant bought at market. In the centre sat a heavy pewter-based oil lamp with a large mottled-glass top and around the table stood three matching chairs. The range was blackened to perfection and on the mantle-shelf stood two brass candlesticks and a few china ornaments, collected by her mother over the years. Beside the range was her father's arm-chair, complete with a bright patchwork cushion, where he always sat after supper. The sight of his empty chair brought home to her the fact that her father was gone from them forever. Her heart ached and tears welled up, but she checked herself. Her family needed her. She would hold back the tears until later ... when she was alone.

Rose, Kate and Annie, tired and drained at the end of the day, made little conversation.

'I think it would be wise if we all had an early night,' Rose instructed her daughters. 'Kate rightly promised Mr Stratton that his order would be on time, so it'll be business as usual tomorrow.' She gave a long hard sigh, as if she had the weight of the world upon her shoulders.

'Come on, Annie, up to bed,' Kate urged. 'If you like, I'll come and tuck you in. We have a hard few days of plaiting ahead of us, if we're to finish the Stratton order.'

Annie, along with eight children from the neighbourhood, aged from five to twelve years, attended Rose Devlin's plaiting school, all working for nine hours, six days a week and paid sixpence a day. Kate was head girl. As she helped Annie into bed, Kate couldn't help but notice how much her sister had changed since the start of her monthly courses ... at just twelve she was beginning to develop the shape of a young woman and with her long chestnut hair, hazel eyes and a healthy countenance, she was too pretty for her own good. She would break men's hearts one day.

'Oh, Kate, I miss Pa so much. I hate the thought of him lying in the cold earth of the graveyard.'

'I know, love. We all do. But you must think of him as being at peace at last. We need to be strong for Ma now ... do you understand?'

Annie nodded.

Kate blew her a kiss. 'Night-night, I'll not be long. I just need to make sure Ma's all right,' she said as she left their shared bedroom.

Kate entered the kitchen to find her mother, her eyes glazed over, staring at the flickering oil-lamp on the table.

'Is there anything you'd like me to do, Ma?'

'No, child, but thank you for taking care of Annie. It's been a long day ... a sad, sad day.' Rose held her head in her hands.

'We'll be all right, Ma. If you're worrying about the plait school, then don't. We've managed well enough up to now. I'll continue to help you all I can, I promise.'

Rose looked up and wiped away the tears from her eyes. 'It's not the school I worry about, but your Uncle Joseph. I wish I knew why he chose today of all days to walk back into our lives.'

'I wonder why he didn't come to talk to us. It feels strange to think that he's my uncle. Of course I've heard of him, but I also know that Pa wanted nothing to do with him. Why was that, Ma?' Kate dared to ask.

'It's a long story ... and if you don't mind, love, one I'd rather not talk about right now.'

Kate nodded. 'That's all right, Ma. I understand.' Of course she didn't, but the anxious look in her mother's eyes was enough for her to drop the subject, at least for now. And, feeling it was what her mother wanted to hear, she quickly added, 'Don't worry about

14

Uncle Joseph. He came ... and now he's gone.'

'I'd like to think so, but I've this feeling that tells me different,' Rose mumbled, almost to herself, as she leaned over to turn out the lamp. 'Come on, let's get ourselves to bed.'

CHAPTER TWO

Early next morning with sunlight spilling on to the flagstones, Kate prepared the kitchen for plait school. The Devlins' school was different to others round about, because they also made plait to order and were contracted to the Stratton Hat Company. Kate began to arrange stools around the kitchen table and at the side of each one, she placed a box to hold lengths of straw.

Even though it was late June her mother had already lit the fire; the grate with its hobs and ovens was needed to boil water and cook. She looked around the room at the nine workstations, all ready for the pupils who were due to arrive at eight o'clock – eager to be taught a trade that would be the making of them. As overseer, Kate's mother always sat in Pa's chair.

It didn't feel right, somehow, to be going about their work so soon after her father's funeral. She gave a deep sigh. With a livelihood to earn, there wasn't even time to mourn. Kate and her mother went about their early morning duties in silence, until they heard the sound of a horse and cart as it rattled over the dirt road. The loud clip-clop of a heavy horse moved ever closer, finally coming to a halt out front – shortly followed by a hard knock on the door.

'Who could that be at this time of morning? Do you think it could be your Uncle Joseph?' Rose's eyes darted toward the door.

'Why don't I go and see?' Kate offered. As she made her way down the passage, she couldn't help but wonder why the possibility of her uncle calling at the house upset her mother so. Kate decided whoever was at the door she would deal with. Taking a deep breath, she opened the door.

'And about time, too!' the man on the doorstep complained, as he secured a large grey carthorse, complete with full harness and padded collar, onto the post outside. It *was* Joseph Devlin.

Kate stood her ground and held the door only slightly ajar. She looked straight at her uncle – a plain man with lank dark hair, small beady eyes and a large misshapen nose, dressed in the same black coat as the day before. On closer inspection, Kate noticed how worn and in need of a good clean it was, although the cut of it spoke of better days. His bowler hat was practically threadbare.

'Who do you think you are staring at, girl?' his surly voice demanded.

Kate remembered the soft Irish brogue of her dear father, so unlike the gruff way her uncle spoke. 'I believe you're my Uncle Joseph,' she answered.

'That's right. And you must be the eldest of my brother's brood.' For a brief moment, his eyes looked into hers in a way that made her skin crawl. Then he seemed to check himself. 'I'm here to see your mother – my *dear* sister-in law.' He forced a smile.

'What's taking you so long, Kate? Who's at the ...' her mother's voice came from behind. The sight of Joseph Devlin rendered her speechless.

'Good morning, Rose. It's been a long time,' he said apologetically as he offered her his hand. When Rose didn't oblige, he simply shrugged his shoulders and let his arm fall to his side, his face giving no reaction to the rebuff.

'What are you doing here, Joseph? Why have you come?' Rose flashed him a look of distrust.

He lowered his head. 'Rose, I understand your reluctance to trust me. After all this time, why should you? I've come to offer my condolences. May I come in?' he asked in a voice that sounded gentle and full of compassion.

Kate couldn't believe it was the same person who had spoken to her so curtly not minutes earlier.

'You don't have to let him in, Ma,' Kate pointed out.

Rose turned to her daughter. 'Kate, what's come over you? This is your father's brother, remember your manners,' she quietly chided.

17

'Joseph, please, come in.' Rose turned and headed for the kitchen.

Joseph Devlin brushed past Kate and into the house.

Kate closed the door and quickly headed down the passage to the kitchen. She didn't want to miss what this man had to say. She entered warily to find her mother standing by the fireplace and her uncle no more than a few feet away from her. Whatever it was he wanted from them, Kate was not willing to see her mother upset by this man. His large presence looked completely out of place in the Devlins' small kitchen, overshadowing her mother's small frame. Kate watched as her uncle's grey eyes went around the room, noting the set up for plait school.

'Well now, this brings back memories. I remember coming here in the days when your parents ran the plait school.' He looked to Rose. 'You've done well for yourself, Rose. William certainly fell on his feet when he married you.'

Kate heard the note of envy in his voice and hoped her mother had, too. It was then she noticed how unsteady her mother looked, so Kate rushed over to her and, placing an arm around her, led her to her father's armchair.

'My parents were everything to each other,' Kate told him with quiet certainty.

Ignoring her, he turned to her mother. 'I'm sure you and William were blissfully happy together – it was never my intention to suggest otherwise.' His voice was soft and apologetic.

'I'm glad to hear it, Joseph. Now, what is it you want? My pupils are due shortly and—'

'I promise I'll not keep you long … may I?' He didn't wait to be answered but, reaching for a stool, dragged it across the stone floor to sit next to Rose. 'As I said earlier,' he continued, 'I've come to offer my condolences and to share in your grief … after all, William was my younger brother.'

'You could have said all this yesterday. We saw you standing behind the tree,' Kate said.

He didn't acknowledge Kate, but kept his eyes fixed on her mother. 'My dear Rose, I felt that yesterday was for you, your children, friends and neighbours. I didn't want to intrude and, truth be known, I wasn't sure if I'd be welcome.' He grimaced.

Rose nodded her head.

Kate couldn't fail to see the look that passed between them, a look that spoke of a shared understanding of something that had gone before, something she knew nothing about.

Joseph gave a heavy sigh. 'For a while now I've been plagued by the memory of what happened between us all those years ago. The guilt I feel is immense.'

'A feeling William and I both shared, and we spent many a sleepless night wishing we'd done things differently,' Rose said, her voice so quiet that Kate had to strain to hear it.

Kate didn't understand – it was as if they were talking in riddles.

'You were both blameless,' he insisted. 'What I did was unthinkable and I hope you'll believe me when I tell you that, for a long while now, I have been building up the courage to call on you, to try to make peace with you and my brother. Sadly, I left it too late. William will never know now how sorry I feel, or how much I've changed.'

An awkward silence followed, only to be broken by the sound of a light tapping on the front door.

'Ma, that'll be the girls arriving for work,' Kate urged.

'Joseph, I'm afraid I'm going to have to ask you to leave us. There's work to be done,' Rose spoke quietly but firmly.

'Yes, yes, of course, I understand, I'll leave at once. But I wonder if I might call back, perhaps at the end of day? I still have so much I want, no – I need to say to you.'

Rose looked to Kate and then to Joseph as if pondering her decision. 'All right, but not tonight. We have a big order to complete and all I'll be fit for at the end of day is my bed. If you must come back, I think it best if you wait until Saturday evening ... say ... seven o'clock?'

'Thank you. Saturday, seven o'clock it shall be,' he said, replacing his hat and coat.

'But Ma—' Kate began.

'Kate, please leave it be. Just show your uncle out and usher the children in,' her mother instructed.

19

Against her better judgement, Kate did as her mother bid. There would be time enough later to air her doubts, but now she had to get to work. As she opened the door for her uncle, he turned to face her.

'If I were you, my *dear* niece, I'd think about changing your attitude toward me. It looks as if we shall be seeing a lot more of each other.'

It was as if he was goading her, but she briskly turned away from him and began to welcome the pupils. Her silence obviously angered him, and as he left the house, he pushed past the children on the doorstep so fiercely that he almost knocked over Dilly Proctor.

'Hey, watch it,' Dilly called after him, and then looked at Kate. 'Who was that?'

'He's my Uncle Joseph, he's only visiting.' As she said the words, Kate truly hoped this to be the case.

'Well, uncle or not, the man's got no manners and a face that could curdle milk.'

'I agree. But you'd best get a move on – we've the Stratton order to finish.'

One by one the girls, dressed in their grey serge tunics, filed into the kitchen. Kate glanced over to her mother.

'Thank you, Kate. We'll talk later, I promise.' Rose forced a smile.

'All right, Ma,' Kate said.

Her mother looked drained. Kate wished she could persuade her to take the morning off, but she knew it would be out of the question. Kate vowed that one day she'd earn enough money to support her family and make life easier for her mother.

With each pupil seated at her station, a small bundle of straw placed under their left arm, ready to begin plaiting, her mother took her place, ready to oversee her pupils at work, a task made easier with only four young 'uns. The older girls in front of her were all accomplished in their work ... even the five-year-olds. Although, as could be expected, their work rate was governed by both age and experience; five-year-olds ten yards, ages six to eight fifteen yards, and over eights seventeen to twenty yards a day. The plait was sold in scores – a score being twenty yards.

Just then the door to the foot of the stairs opened and Kate's sister, Annie, burst into the room. Unlike Kate, Annie was not a natural when it came to plaiting; her job was to keep the work areas tidy and sweep the floor of straw cuttings – this was crucial to their safety because straw acted like a tinder-box to sparks from the fire.

'It's good of you to join us,' Kate quipped.

'Sorry, Ma, I overslept,' Annie said.

'Take yourself to the scullery for a glass of milk, child – yet again, you've no time for breakfast.' Rose shook her head. 'What am I to do with you?'

With the children all ready to start work, Rose welcomed them.

'Good morning, girls. I hope you're all well rested and ready for a good day's plaiting. Pick up your work. Kate, you can begin singing the first lesson of the morning. You all know the rules. Any problem, stop plaiting, raise your hand, and Kate will come to you.'

Everyone picked up five strands of straw and, to make them soft and easier to work with, ran the straw across their mouths, coating it in saliva, which often caused sore and blistered lips. A practice Kate chose to avoid. She had long ago decided that sore hands were better than sore lips. It was time to start work.

Kate began to sing, 'Under one and over two ... pull it tight and that will do.' These were the instructions to achieve a simple flat plait. Another more elaborate plait was, 'Criss-cross patch and then a twirl ... twist it back for English Pearl.' Soon all the class was singing and plaiting. Kate tried to put all thoughts of Joseph Devlin out of her mind – a mind still struggling to come to terms with the loss of her dear father. But try as she may, she couldn't shake away the feeling of foreboding.

For the rest of the morning the girls continued singing and working – it took nimble fingers to achieve sellable plait. As well as working her own plait, every hour Kate would check the yards of worked plait in each of the girl's boxes. She then had the delicate job of clipping any sharp ends sticking out of the joins from the back of the pattern.

At twelve o'clock, Rose Devlin raised her hand. 'Stop plaiting, everyone. It's time for lunch and your school lesson.'

The girls stopped plaiting and proceeded to open their packed lunch, usually just a slice of bread and dripping. Rose Devlin provided them with a drink; cold in summer, hot in winter. As Annie and the girls mischievously huddled together sharing stories, Kate took her mother to one side.

'Ma, can you spare a moment? I need a word.'

'Yes, Kate, love. Why don't we go outside where we can talk in private?' Rose suggested. Then, turning to her younger daughter, 'Annie, when the class have finished their lunch, please open the Bible and have them practice reading the twenty-third psalm, "The Lord is my Shepherd I shall not want", your dear Pa's favourite.'

'Yes, Ma, we all like that one, and today we'll recite it just for Pa,' Annie promised, her voice quivering with emotion.

Rose gently touched Annie's shoulder before following Kate outside. Kate made for the wooden bench, lovingly made by her pa and situated close to the draw-well – a deep well shared by every cottage in the hamlet, each drawing three to six buckets of water every day for their needs. Rose sat next to Kate.

For a while they sat in silence then Rose prompted, 'Well, come on, tell me what's troubling you. Your mind has not been on your work all morning.'

Kate noticed how pale her mother's skin looked with dark rings under her eyes – eyes that had lost their brightness.

'Ma, I don't want to add to your troubles but, it's Uncle Joseph … I just can't take to him.'

Her mother pondered for a while. 'Your uncle says he's changed,' she said, her voice full of uncertainty. 'I keep asking myself what your father would do if he were here.'

'Ma, I might not know what happened between Pa and Uncle Joseph – I understand it was way before I was born. But I remember when I was younger someone mentioning Joseph's name in this house … and I never saw Pa so angry.'

'Your father and Joseph were close once, until—'

'What happened between them must have been really bad.'

'Yes. Way back then, your father swore he didn't want him in this house and vowed never to speak to him again.'

'Well then, if that was Pa's wish, why go against it now?'

'Kate. Your father's passing has filled my heart with so much grief, there's no room left for any other emotion – especially hatred. What happened with Joseph was a long time ago and … it's best forgotten.'

'Perhaps, but there's just something about him....'

'I truly believe Joseph has seen the error of his ways. He was always a proud man. I know how hard it must have been for him to come here with cap in hand. He has the look of a broken man.'

Kate didn't agree. While her mother might have been taken in by his words of compassion, Kate certainly hadn't. She had seen another side to him.

'Have you thought it might be an act?'

'No, and you might be right. But I'm sure your father would want me to make my peace with him.'

Kate could hold back no longer. 'Ma, you didn't hear the way Uncle Joseph spoke to me, or see the way he almost knocked poor Dilly to the floor as he was leaving, he's a—'

'Kate, love, please, I've made my decision. When Joseph calls back on Saturday evening, I *shall* hear him out – and that's the end of it. Now, go make sure the children have read their lesson. It's time we got back to work.'

It was almost four o'clock, half an hour before the official end of the day, and they had fully completed the Stratton weekly order of fifty score.

Rose stood up from her chair. 'Girls, I'd like to thank you all for your hard work and to tell you there'll be an extra thrupence in your wage packets this week.'

The girls all let out a squeal of delight.

Kate proceeded to collect the plait from each of their boxes. She then had to press each length through a wooden plait mill, with rollers to ensure the finished pattern was not flattened, and check each one to make certain it was up to the right standard and length for a sellable product.

'I know it's early, but why don't you all head for home? Annie and I can box up the Stratton order,' Kate offered.

'Ta, Kate. That'll mean we can take a breather before us older ones have to head off to Mrs Tucker's workshop – no rest for the wicked, eh?' Dilly scoffed, as she led the girls out the door. 'Kate, we're all going to miss your pa. He was always so good to us.'

'That's kind of you, and I shall let Ma know what you said,' Kate said.

'So-long, Mrs Devlin, see you in the morning,' the girls all called out as they left the house.

Kate breathed a heavy sigh. They were all such good, hard-working girls. It didn't seem right that this was not the end of their working day. And it wasn't just the older girls who had to work another shift. Even the younger ones were expected, along with other members of their family, to carry on plaiting in their own homes well into the night – making plait to sell at George Street plait market in the centre of town. It was no secret that the wife and children could earn more than their menfolk could, working the land. To enable her pupils to attend the market, there was no plait school on Monday morning, opening at 12.30 instead, on the understanding that they made up the four hours over the rest of the week. This they did willingly.

Kate thanked her lucky stars that she didn't have to go out to work in the evening. After helping her mother make the supper, she could spend her evenings doing what she loved best … making ladies' straw hats – made to her own design. In six weeks she could make six hats, which she would then endeavour to sell for the princely sum of one shilling each on Dilly's mother's market stall; she paid Maude Proctor a small commission on every sale.

Daniel Groves awoke long before dawn. With time to spare before he picked up young Liam Devlin for their weekly trip to the thatcher in Dunstable, he lay in his bed reflecting on the conversation he'd had with the boy as he, along with the rest of the workers, returned from the fields at the end of the previous day. Everyone had been in good spirits ... everyone except Liam.

'Liam, I just want to say how pleased I've been with your work this week. It can't have been easy for you,' Daniel had said to his young employee.

'Working in the field has helped keep me going and stopped me dwelling on what's happened. If I'm to be honest, watching my pa go from a strong, healthy man to a weak invalid saddened me more than his actual death.'

'Your father will be sorely missed. He was a good man.'

'Yes. I know. But the truth is, the man I remember as my father was lost to me months ago. I only wish I was older and able to look after my ma and the girls more.'

'You see them every Sunday. I'm sure they understand.'

'They might. But what good am I to them, when I only get to see them a few hours a week? It shouldn't all fall on Kate.'

'And it doesn't. I know for a fact that you give most – if not all of your wages to your ma, so you do more than your bit to help. Take heart, your Kate's a strong young woman and she'll always do right by the family.'

'You like my sister a lot, don't you?' For the first time since the funeral, Liam flashed his boss one of his wicked grins.

'I admire her hard work and loyalty to her family, if that's what you mean.'

'And, I suppose, the fact that she's a real bobby-dazzler has nothing to do with it?'

Daniel reached over and ruffled Liam's mop of dark hair. 'You cheeky young devil. I'll not answer that. That's for me to know and for you to wonder about.'

Now, as Daniel lay in his bed, he pictured Kate standing proud on the day of her father's funeral. Her long hair, the colour of roast chestnuts, tied back under her straw bonnet, her brown eyes full of sadness, her face showing the care she felt for her family at such a sad time. How he longed to see again her smile ... a smile that warmed his very being. Oh yes, Kate Devlin was a real beauty and the type of girl any man could love.

*

It was Saturday morning and, with the Stratton order duly boxed and ready for collection, the plait school had a 'stock' day – any plait made today would be held for future orders or sold at the market. Kate suggested that today the older girls should work the more elaborate and more expensive plait, and she proceeded to lead the singing. 'Criss-cross patch and then a twirl ... twist it back for English Pearl.'

It was midday and everyone had stopped for lunch when the sound of the Strattons' heavy cart arrived to collect the order. Jonas Miller, the regular driver and storeman, after checking the contents of each box, handed Rose Devlin the agreed payment and confirmation of the same required length of plait for the following week.

By the end of day, the pupils had between them completed three score of sellable plait to be placed in the stockroom. The pupils headed for home.

It was coming up to 7.30 and Rose, Kate and Annie had just sat down for supper, when they heard the arrival of Joseph's horse and cart.

'Go let your uncle in, and Kate, do try to at least be polite to him,' her mother urged.

Reluctantly, Kate went to the door and opened it. A cool wind swirled in from the street where her uncle stood with his back to her, unaware of her presence as he tended his horse. It was growing dark outside and, as she watched him fumble to tie his horse to the post, she wondered how the poor animal would manage to find its way back later to wherever they lived.

'There we are, old boy,' Joseph murmured to his horse as he gently patted the horse's flank. 'You did well getting me here – but then you always do. If you hang on for a while, I'll see if I can find you a tit-bit ... perhaps a nice juicy carrot, eh?'

The way her uncle spoke to his horse surprised Kate – as if man and horse had a special bond. She checked herself, refusing to let her opinion of her uncle be influenced by a conversation with a horse.

Joseph turned and caught sight of her in the doorway. 'Good evening, Kate. I believe that's your name.' His voice was gentle and respectful.

'Yes, that's right,' she answered, as politely as her suspicious mind would allow.

'Well, Kate, I do believe that you and I may have got off on the wrong foot. What say we give ourselves a chance to get to know one another before making any hasty judgements, eh?'

Caught by surprise, Kate didn't answer. She just stood aside to let him enter. 'You'd best come in.'

He flashed a wry smile before entering the passage that led to the kitchen.

'Good evening, Rose,' he said, removing his bowler hat. 'Here, I've brought you a quarter-pound of tea leaves, a little thank you for letting me call this evening.' He handed her a small brown paper bag.

'That's very generous of you and much appreciated.' Rose took hold of the brown earthenware tea pot. 'The leaves in this pot have been used so many times they've lost their taste. I shall enjoy a fresh brew,' she said warmly, then, turning to her daughter, she added, 'Kate, love, take your uncle's coat, while I set an extra plate at the table for supper. I'm guessing you haven't eaten yet, Joseph?'

'N-no and, thank you.'

As Kate took his smelly old coat, she felt powerless to stop what was happening in front of her. Her uncle – the man her father had never wanted in his home – was now sitting between her mother and Annie at the family table.

'Kate, love, do come and sit down,' her mother prompted.

Kate took her position at the table. Unfortunately, her chair was positioned directly opposite her uncle. To avoid looking into his bulbous eyes, she fixed hers down on her supper plate. Rose began to serve their meal, a hearty stew of boiled beef and carrots which they ate in awkward silence.

Kate struggled to finish hers – she'd suddenly lost her appetite.

'Thank you, Rose. That was a lovely supper. It's been a long time since I've sat at a family table.' Joseph's voice began to break up. He put his hand to his mouth and coughed in an effort to hide any show of emotion.

'Joseph, is something wrong?' Rose asked.

'No – I mean, yes.' He quickly composed himself. 'The thing is, earlier, I promised old Samson that I'd try to rustle him up a carrot.'

'Old Samson – you mean to say you still have the same horse you had when—'

'Yes, we've been together for so long now he's like a second skin.'

'Oh, Ma, can I take the horse a carrot from the vegetable box?' Annie pleaded. She looked directly at her uncle. 'If I take your Samson a carrot, do you think he'd let me feed it to him?'

'Oh yes, I'm sure he would, child. That's if your mother will allow it ... and who might you be?' he asked.

'My name's Annie. I'm the youngest. First there's Kate, then my brother Liam and then me,' Annie chatted easily.

Kate couldn't believe how comfortable Annie seemed in his company and began to wonder if it was only *she* who saw him as someone hell-bent on taking advantage of a family in grief.

'I'm very pleased to meet you, Annie. I'm your Uncle Joe, your father's older brother.' His eyes lingered just a little too long on her pretty face.

Kate fidgeted in her chair, there was something about the way he was looking at her younger sister that made her feel uncomfortable and she looked to her mother, wondering if she'd seen it, too. She saw no response.

Annie screwed up her face. 'If you're my uncle, then how come I've never seen you before?' she asked in all innocence.

'Well ...' he began.

'Well, it's a long story and one we'll not go into at this late hour,' Rose insisted. 'Annie, if you like, you can take a carrot to old Samson, but only after you've done your chores. Kate, there's hot water in the kettle, so if you girls can see to the dishes, then Joseph and I can have our chat.'

Kate walked over to the fireplace and lifted the heavy, cast-iron kettle from the hook that hung above the open fire. 'Annie, you collect the dishes and follow me,' she said as she headed for the scullery, a tin-roofed extension off the kitchen.

As Kate emptied the contents of the kettle into the large earthenware sink, she felt agitated. The last thing she wanted was to leave her mother alone with Joseph Devlin. She knew that, having lost not only the man she loved but her best friend, she wasn't thinking straight. It was up to Kate to prevent her from making any hasty decisions, at least where her uncle was concerned.

Minutes later, Annie entered the scullery carrying a tray stacked with dishes.

'Kate, here's the dishes. Now please can I go feed Samson?'

'All right, take the bucket and fill it at the pump at the same time. But be quick, there's something I need to do.'

'I won't be long, I promise,' Annie said and, with bucket in hand, bent down to pick up not one, but two carrots from the vegetable box in the larder. 'I'll go out the back way and nip around the side.'

Kate's thoughts went to her mother and wondered what yarn her uncle was spinning. She didn't trust him and wished with all her heart that Pa was here to talk to.

By the time Annie returned, Kate had almost finished washing the dishes.

As she rushed through the back door carrying the bucket, water slopped over the side. 'Oh, Kate, you should have seen the way old Samson ate the carrots from the palm of my hand. He was that gentle. He even let me stroke his neck and mane,' she said as water from the bucket spilled over the flagstone floor, made smooth by generations of feet.

'For goodness' sake, set that bucket down, Annie, before you empty the contents over the floor. And, as pleased as I am to hear about Samson, I've more pressing things to attend to.'

'Like what?'

'Like … never you mind. Annie, love, if you clear away the dishes, I promise to read you a story later.'

Kate knew how much Annie enjoyed her reading by candlelight late into the night. Annie might be twelve and looked so grown up but in many ways she was still a child.

'You promise? And you won't say you're too tired or that your eyes hurt?'

'I promise,' Kate said, moving aside to make way for her sister at the sink. She tiptoed across the stone floor and positioned herself with her ear pressed against the kitchen door, eager to find out what her uncle had to say for himself.

'What are you doing?' her sister asked, wide-eyed.

'Shush! I'm trying to listen,' Kate whispered.

'Pa always said it was wrong to eavesdrop,' Annie said in a quiet voice.

Kate shook her head. How could she begin to explain to her sister that this was different? This was looking out for Ma.

'Rose, I expect you're wondering why I asked to come back this evening.' Joseph's voice sounded gentle and caring.

'I am. What have you been doing with yourself all these years? The last we heard, you were living and working in Clophill.'

'Yes. That's right. I'm a carter – carrying small goods for the people of Clophill. Over the years I've shifted furniture, apples and shop-goods of all kinds, from one place to another with my horse and cart. In Clophill I'm known as Carter Joe. It's true to say that, over the years, Samson and I have done well ... until now, that is. Of late, business has been slow; people just haven't got the money it costs to hire me ... which is why I thought I might offer my services to you.'

Kate held her breath, willing her mother to say no.

'I don't understand, Joseph.' Her mother's voice sounded puzzled.

'If I'm not mistaken, as it stands, you have to pay your supplier to deliver the cut straw used for plaiting.'

'Yes. I have a load of ready cut straw delivered every Tuesday and Thursday from the thatcher in Dunstable.'

'Well then, if Samson and I were to collect it, it would save you the cost.'

'But then you'd need paying, so I'd be no better off.'

'Now Rose, what if I was to say that the only payment I'd want is a meal for me and Samson on the day of the delivery?'

Kate's mother stayed silent, obviously pondering his offer.

'Surely there's no harm in giving it a try,' Joseph pressed. 'When's your next delivery due?'

'Tuesday morning, but—' Rose's voice sounded unsure.

'I can be at the thatcher's first thing and have your straw delivered to you by say ... seven thirty in the morning. How does that sound?'

'Joseph, there's something I have to ask you.'

'Ask away.'

'What about your taste for the drink?'

'Rose, dear, I promise you, I haven't touched a drop in years. I now lead a life of temperance. So you have no worries on that score.'

'I'm glad to hear it. And I know how pleased William would have been, too.'

'So does that mean you'll take me up on my offer?'

Rose nodded. 'I suppose it's worth a try.'

'Good. Then I'll say goodnight. And Rose, thank you for giving me a chance to make amends. You'll not regret it.'

Kate waited until he'd gone before entering the kitchen.

'Ma, what have you done?'

'I gather you've been listening at the door.'

'Yes,' Kate openly admitted.

'So you'll have heard Joseph's offer.'

Kate nodded. 'Ma, I beg you to think again. You've just lost Pa ... and we all understand you're not thinking straight. We've managed well enough till now. We don't need Joseph ... or his horse and cart!'

Rose Devlin shook her head. 'Kate, what's got into you? Why are you so against your uncle?'

'Ma, I just ...' Kate didn't know what to say. There was nothing specific, she just had this overwhelming feeling that he was up to something but she didn't know what.

'I know. None of us like change. But we have to look to the future now. It's what your father would have wanted.'

Kate knew she'd lost. Her uncle's words had been proven right: 'from now on we'll be seeing a lot more of each other'. It was obvious to Kate that he had planned this from the start and she could imagine how smug he must be feeling. Resigned to the inevitable she put her arm around her mother.

'At least we have tomorrow and Monday free of his presence. I just hope the wheels drop off his cart and then that would be the end of it.'

Her mother simply shook her head and sighed.

The next morning Kate and the family awoke to a fine day, although the dark clouds in the distance or as her dear pa used to say, 'dark clouds over Aunt Fanny's grave', – promised rain later in the day. It was the first day of July and with June being the driest for many a year, the farmland was desperate for rain.

Kate, along with her mother and Annie, having already held a pre-plait school class for the under fives, had changed into their Sunday best outfits and attended morning service at the local church. Kate's father had been brought up in the Catholic faith but over the years, had relaxed his beliefs and impressed on those close to him to accept – as their God-given right – the choice of worship of their friends and neighbours. Back in Ireland, his fore-bears had witnessed first-hand the 'conflict' caused in the name of religion. For William and Rose, attending church, be it Catholic or Protestant, was simply a way of giving thanks to God for their con-tinued good fortune – three healthy children, food on the table and a roof over their heads.

Kate, Rose and Annie waited at the crossroads, each hoping to catch the first glimpse of Liam as he came into view, whether he was perched atop Daniel's horse and trap or – as was mostly the case, on foot. His visit was the highlight of the week.

'There he is,' Annie squealed with delight, as she spotted him walking toward the crossroads. 'Liam!' she called, as she ran to meet him, launching her body into his arms.

Liam hugged her, lifting her into the air before setting her down beside Kate and his mother.

'Hello, Ma, Kate. It's so good to see you. This week has just dragged by. I hated leaving you at Pa's graveside.'

'I know, son. But your job must come first. Daniel and his family have been good to you. It wouldn't do to let them down.'

'I suppose not.'

'Anyway, you're here now, that's the main thing,' Kate enthused. Looking up at the dark clouds above their heads, she added, 'It looks as if we're in for a downpour, I think we should head for home.'

They arrived at the house minutes before the heavens opened, and sat down for a hearty meal. Rose Devlin was always up at the crack of dawn on Sunday, baking bread and oatcakes, and pot-roasting pigs' trotters – a special meal for the son she saw so little of.

'I hope this weather isn't set in for the day. I'll get drenched going back to the farm later.'

'It's a pity Uncle Joe and Samson aren't here. I'm sure they would have given you a lift back,' Annie said.

'Uncle Joe? Samson? And who might they be?' Liam looked first to his mother and then to Kate for an answer.

'He—' Kate started to explain.

'Uncle Joe – Joseph Devlin is your father's brother,' Rose interrupted. 'He paid us a visit the day after the funeral. He was there on the day but didn't want to intrude on our grief.'

'How come he's never been to see us before?'

'He and Pa fell out years ago. Pa wanted nothing to do with him and—'

'That's enough, Kate. As far as I'm concerned, your Uncle Joe has made his peace. I'll not have you opening old wounds, do you hear?'

'Yes, Ma,' Kate answered reluctantly, before adding, 'Uncle Joe's going to be in our employ.'

'Is that so, Ma?' Liam asked.

'Well, yes ... and no. Your uncle is a carter, and he's offered to collect the cut straw from the thatcher in Dunstable for us, in exchange for a meal for him and his horse.'

'It was only yesterday that me and Daniel dropped off a load of freshly hewn straw to the very same thatcher. He's a good customer of ours,' the lad boasted. 'This arrangement with Uncle Joe sounds a good offer.'

'Perhaps *too good*,' Kate quipped.

'Not if he's family, it's what families do for one another, isn't it, Ma?'

'Yes, Liam. You're right, it is,' Rose agreed, flashing Kate a stern look.

'I fed old Samson a carrot. He was so gentle,' Annie enthused.

'I'd like to meet my Uncle Joe ... and Samson. Do you think you could arrange it, Ma?'

'I'll see what I can do, son,' Rose said.

Liam smiled. 'You won't believe how much happier I feel, knowing that Pa's long lost brother is here to look out for you all. I've been that worried.'

'You needn't worry your head about us, lad. We're fine, aren't we, Kate?' Her mother's eyes willed her to agree.

Kate smiled and nodded. What was the point of speaking out when the whole family seemed keen on welcoming her uncle into the fold?

After lunch, while Kate, Annie and her mother washed the dishes, Liam swept and cleaned the backyard and drew six buckets of water from the draw-well, before chopping a pile of wood for the fire. These chores he insisted on doing every week. It was his way of helping his mother and sisters; he only wished he could do more.

With the chores done, they returned to the kitchen.

There was a knock on the door. 'I'll get it, Ma,' Kate said, already heading down the hallway.

She opened the door to find Daniel Groves standing on the doorstep, his horse and trap tied up to the post. Thankfully, the heavy rain had now passed, replaced by a fine warm drizzle – the afternoon sun trying its hardest to break through.

'Daniel, what a nice surprise.' She moved aside. 'Come on in. Give me your coat. You look wet through.'

'Yes, I got caught in that heavy shower. I don't mind, though, a drop of rain never hurt anyone and it's good for the land,' he said, removing his rain-sodden cap and tweed jacket.

She stared at him; with the rain glistening on his blond hair, and his tanned, weather-beaten complexion, he looked a picture of health. Daniel was not a tall man, but he was broad-shouldered and strong.

Aware that she was staring at him, he beamed a smile. She felt

34

her colour rise.

'Kate, I was wondering if I might pick you up one evening after plait school and take you for a drive to the lavender fields. It's in full bloom and looks grand at this time of year. Then I thought maybe we could call at our farm for tea and meet up with Liam,' he spoke quickly, hardly taking a breath.

She was touched. And a trip to the lavender fields did sound fun ... now there's a word she seldom used.

'Daniel, I'd like that very much. Although, most evenings, I usually stitch bonnets, but I dare say one evening out won't hurt.'

'That's grand. What day is best for you?'

'We end our week at plait school four thirty on Saturday, so if—'

'Half past four on Saturday is fine with me,' he quickly interrupted, his boyish good looks beaming with anticipation.

'Good. I shall look forward to it.'

A few seconds of silence followed. 'Liam's in the kitchen with Ma and Annie,' she eventually said. 'Come on through. I know they'll be pleased to see you.'

'Daniel, how lovely to see you, what brings you to town? Have you eaten?' her mother asked all in the same breath.

Daniel smiled. 'Yes, thank you, Mrs Devlin. I had a bit of business over at the Red Lion, and I managed to grab a sandwich and a porter of ale there. When my business finished early, I thought I'd call and give Liam a lift back.'

'That's very thoughtful of you. I know he wasn't looking forward to getting caught in the rain.'

'That's what I thought. While the trap offers little protection from the weather, it's a lot quicker than walking.'

'You're not just a good boss, you're also a good mate,' Liam said, and meant it.

Kate smiled. While in no doubt of Daniel's good intentions, on this occasion, she did wonder if his calling might have been more to do with his invitation to take her for a drive.

'I've just been hearing about my Uncle Joseph – Joseph Devlin, my pa's brother,' Liam enthused. 'He's a carter in Clophill and he's going to be helping Ma and the girls. I'm that pleased they'll have a man around.'

Kate couldn't help but notice the sudden frown that appeared on Daniel's forehead. 'Would that be Carter Joe?' he asked.

'Yes, the very same,' Liam said. 'Do you know him?'

'No, but I know *of* him. Your uncle, you say?' He looked directly at Liam. 'I can't believe I never made the connection. I—' He hesitated as if trying to find the right words. 'I'm pleased for you,' he finally said. 'Now, Liam me lad, it's time we were heading back.'

Kate sensed his discomfort and suspected it might have something to do with Joe Devlin. She made a mental note to broach the subject during their drive out on Saturday.

It was just coming up to four o'clock when Daniel and Liam set off for the Groves' farm. Thankfully the rain clouds had moved on and the air was warm and still, giving promise of a balmy summer evening.

'I can't believe that I've had an uncle living in Clophill all these years. Don't you think it strange that my parents never mentioned it?' Liam didn't wait for an answer. 'I do. Kate seemed to think there was a family feud. I think she's been listening to too much local gossip. You know what folk are like. Well, whatever the reason might be for the distance between my uncle and our family, I'm just pleased he's seen fit to make himself known to us and offer his help to my mother and the girls. After all, he *is* a carter and who better to take delivery of our straw from the thatcher. Don't you agree, Daniel? Daniel, have you heard a word I've said?'

Daniel gave a heavy sigh. They were almost at their destination and throughout the journey, young Liam had been droning on about his new-found relative. After the first few minutes Daniel had switched off, lost in his own mixed thoughts. For a while, obviously excited at the prospect of taking Kate out for a drive, the gloss had been somewhat tarnished by his suspicions concerning Joseph Devlin. If the stories Daniel had heard were true, then his concern for Kate and her family would be justified. This man did not have a good reputation. He was known throughout the area as a drunkard, a gambler and a womanizer. There were even rumours that he had taken his hand to the few women who dared cross him. Daniel vowed to make enquiries the next time he visited Clophill.

'Yes, lad, of course I've been listening,' Daniel lied.

CHAPTER THREE

It was just after 7.30 on Monday morning and a golden sun glowed above the horizon, promising a fine summer's day. Kate, dressed in a clean shift dress, well-worn, lace-up brown leather boots and wearing one of her handmade straw bonnets, carefully packed four such bonnets into her basket and with several score of the ever popular lengths of English Pearl hooped over her arm, she crossed the kitchen. Today was plait market day and Maude Proctor would be leaving her house soon. She always had her stall set up with an array of plait before eight o'clock.

'It's an early bird,' Mrs Proctor always said.

Before leaving to call for Mrs Proctor and Dilly, Kate went to see her mother in the scullery, where she found her busily washing bed-linen in the large tin wash-tub.

'I'll be off now, Ma. What time can I expect to see you and Annie?'

'I'm not sure, love. It all depends how long the household chores take us.'

Kate stared at her mother's thin frame bending over the wash-tub. 'Ma, just leave the washing. I'll do it this evening. Come down to the market, a bit of fresh air might help put some colour in those cheeks of yours.'

'Don't be daft, this is the only free morning I get, and anyways, you already do enough.' She stopped and stared into her daughter's eyes. 'Look, love, I know you mean well, so I tell you what … I'll give our Annie a call shortly and as soon as she's up and breakfasted, I'll have her peg this washing on the line – it would be a shame to miss what looks to be a good drying day, and then I promise we'll head down the market to see you.'

'Good,' Kate said. 'You might want to bring along a few more score of English Pearl for me to sell. With a bit of luck, by the time you get there, I'll have sold out of everything in my basket.'

Her mother managed a smile. 'I like your confidence. And yes, Annie and I will bring what we can. Now be off with you. You know you'll get the wrath of Maude's tongue if you're late.'

Kate headed next door to the Proctors' house, only to find Mrs Proctor, a woman in her mid-forties, standing on the doorstep waiting for her. She was dressed in her usual dark green, paisley wrap-around pinafore, her brown hair streaked with grey, strained back in a bun at the nape of her neck. Maude Proctor was a tall, large-framed, attractive woman with a kind and friendly disposition until you crossed her.

'Good morning, Mrs Proctor,' Kate said.

'I'm glad you're here, ducks. It's time we were on our way.'

Mrs Proctor strode off towards Bridge Street. They crossed the ford over the River Lea which ran through the centre of town, leading to the top end of George Street where the market was always held. With seemingly little effort, Maude Proctor pushed her heavy barrow containing a trestle-table, numerous score of plait and some home-cooked oatcakes, all to be sold at the market.

'Where's Dilly? Isn't she coming today?' Kate asked. She missed the cheeky young girl.

'I've left her in bed. The poor lamb is fair done in. It was near midnight when she came home from work last night. That old witch, Ada Tucker, certainly gets her pound of flesh from her workers.'

'That woman should be reported. Her place gives plaiting a bad name.' Kate's voice relayed the frustration she felt.

'I do agree with you, ducks. I admit that, on more than one occasion I've been tempted to report her to the Board. But then, if they were to close her down, Dilly and the girls might find it hard to get another place.'

'Mrs Proctor, it's so wrong,' Kate protested.

'I know. Anyways, I told Dilly to have a lie in and come down with her dad and the young 'uns in an hour or two. No doubt Mr Proctor will want to join his fellow farmhands in the Red Lion for a porter or two of ale.'

'Yes, my dad always enjoyed meeting up with them all on market day.' Kate fondly remembered how he used to tease her mother, saying he might stay out all night ... of course, he never did.

'I'll challenge anyone who'd begrudge our men a drop of ale. They give their blood, sweat and tears to work the land and some, like your dear father, even give their life.'

Kate nodded her agreement and choked back the tears that threatened.

It was just approaching 10.30 when Dilly and her family arrived. Kate noticed how pale and tired she looked, and once again counted her blessings that she didn't have to attend Ada Tucker's evening plait school.

'Looks like you've had a good morning,' Jake Proctor said.

Maude looked pleased with herself. 'Yes, trade has been good. As you can see, I've already sold half of my plait and almost all of my oatcakes.'

'What about you, Kate?' Dilly asked.

'Like your ma said, it's been better than I could have hoped. I've already sold out of English Pearl and even sold one of my straw bonnets – to a well-to-do looking lady, who didn't even haggle the price.'

'That's wonderful. Sorry I wasn't here to help,' Dilly said.

'That's all right. Me and your ma managed fine.'

'Kate, I'll take my break now to share a picnic and a jug of ale with my brood. I shall keep you a slice of bread and dripping ... and a pipe of my tobacco if you want.' Maude gave a loud belly laugh.

Kate shook her head. 'I'll settle for just the bread and dripping, please. I'd probably cough my lungs up if I smoked one of your pipes.'

'You don't know what you're missing, girl,' Maude teased, as she led her family toward the large wooden settle outside the Red Lion, an old hostelry situated on the corner of George and Castle Street. It was a popular inn, frequented by travellers and locals alike, especially on market day.

They had been gone only a few minutes when a female voice asked, 'Hello. How much are these bonnets, miss?'

Kate looked up to see an auburn-haired young woman dressed in a blue serge dress with an extremely low neckline, and on her head an eye-catching straw bonnet adorned with dried flowers and feathers. She looked to be in her early twenties and she was holding up one of Kate's bonnets.

'Well?' the young woman prompted.

'The bonnets are all priced at one shilling each,' Kate informed her.

'S'pose that's a fair price,' the young woman said, as she closely examined Kate's work. 'Haven't I seen you on this stall afore?'

'It's possible, although I'm not here every week.'

'And is this your stall?'

'No, it belongs to my neighbour, Mrs Proctor.'

'And are these hats hers as well?'

'No, they're mine – they're all my own work,' Kate assured her, becoming slightly irritated by all the questions.

For what seemed like an age, the young woman studied Kate's handiwork, before setting the bonnet back down on the stall. Then she smiled and asked, 'What's your name?'

'Kate – Kate Devlin.'

'Do you work, Kate?'

'Yes, I help my mother run our plait school. We supply the Stratton Hat Company,' Kate proudly told her.

'Well, I'll be damned! That's where I work. My name's Ruby Cooper and I'm one of Stratton's best hat-makers,' she boasted, 'and I can spot another expert hat-maker when I sees one.'

Kate felt her colour rise at such praise. 'Thank you, that's very kind.'

'Kindness has nothing to do with it. It's the truth.'

Just then a few potential customers began to surround the stall.

'Look, I'd best leave you be, but if you ever think of looking for a job at Stratton's, then I'll be only too glad to put a word in for you.' And with that she turned and left, leaving Kate feeling as if she was floating on air.

'I'll take a few lengths of this plait,' an elderly lady said, as she fingered Maude's plait, 'and make sure there's no loose joins, do you hear?'

Her voice instantly brought Kate back down to earth.

'It's all right, ducks, I'll deal with this,' Maude said, taking her place behind the stall. 'I've asked our Dilly to take charge of the young 'uns so that their pa can take himself off to the inn. She's taken them for a stroll around the market. She looks much better for her lie in. I so wish she didn't have to do two shifts.' Maude's eyes looked sad.

'Mrs Proctor, look,' Kate pointed, hoping to change Maude's mood, 'there's my mother and Annie.'

'I'm right pleased for you, child. Now, why don't you take a few minutes off and treat them to a cup of cha?'

'Thanks, Mrs Proctor. Once I offload the plait they're carrying, I'll do just that.'

'Hello, you two,' Kate greeted her mother and younger sister. 'I'm so glad you made it to the market. It's such a lovely sunny day – too nice a morning to be cooped up indoors.'

'I couldn't agree more,' a friendly male voice said.

Much to her surprise, Kate saw Luke Stratton standing at her stall. He was dressed in a striped jacket, light grey trousers and waistcoat with a pale grey stock knotted beneath a white, wing collar. On his head a Luton straw boater at a jaunty angle. She had never seen anyone dressed as stylishly – he certainly stood out from the crowd.

'Why, Mr Stratton, how nice to see you,' Rose Devlin said.

'And you, Mrs Devlin. I'm so pleased to see you here today. I've been meaning to call on you to praise you for the prompt delivery of last week's order. Under the circumstances … with your family still mourning the sad loss of your husband, I didn't expect—'

'I told you on the day of my pa's funeral that your order would be on time,' Kate interrupted.

'Yes, Miss Devlin, so you did.' He looked mildly put out by the reminder, and for a moment there was an awkward silence between them.

'I do admit to being somewhat surprised to see you here, Mr Stratton,' Rose Devlin said to break the silence.

'What, at the market, you mean? As a matter of fact, I come here quite often. I'm always on the lookout for potential suppliers – and I must say, the quality of plait on sale here often surprises me.'

'You'll not find better quality than we produce at 10 Plaiters Way,' Kate was quick to point out.

'I'm sure you're right, but as I use several different suppliers, it pays to know where the best product lies.' He flashed a warm smile, as if to reassure her. Then his eyes went to her bonnets, and, leaning over, he picked one up off the stall. 'Did you make this?' he asked, as he inspected her stitch-work.

'Yes, I make them to my own design,' she said proudly.

'Mmm, is that so? I see,' he murmured before turning to her mother. 'Mrs Devlin, I've a feeling your daughter's talents might be wasted on straw-plaiting. She appears to be a born hat-maker ... she might want to think of applying to work at my factory.'

Kate, although flattered by the compliment, couldn't help but feel annoyed by the way he chose to address her mother and not her.

'That's praise indeed, Mr Stratton, I'm sure it's something Kate and I will discuss at some time.'

'Good. Then I shall bid you good day.' And with a quick doff of his straw boater, he turned and walked away.

As Luke Stratton walked away from the stall he couldn't help but smile to himself, he was in no doubt that Kate Devlin was a strong-willed young woman ... and a good-looking one with an obvious talent for hat-making, but one he instinctively knew he should give a wide berth. But there could be no denying that he *was* attracted to her: the way her soft curls escaped from under her straw bonnet encircling her pretty face, her dark brown eyes so full of life, her fulsome yet petite figure, a shape that could make even the simplest garment look tailor-made. Just the thought of what might be hidden beneath aroused him more than he knew it ought. With this thought in mind he strode quickly away in an effort to put distance between him and his weaknesses.

As he did so he almost bowled over the young woman walking ahead of him.

'Hey, watch where you're going, where's the fire?' the young woman called after him.

Again he smiled, this time with relief. It was Ruby Cooper, such a welcome distraction from his dangerous thoughts about Miss Devlin. With Ruby he could feel safe. She understood a man's needs and she asked for no more than to be treated fairly; to have his company occasionally, to visit the same ale houses as her so called 'friends' and to be thought of as 'his girl'. They both knew this could never be the case – but where was the harm in pretending? No ties, no promises, no commitments, just two people enjoying the pleasures of the flesh. But shouldn't she be at the factory?

'Ruby, as pleased as I am to see you, I do hope you have a good excuse for not being at work,' Luke said sternly.

'Lu – Mr Stratton, I can explain. I-I—'

'Let me guess. I'll wager the draw of a morning at the market proved too much of a temptation.'

'You always could see right through *your* Ruby. But I will be heading back to the factory soon, I promise. I was just going to the Lion for a porter of ale … a bit of Dutch courage before having to face Mrs Hobson. Your forewoman can be a right tartar when she wants to be, I can tell you.'

'I'm glad to hear it,' he said seriously. Then, rubbing his chin, he flashed a smile. 'I've had a very tempting thought. We both know that it's well within my power to make things right with Mrs Hobson. I could quite easily say that you had my permission to take the day off.'

'I know you could … but will you?'

'That depends. What do you say to my joining you at the Lion, and then this evening we could perhaps visit the Gaiety Theatre and make a night of it?'

She gave a wicked chuckle. 'I knew you couldn't stay away from your Ruby for long,' she said, taking his arm. 'Come on, let's head for the tavern. I'm so in need of a porter of ale, my throat is as dry as a bone.'

On Maude Proctor's insistence, Kate took her mother and Annie to sit on the bench at the end of George Street and, while her mother opened the parcel of bread and dripping, Kate went to find the stall selling home-made lemonade. She thought her mother might enjoy a glass of stout, but knew it would be frowned upon by the locals if she, or any other woman for that matter, deemed to enter an ale house unaccompanied.

Later, as the three of them sat enjoying their break and watching the goings on around the lively market place, a young lad with a bad limp walked towards them, closely followed by a few local children. It was Simon Dobbs, known to the village as being a ward of the Stratton family.

'Good morning, Simon, how nice to see you,' Kate's mother greeted him warmly.

'Good – morning, Mrs – Devlin,' the lad replied. His speech was slow and laboured.

The children behind him, who were cruelly imitating his limp, began to taunt, calling out, 'Simple Simon, Simple Simon,' over and over again.

The lad looked distraught.

Kate leapt to her feet. 'Get away with you. Leave the lad alone, or you'll have me to deal with.'

It worked. The youngsters turned on their heels and ran.

'You're all right now, Simon, they've gone and you can safely go about your business.'

'Thank – you, Miss – Devlin,' the lad said, touching the peak of his cap.

Kate noticed that the lad's eyes had not left her sister, Annie. He obviously had a soft spot for a pretty face.

'Children can be so cruel,' Kate's mother said. 'They're wrong to treat him like an imbecile – I know for a fact that despite his slow speech and awkward gait, the boy's mind is razor sharp. Your pa often had a yarn with him over a porter of ale.'

'What's wrong with him, Ma?' Annie asked.

'When he was little, he was run over by a horse and trap being driven by the proprietor of the Stratton Hat Company. A truly dreadful accident and it was touch and go whether the boy would survive – but survive he did. Old Mr Stratton blamed himself, but in truth he was not at fault. He took the boy, an orphan, from the care of the parish and gave him a home up at Leagrove House – the Strattons' estate.' She pondered for a while. 'There can be no denying that the Strattons are good folk.'

Kate thought this might be a good time to broach what she knew would be a difficult subject.

'Ma, what do you think of what Luke Stratton said about my bonnets? He isn't the first to make such comments. Earlier, a young woman called Ruby, an expert hat-maker for the Stratton's, said how much she liked them.'

'I'm so pleased for you, Kate, dear, and for what it's worth, I think their praise is well-deserved.'

'Do you, Ma?' Kate asked.

'Yes, I do, but—'

'Ma,' Kate interrupted. She didn't want to hear whatever her mother's 'but' was. 'I've been thinking I might take Mr Stratton up on his offer and apply for a position at his factory.'

Kate's mother stopped eating and gave a heavy sigh. 'Oh, Kate, love. I'm sorry, but while I understand you have ambitions to become a hat-maker, with your father gone … well, suffice to say, I need you at the plait school. Perhaps later on when—'

'When what, Ma? When I'm too old to learn a new trade? You could easily take on another pupil or … what about Annie? If she were to start plaiting, then I could train Dilly to do my job.'

'I don't think so,' Annie blurted out. 'You know how hopeless I am at plaiting. How many times have you tried to teach me? My fingers just aren't nimble enough, and anyway, I have a job.'

'What, sweeping the floor? Why, anyone can do that!' As soon as Kate had said the words she wished she hadn't, the hurt look on her sister's face told her she'd gone too far.

'Kate, that's quite enough,' her mother scolded. 'My decision is final. I'm afraid you have to be content to make your bonnets in whatever spare time you have. Now apologize to your sister.'

Kate knew that she may have lost the argument but she had in no way lost the battle. Deep down she truly believed she would one day fulfil her ambition to become a hat-maker. With this thought firmly imprinted on her mind, she looked to her sister.

'Sorry, Annie. You know I didn't mean it. Why, if it wasn't for the way you keep the floor clean, who knows how many unwanted fires we'd have had.'

Annie smiled. 'That's all right, sis. And Ma's right, you can still make your bonnets. And if I'm not mistaken, there's a woman eyeing up one of your hats right now.'

Kate looked across at her stall. 'You're right. I'd better get myself back to work.'

'Yes, child, you go. I'll pack up here, and then Annie and I will take a look around the market, before heading back to put the tea on.'

Kate reached into the pocket she'd sewn into her homemade dress. 'Here, Ma,' she said, handing her mother a shiny one shilling piece. 'Why not pick us up some pie and mash from Evans the baker for tonight's supper? A special treat from the proceeds of one of my hats.' Kate was pleased to see that there was already some colour back in her mother's cheeks now that she was out in the fresh air.

'Thanks, dear, you're a good 'un,' her mother said, placing a tender kiss on Kate's cheek.

It was a successful day at the market – all stock sold. Kate and Maude began to pack up and they had almost finished when Kate's eyes were drawn to an attractive young couple entering the Red Lion. The man was wearing a striped jacket and straw boater, and had his arm around the woman's waist. Kate instantly recognized them as Luke Stratton and Ruby Cooper, the woman who had been so interested in her bonnets and who had mentioned that she worked for the Strattons. Well, from where she was standing, they looked to be a lot closer than employer and hat-maker.

Kate remembered how there had been talk around the town a little while back that 'old' Mr Stratton, having heard of his son's reputation with women, had given the young man an ultimatum – one that was obviously being ignored.

Luke Stratton stared into the porter of ale that Ruby had set in front of him, wondering how he could extract himself from the situation he'd got himself into. Ruby was up at the bar, laughing and joking with a couple of the regulars, delighted to be released from the factory's daily grind. He didn't really like the company she kept but it was part and parcel of what she expected when they were together. Well, no more. He would finish it for good this time. His mind kept going back to earlier in the day when he'd seen Kate Devlin and remembered the feelings she had aroused in him – feelings so different to any he'd felt with others. His invitation to Ruby had been to take his mind off it and be a distraction, but it hadn't worked. He looked to Ruby and he beckoned her to join him.

She sauntered over to him. 'Are you missing *your* Ruby, then?'

'Sit down, Ruby. I was wrong to suggest that you – we ... look, we've had some good times together, you and I, but I'm sorry, it's got to stop.'

'Why? We have such fun.' She was still smiling but her green eyes had become guarded.

'Come on, Ruby, you've always known it wasn't serious.'

She stood up with an easy laugh that didn't reach her eyes. 'It was fun while it lasted, wasn't it?' She chuckled brightly. 'So I'd best head back to the factory now, I suppose.'

'I said I'd make it all right with Mrs Hobson and I will. You just tell her I gave you permission to take the morning off with pay.'

'With pay, you said?'

He nodded. 'Yes.'

'Well, I'll say cheerio, then.' As she turned and left, she gave a loud gruff laugh. 'Plenty more fish in the sea, eh?'

Luke smiled to himself, but he couldn't quite suppress a tinge of guilt. One of the qualities he admired in Ruby was that she never held a grudge.

CHAPTER FOUR

O VER THE NEXT two weeks, although Kate was loath to admit it, her Uncle Joe had proved a great help. It started that first Tuesday morning when he had arrived as promised at 7.30 to deliver the cut straw from the thatcher. Her mother had instructed Kate to help unload his cart. It was a fine morning with a clear blue sky and bright sunshine, a perfect day for drying straw.

'Good morning, Kate, and what a lovely morning it is,' her uncle said, his voice much softer than she remembered.

She was a little taken aback. 'Yes. It looks to be a grand day,' she politely answered.

'Tell me, child, where would you like these bundles of straw?'

'If you could hand them down to me two at a time, I'll take them to the yard and then come back for more.'

'I'll not hear of it. If I were to let a young lady carry such a load, I'd be the talk of the village,' he protested, before taking not two but four bundles of straw in his hands and jumping down from the cart. 'You just lead the way and I'll do the rest. I've my reputation as a carter to think of.'

Kate's first instinct was to object. Who was this man? He certainly looked like her uncle, but his actions and whole demeanour had changed. She was confused. Had she got it so wrong? Had they, as her uncle had earlier suggested, got off on the wrong foot?

'Well, are you going to lead the way? These bundles won't unload themselves, now, will they?' He flashed what she thought to be a kindly smile ... or was it a smirk?

'Thank you. If you can place them in the yard, I'll untie them ready for bleaching.'

'Consider it done,' he said.

Kate watched him carry the cut straw with ease. There could be no doubting his obvious strength, even for a man of his age.

'What's that awful smell?' he asked, raising one hand to cover his nose.

'It's the bleach in the tubs. Everyone says how bad it is, but I'm used to it.'

As her uncle slowly lowered the bundles to the floor, Kate made to untie them and placed the straw into the tubs of bleach.

'Here, let me help you,' he offered.

'It's all right, it's my job,' she insisted.

'And I suppose you're too proud to let your old uncle help you, eh?' He smiled and gestured with opened hands. 'These hands have been roughened from years of hard work and toil. I'm sure they could cope with the bleach better than those pretty hands of yours and anyway, I'd feel I was doing more to warrant my free supper.'

Kate stepped aside. 'Thank you. If Ma finds you helping like this, I'm sure she'll insist on you staying for lunch as well, with an extra carrot for Samson.'

'Now there's an offer no man could resist. How long does the straw need to lie in this concotion?'

'For several hours, before it's laid out to dry.'

He nodded. 'I see, there's more to this straw-plaiting than I thought.' A fact he seemed to ponder for a while, before saying, 'Now, why don't you go about your business, and leave this to me?'

On his insistence, Kate reluctantly left him to the job in hand. She made her way to the kitchen and began to prepare for plait school, unaware of the way his eyes followed her or the look of triumphant satisfaction on his face.

'I heard you and Joseph in the yard. It's good to see the pair of you getting on,' her mother said.

'I wouldn't say that exactly, but he does seem keen to help.'

'If that's the case, then I think we should let him.'

And so it was decided that, for two meals a day, Joseph Devlin would become their handyman, carter and general helper. The fact that he would now call at the house every day pleased Annie no end. She so loved Samson and eagerly fed him his carrots and other tit-bits. And, much to the surprise of those around her, was now out of bed at dawn, eagerly awaiting Joseph and Samson's arrival.

Toward the end of the week, Rose Devlin gave way to Liam's request and invited Joseph to join the family for Sunday dinner. 'I think it's time you met our Liam,' was all she'd said.

'Thank you, Rose, I shall look forward to it,' he politely accepted.

Joseph was due at two o'clock, thus giving the family a few hours alone with Liam before he joined them.

'Why does he have to come to dinner?' Kate asked. 'We don't get Liam to ourselves much as it is, it won't be the same having someone else here.'

'It's not just "someone else", Kate, it's our Uncle Joseph, our father's brother. And I can't wait to meet him,' Liam gushed.

Kate looked at her brother, his face beaming with excitement. He was right, Joseph was family after all and, so far, where work was concerned, the man had more than proved his worth. So why did she still have this feeling of apprehension? A feeling she decided to keep to herself ... at least for today. She didn't want to spoil the moment for Liam. This was the first time since her father's death she'd actually seen her brother smile.

'You're right,' Kate said, 'I'm sorry. If the truth be known I want you all to myself. I'm just being selfish.'

'That's all right, sis. I understand, I have that effect on lots of girls.' He laughed aloud, such an infectious wicked laugh that the rest of the family joined in.

'Anyway, you'll not just be meeting Uncle Joseph, there's Samson too,' Annie reminded him. 'Oh, Liam, Samson is so big, yet so gentle, you'll just love him.'

'I'm not sure I'll go as far as that. Although for a while now, I've been itching to take the reins of Daniel's horse and trap maybe.'

'I have to tell you that Samson is not your normal horse – this horse is almost as big as a house,' Kate told him. Where Samson was concerned she had always opted to keep her distance.

At precisely two o'clock, the sound of the horse and cart pulling up outside the front door echoed around the kitchen.

'He's here,' Liam said.

'Kate, go let your uncle in, and please ... try to smile,' her mother instructed.

'Good afternoon, Kate. Now don't you look grand in your Sunday best? I hope I'm not late,' he said.

'Thank you, Uncle, and no, you're right on time,' she said, forcing a smile. As she waited for him to tie Samson to the post, she reminded herself that today was for Liam.

'Well now, look at you,' Joseph said, as Rose introduced him to Liam. 'Why, you're the image of your father ... my dear brother when he was your age. Your pa must have been very proud of you. It's every man's dream to have a son to follow in his footsteps.'

Liam bit his lip, obviously choked with emotion.

'Yes, he was,' Rose answered for him. 'Now come on, get yourselves to the table, lunch is ready.'

Liam made sure he sat next to Joseph, and all through the meal they chatted like two old friends – Joseph asking all the right questions about Liam's work at Groves' Farm and Liam eager to know all about his uncle's work as a carter. On more than one occasion during the meal, Joseph smiled at Kate across the table. She didn't respond. The trouble where Joseph was concerned was, she could never be sure if his smile was genuine.

After the meal Liam asked if he could go out and meet Samson. 'Certainly, that's if your mother doesn't object,' Joseph said, looking to Rose.

'I don't mind at all. In fact, I've left some vegetable peelings in a bowl out in the scullery. Annie, why don't you and Liam feed them to Samson?'

Annie headed for the scullery, closely followed by her brother.

'And Liam,' Joseph called after him, 'if you've a mind to take up the reins one day, then I'm the man to teach you.'

'Thanks, Uncle Joseph, I'd really like that.'

CHAPTER FIVE

IT WAS 4.30 on Saturday – the end of the plait school's working week and everyone looked forward to Sunday's day of rest. As the girls prepared to leave for home, Kate reached for her bonnet and straightened her tunic before heading down the passage to the front door. She held it open and one by one the girls filed past, bidding her good day. Dilly Proctor held back and stayed close to Annie; they huddled together trying to suppress their giggles. Kate guessed that she might be the butt of their childish behaviour.

Outside, Kate struggled to hide her excitement. It was such a lovely summer's day, perfect weather for a trip out to the lavender fields. She looked toward the end of the street, hoping to catch a glimpse of Daniel's horse and trap, but he was nowhere to be seen.

'I'm sure young Daniel will be along shortly,' her mother said, stepping out on to the dirt road and into the bright sunshine. 'It was so good of him to ask you out to tea. Be sure and send my regards to his parents and tell our Liam I'll see him tomorrow.'

'I will, Ma.'

Just then Maude Proctor came out of her door and made her way to number 10. 'Hello, Rose, I thought I'd join you for a brew and a chat. Dilly, the little ones are playing in the backyard, keep an eye on them, there's a love.'

'Me and Annie will go in a mo, Ma, I promise. We just want to see Daniel Groves arrive. He and Kate are going out, he's taking her to the lavender fields and afterwards to tea at Groves' Farm. Kate's got a beau,' Dilly and Annie sang out.

'Will you girls behave yourselves? Daniel's a friend and tea at the

Groves' is just a chance to catch up with Liam.' Kate hoped she'd nipped their silly thoughts in the bud.

She wished she could have kept her outing with Daniel a secret but she'd felt it only a courtesy to ask Ma's permission.

'I think it's a splendid idea. It's about time you let your hair down a bit,' her mother had said.

Of course her sister, Annie, had overheard their conversation and couldn't wait to tell Dilly, hence the giggles.

'A friend, is it?' Dilly said. 'Well, here he is, and doesn't he look handsome sat atop his horse and trap, dressed in his clean white shirt, waistcoat and britches? What I wouldn't do for a *friend* like that.'

Kate looked down the street just in time to see Daniel pull his horse to a halt. As he dismounted, he removed his flat cap and beamed a smile. 'Hello there. What a welcoming committee.'

'We're just waiting for you to arrive,' Kate's mother said. 'Now that you are here, I'll put the kettle on for a brew. Maude, come on in when you're ready. Have a good trip, you two. I'll see you later.' And with that she turned and went inside.

'What a lovely evening for a trip to the lavender fields. It brings back memories of when my Jake and I used to take trips out.' Mrs Proctor sighed. 'Sadly those days are now long gone.'

'Just say the word, Mrs Proctor, and I'll be happy to take you for a ride out,' Daniel said, flashing a wicked grin.

She gave a loud belly laugh. 'If I were to do that, the gossips would have a field day. Why, we'd be the talk of the village.'

'That wouldn't bother me. So, anytime you fancy it, Mrs Proctor, just let me know,' Daniel teased. Then, straightening his tweed waistcoat, he walked over to Kate.

'Hello, Kate, I hope you're looking forward to this trip as much as I am.'

'Yes, I am. I've managed to make three new bonnets this week, so I'll not feel guilty about having an evening off.'

'Well, if the ones you've made are half as pretty as the one you're wearing, you'll have done well.'

Kate felt her colour rise. 'Thank you, Daniel, it's always nice to get praise for my hats.'

'Get away with you, girl. That was the lad telling you how pretty *you* looked,' Maude scoffed.

Daniel smiled. 'I can see there's no fooling you, is there, Mrs Proctor?'

'I've always been one for plain speaking. Folk know where they are with me. Now come on, lad, don't stand there all day, it's time to help the girl with the pretty bonnet up into the trap.'

'Sorry – yes, here, let me take your basket, Kate. I'll set it in the back of the trap along with your shawl. You may need it later, when the sun goes down. Now if you take my arm, I'll help you up.'

Before taking his arm, Kate leaned across and placed a kiss on her neighbour's cheek. 'You're a real gem, Mrs Proctor, thank you.'

'Get away with you,' the woman replied, but her smile said otherwise.

With Kate firmly in her seat, Daniel jumped up and took his place at the reins, then with a click of his tongue and a gentle, 'Walk on' to his horse, they set off. As the horse and trap moved along the rough road, Kate was aware of Liam's closeness alongside her, felt both strange and yet … comforting, to have him so near.

They travelled for a while in silence, each taking in the vast countryside.

Daniel spoke first. 'It's so nice to take a trip out in the trap when the weather's this good and even nicer when in the company of such a pretty girl.' He flashed a wicked smile.

'Daniel Groves, are you trying to make me blush? I never had you down as a sweet-talker,' Kate joked.

'I'm taking heed of what Mrs Proctor said and speaking the truth. If that's what's considered sweet talking, then so be it. Either way, I'm glad you agreed to come out with me today.'

She beamed a smile. 'Me too, I've been really looking forward to it and can't wait to see the lavender fields.' Just then, a gust of warm air, laced with the smell of lavender made Kate catch her breath. 'I'm already getting a whiff of its heady perfume and look, there are the fields.'

Ahead of them, stretching out as far as the eye could see, was acre upon acre of purple lavender blossom. 'The smell of lavender is so soothing. It's no wonder people swear by its healing powers,' Kate said. 'Oh, Daniel, I'd forgotten their deep colour and natural beauty, a sight that so lifts my spirits.'

'Mine, too. These fields run parallel with my family's farm. Have you heard that all this land – along with a good size farmhouse – is up for sale?'

'No, I haven't. Why would anyone want to sell such a lovely place?'

'Farmer Perkins is well into his eighties and since his wife passed on last year he's not got the heart for it. His only daughter, married to a doctor with two children, lives somewhere in Devon, and he wants to move to be closer to her.'

'Makes sense, I suppose. Will there be an auction for the farm? I haven't seen any billboards.'

'No, the thing is, he's given me – well my family, the first option to buy. Farmer Perkins has always known my love of lavender and the farming of it. When I was younger, I would spend hours helping him plant seed and later harvest the crop.'

Kate smiled. 'Farmer Perkins obviously wants his farm to go to someone with the same passion for lavender as he has.'

'I'm sure you're right. My father and I have been discussing the prospect of my taking it on. The good thing is that my younger brother, Stephen, having worked alongside me for so long, is now ready to take my place. I have some savings and my father has agreed to loan me the rest to be paid back over ten years.'

'Oh, Daniel, I'm so pleased for you.'

'I knew you would be, that's why I wanted you to be one of the first to know. My goal is to make lavender farming an industry equal to wheat-farming and hat-making.'

'I admire your ambition.'

'And now, if you're ready, we'll head over to my farm; it's almost time for tea.'

'I'm ready when you are, it'll be nice to see your parents and the farm again. It's been a long while since I first brought Liam to meet them, with a view to him being taken on as a farmhand.'

'Can you believe that was almost two years ago? And I have to say, I did have my doubts when my father took him on. I thought he had a bit of a chip on his shoulder, but he's turned out to be a real asset, a loyal, hard-working … friend.'

'It's nice of you to say that. And I'm sure he has you to thank for that. My father was so proud of him.' She gave a heavy sigh.

'Are you all right?'

She nodded. 'I miss my father so much, he was so loved by us all – and now there's my Uncle Joseph. It's just not the same.'

'Why, don't you like him?'

'I'm not sure. It's all happened so fast. In under a week he's gone from delivering cut straw from the thatcher two days a week, to suddenly becoming our daily general helper, over-keen to learn the workings of the plait school.'

'I see what you mean.'

'Daniel, don't you think it strange the way my uncle suddenly appeared from nowhere on the day of my father's funeral?'

'Kate, I can't answer that. I don't even know the man.'

'But you said the other day that you knew *of* him and, did I imagine how uncomfortable you seemed?'

'It's true I've heard of him, but that's all.' Daniel had decided to say nothing about his suspicions concerning her uncle. After all, he had no real proof – only rumours. He needed to wait until he had the full facts and, to this end, he planned to make it his business to find the truth about Joseph Devlin. 'Kate, I promise, I will make some discreet enquiries and get back to you.'

It warmed Kate to feel she had someone on her side, a friend she could confide in. 'Thank you. I'd appreciate that. My mother thinks I'm being silly, she believes he's simply trying to make amends and do the right thing for his brother's family. I'm not so sure.'

'Mothers have a way of seeing things differently and, talking of mothers, there's mine stood on the doorstep waiting to welcome us and look, here's your Liam running to greet you.'

The welcome Kate received at the Groves' farm was second to none. It was a much bigger place than she'd remembered, with acres of wheat fields and a large farmhouse.

Daniel's parents greeted her with open arms.

'Welcome to our farm.' Daniel's mother beamed a warm smile.

'Yes, it's a rare thing to have Daniel invite one of his friends for tea – especially a lovely young lady like yourself,' his father said, as he gave her a fatherly hug. 'We're so used to having your brother with us – he's become part of the family.'

'That's very kind of you. I know Liam loves living and working here. Of course, we all miss him at home but to know he's happy is such a comfort, especially to my mother, who sends her regards by the way.'

'And how is your dear mother? We heard the sad news about your father's demise. It must be very hard for you all. Although Liam tells us that your uncle is now helping you. But if there's anything we can do, just ask,' Mrs Groves said.

Kate flashed Liam a look of disapproval. 'Thank you again. I'm sure, as long as we have the plait school to keep us busy and pay the bills, we'll be fine.'

'I'm glad to hear it, now come on into the kitchen, I've laid up the table and all I need to do is mash the tea.'

Mr and Mrs Groves led the way into the kitchen – a large farmhouse kitchen with a high ceiling and a huge black cooking range. In the centre of the room stood a long wooden table which was groaning with food. Mrs Groves had obviously been busy.

'Don't stand on ceremony. Daniel, Liam, why don't you sit either side of Kate? Father,' she said, warmly addressing her husband, 'you make sure they all tuck in to my home-baked bread, cold cuts and fresh vegetables. I'll have the tea brewed in no time. There's apple pie and custard to follow.'

'So, how did the trip to the lavender fields go? Did Daniel tell you of his plans?' Mrs Groves asked, as they were all tucking into the wonderful spread.

'It was lovely, and just as I remembered it. And yes, Daniel told me about the forthcoming sale and his plan for the future. It all sounds very exciting,' Kate enthused.

'A lot of hard work too, I think. And not a task to be taken on single handed,' Daniel's father pointed out.

'I'm well aware of that and, if all goes to plan, I've a few ideas up my sleeve to establish a workforce,' Daniel said.

'Well, thank goodness our Stephen is ready to take your place here. Mind you, I'm not looking forward to the transition. I don't like change.'

'But it's not change for change's sake – think of it as expanding the family business. We've talked about this at length and I thought we'd agreed that it is time for me to move on,' Daniel spoke with confidence.

'Aye, I know, son. And perhaps I shouldn't have brought it up while we have a guest. I'm sorry, Kate.'

'That's all right, Mr Groves. I know how hard it can be to accept change.'

'Of course you do, child. And ours doesn't begin to compare with yours. But I think my husband's worry is that—'

'That he should have a partner – a wife to help him through the good and … bad times,' Daniel's father interrupted. 'There's a grand farmhouse that goes with the property, I'll admit it needs a bit of work doing. Farmer Perkins hasn't done anything to it for years. Daniel, perhaps, on your next trip out, you could take Kate to see it. I'm sure she'll love it – any woman would jump at the chance to live there as your wife.'

'Pa, will you stop it? You're embarrassing Kate.'

'I think it is a great idea. To have my two most favourite people tie the knot,' Liam piped in.

'Liam! How could you even think such a thing? You of all people know that Daniel and I are just friends,' Kate scolded.

An awkward silence followed.

'I'm sorry, Kate, love. I can see by your reaction that it was just wishful thinking on our part,' Mrs Groves eventually said. 'The thing is with you being such a lovely, hard-working girl – you're the answer to every parent's prayers. Please don't hold this against Daniel, he had no idea our minds were working overtime. Now is anyone ready for another cup of tea?'

Kate and Daniel's journey back to Luton town was undertaken in silence, both too embarrassed to say anything. They were almost at their destination when Daniel decided to speak – desperate to make things right between them before he dropped her off.

'Kate, I'm so sorry. I had no idea my parents thought that you and I were—'

'I was mortified. What made them think it?'

'I honestly don't know. But … maybe it's not such a bad idea after all.' As soon as he'd said the words he wished he hadn't. The look on Kate's face was one of sheer disbelief.

'Daniel Groves, are you saying you have feelings for me? If so, then I hope you're not suggesting that I've been leading you on. I've only ever thought of you as my … akin to having an older brother. I don't want that to change, do you hear?'

Daniel felt sick to his stomach. All his hopes and dreams of them having a future together as man and wife shattered in one heartfelt outburst. Well, if he couldn't have her as a wife, he would have to settle on keeping her as a friend.

'Daniel, answer me, please!'

Daniel feigned a laugh. 'Look at your serious face. I sure had you going there for a while. I hope you were suitably impressed by my love-sick out-pouring. You daft ha'peth – of course I don't think of you in *that* way. You're my best friend and nothing will ever change that. Now come here.' Daniel placed an arm around her, pulled her to him and gave her a friendly hug, then, all too quickly he released her to hold the reins with both hands.

There was another horse and trap heading toward them and he needed to manoeuvre his horse to the side of the lane to let it pass. As the driver came into view, Daniel recognized Luke Stratton at the reins. As he made to pass he gave Daniel a cursory nod of the head by way of recognition, then the man turned his full gaze on Kate and kept it there for what Daniel felt was an ungentlemanly length of time. Daniel was glad when he'd passed. Men like Luke Stratton with a reputation as a womanizer think they can make free with every woman they see – well, he had another think coming if he had designs on Kate.

'Whoa, boy,' Daniel ordered, as he pulled the horse to a halt. It was just after 6.30 and they'd arrived back at Plaiters Way.

As Daniel helped her down from the trap, he looked at her, 'Are you all right? You've not said a word for the last ten minutes,' Daniel asked. 'Are you still mad at me?'

'No, of course not. Don't worry, we're still the best of friends. I'm just tired. It's been a long day. I've been up since dawn. I'll be ready for my bed tonight and that's for sure.'

'I'm sorry. I'd forgotten you'd done a day's work before I picked you up. You get yourself indoors, I'll bring your basket and shawl.'

'No, really, there's no need. I can manage them. I'd rather you get yourself back to the farm before dark. And tell Liam I'll see him tomorrow.'

'All right, if you're sure. And as tomorrow's Sunday, don't be surprised if you see me, too.'

'That would be nice. You know how Ma loves you to call in.'

'Yes, I do,' he said softly, 'your *mother* is always pleased to see me.' He sighed then leaned over to give her a peck on the cheek. 'Thank you for a lovely day.'

'No, *thank you*. And good luck with your plans for the Perkins' farm. It's all very exciting.'

But she hadn't told Daniel the real reason for her silence. The way Luke Stratton had looked at her when he passed them in the lane had caught her by surprise – a look that seemed to last for an age, a look that had no explanation. She had tried to fathom it and failed, hence her silence for the latter part of the journey home.

Luke Stratton had left Leagrove House, the family estate, in good time for his secret meeting with a young lady in Luton. During the first part of his journey, his forthcoming liaison had been the only thing on his mind, wondering what pleasures lay in store for him. Now, much to his annoyance, his thoughts seemed full of young Kate Devlin. He'd been more than a little surprised to see her so close to the Groves lad. Whenever Luke met her, she had always acted so chaste and gave the impression of being a girl with high morals. And now there she was, not only sat atop the lad's horse and trap but, on his approach he'd definitely seen the lad's arm around her, embracing her. So, obviously, she was not the paragon of virtue she made out to be. He hoped his gaze had made her feel suitably uncomfortable. For some reason seeing her with this lad made him feel ... what exactly? Was it anger, disappointment or maybe jealousy? No ... surely not? What did it matter? Why was he letting this slip of a girl affect him so much? As he approached the George, he smiled to himself and forced all thoughts of the Devlin girl out of his mind. A generous payment to the landlord of the inn had secured him a room – far away from prying eyes, a bed, a bite to eat, two glasses, a jug of ale and a bottle of brandy, and that's where he would find a full-bodied woman waiting for him, eager, willing and – he chuckled to himself – more than able.

CHAPTER SIX

IT WAS LATE afternoon when Daniel approached Plaiters Way, only to find Joseph Devlin's horse and cart already tied up outside. This was the last thing he expected, and knew it would make it difficult for him to tell Kate what he had managed to find out about her uncle. He gingerly knocked the door. Kate answered and instantly beamed a smile that warmed him.

'Daniel, it's nice to see you. I was beginning to wonder if you were going to call. Come into the kitchen, Ma's just mashed the tea.'

'Kate, what's your Uncle Joe doing here? I need to talk to you in private.'

'He's come for Sunday dinner.'

'Did I hear my name mentioned?' Her uncle's loud voice called from the kitchen.

Kate put her fingers to her lips. 'Later.'

The scene in the kitchen was one of family bliss, with Mrs Devlin, Liam, Annie and Joe all seated around the table and yet something about the smug look on the man's face didn't sit well with Daniel, especially knowing what he now knew.

'I was just telling Daniel how you've come for dinner, Uncle, and how you two must meet each other,' she lied.

'Good afternoon, sir. I'm Daniel Groves. It's good to meet you.' He offered his outstretched hand.

'Likewise, I'm sure,' Joe Devlin said, as he shook Daniel's hand, squeezing tight. 'I do believe you're my nephew's employer.'

'Not just an employer, Joseph, he's also a true friend of not just Liam, but of this family,' Rose Devlin was quick to inform him.

'Is that so? And I do believe you took young Kate here out for a drive last week?'

'Yes, sir,' Daniel answered, removing his hand from the man's grip.

'Sit yourself down, Daniel,' Rose Devlin said. 'Kate, pour Daniel a cup of tea while it's still fresh in the pot,' Rose instructed.

'Before you sit down, lad, I was about to take myself out to the yard for a smoke – why don't you join me? We can have a chat ... man to man, like, what do you say?' Not waiting for an answer, Joe headed for the back door.

'Daniel, you don't have to go with him, you know. I get the feeling he's up to something,' Kate whispered.

'For goodness' sake, child, can't a man ask another out for a chat without you reading something into it?' her mother chastised.

'It's all right, Kate, I'm sure it's nothing for you to worry yourself about,' Daniel said, softly touching her arm as he passed her chair.

Daniel found Joseph Devlin at the far end of the yard. It crossed his mind that he had chosen a spot well out of earshot of the family.

'Now, lad, it's time for some plain speaking,' Joe Devlin said. 'I've never been one for pussyfooting around, so I'll come straight to the point. In future, if you have thoughts of taking Kate – or anyone else from this family out for a jaunt, then I'll thank you to ask my permission.'

'I think you'll find, sir, that as a trusted friend of this family, I have always—'

'That was then – this is now. And I would also ask you not to just turn up at this house on a whim.'

'Sir, I object to that,' Daniel interjected, suppressing a ripple of anger. 'I have always had an open invitation from Mrs Devlin to call anytime I was passing.'

'Again I'd say that was then. And what, may I ask, brings you here today?' Joseph threw him a knowing look.

Daniel wondered if Kate's uncle had wind of his enquiries earlier. 'I called to offer Liam a lift back to the farm.'

'And I suppose you were just passing this way?'

The look on the man's face told Daniel he definitely knew

something – but how much or what, he couldn't be sure. His instinc-
tive dislike of Joseph Devlin made his tone curt. 'I had business in
Dunstable: this is on my way back to the farm.'

'Well, you're not needed today ... or any other day for that
matter. I've already suggested that Liam take the reins of my horse
and drive himself back to your farm – obviously with me at his side
to show him the ropes.'

'I see.' Daniel stared coldly at the small restless eyes. Now was
not the time to linger. 'Well, in that case I'll be on my way.'

'I think that wise. I'm so glad we had this little chat. It's always
best to know where we stand, don't you think?'

Daniel didn't answer. He just turned and made his way to the
kitchen.

'At last, you're back, come and sit yourself down, lad, and drink
your tea.'

'If you don't mind, Mrs Devlin, I'll not stop. I'm running late. I
only called to give Liam a lift and I've just been told he'll be driving
himself back.'

'Yes, I'm really excited about it,' Liam said in a rush. 'A bit
scared, though.'

'Don't you worry, lad. I've every faith in you. You've sat beside
me often enough to know what to do. If I'd have thought of it, I
should have had you driving long since,' Daniel said.

'Well, maybe once I've learned, you'll let me drive you one day.'

'That I will, lad. Now, I'd best be on my way.'

'All right, if you're sure,' Rose Devlin said, adding, 'Kate's in the
parlour counting stock. Why don't you put your head around the
parlour door on your way out?'

Daniel was about to do just that, when Joe Devlin's untimely
return from the yard stopped him.

'I see you've decided to be on your way, Daniel,' the man said.
'Liam, lad, if I'm to let you drive yourself back to the Groves' farm
and then make my own way back to Clophill, I think we should be
making a move, too, don't you?'

'Yes, Uncle Joe, I'm ready when you are.'

After saying their goodbyes, Daniel, Joe and Liam headed for the front door at the same time, making it impossible for Daniel to talk to Kate alone. Having talked to a few of his allies in Clophill and Dunstable, Daniel was now sure that the rumours about Carter Joe were true. He was definitely not a man to be trusted.

Just then the parlour door opened. 'Daniel, Liam, are you both leaving? Don't tell me you were thinking of going without saying goodbye,' Kate reproved them.

'Of course not, sis,' Liam laughed. 'It's just I'm that excited about taking the reins. Why don't you come and wave us off? Daniel, if you lead the way back to the farm, then all I need to do is follow.'

'Now there's a crafty move,' Daniel joked. He turned to Kate and found her watching him. 'See you soon, Kate,' he whispered. He needed to tell her of his findings ... and sooner rather than later.

CHAPTER SEVEN

D ANIEL LOOKED ACROSS row after row of deep purple blooms of the lavender fields – *his* lavender fields, with pride. It had all happened so fast because Farmer Perkins had wanted a quick sale – Daniel's father had agreed the loan and the deal had been settled in less than a week.

'Well, lad, now the hard work begins. I think you were wise to keep the workforce on. They are obviously well-practiced in the cultivation of lavender. I'd let them get on with it, at least until you've found your feet,' Daniel's father advised.

'I intend to do just that. For the first few weeks I will oversee their work, but in the main I'll let them continue as they've been doing for years, while I concentrate on doing up the farmhouse.'

'I think that's wise, son.'

'Pa, are you sure you don't mind me taking Liam with me?'

'Of course I'm sure. Ever since he started working for us, the lad has been like kin to you. You work well together. It'll be up to your brother to find his own trusted workmate.'

On the day of purchase, Daniel and Liam moved to the newly named Groves' Lavender Farm.

'Daniel, I'm glad you asked me to work for you, but I know absolutely nothing about harvesting lavender. I hope I don't let you down,' Liam said, his voice full of concern.

'I *know* you won't let me down. You're a born farmer. All you have to do is watch the workforce ... look and learn. Liam, that's the order of the day for both of us. Although it wouldn't do to let the workers know what we're up to. So for the first few weeks we'll have to bluff it … agreed?' Daniel offered Liam his hand.

'Agreed,' Liam said, vigorously shaking it.

'Right, let's get to work on the farmhouse. I'm afraid there'll be no days off for us until it's done.'

'That's all right by me. I feel a lot happier now that my Uncle Joseph's helping Ma and the girls.'

Daniel winced. With his new purchase came responsibility, which meant that he wouldn't be able to see Kate for a few weeks. He needed to get the farm sorted, his livelihood depended on it.

With the Devlin plait school doing so well and Kate regularly selling her bonnets at market, the family had begun to see the benefit.

'Carry on like this and we might approach Mr Stratton with a view to increasing his order.'

'With the quality of plait you provide, I'm sure they'd jump at the chance – you might even push for a better price. Since I've taken to delivering their weekly order, I've seen first-hand how the Strattons get rich on the likes of you.'

'We're quite happy with the arrangement, aren't we, Ma? Over the years the Strattons have always been more than fair to us. It wouldn't do to rock the boat.'

'You're right, Kate, let's not be greedy, eh?' Rose said, looking directly at her brother-in-law.

He gave a loud grunt. 'Well, if that's it, I'll get myself off to my digs. Thanks for the meal, I'll see you tomorrow.'

Kate always breathed a sigh of relief when he left the house. She liked it best when it was just her mother, Annie and herself there. Although to be fair, Joseph had stuck to his word. He arrived on time every morning and left after his meal every night.

The news that Daniel Groves had indeed purchased the Perkins' farm came to Kate via local gossip; it was the talk of the town – folk seemed pleased that the new owner had kept the workforce and that Liam Devlin was now working the lavender field alongside him. This explained why she hadn't seen Daniel or her brother for weeks.

*

Kate wrapped her shawl tight around her. It was early September and the weather was bright and dry, but had a fresh, autumnal feel to it. It was the end of her morning at the market – another success-ful one for Kate and Maude Proctor. With four bonnets sold, Kate would have to work every evening to replenish her stock. Maude and her brood were heading home and Kate was about to follow when out of the corner of her eye, she saw Luke Stratton walking towards her, a brightly coloured woollen muffler draped around his neck.

'Good afternoon, Miss Devlin,' he said, doffing his straw boater.

Kate gave a small nod of her head. She didn't know why, but she felt self-conscious around him.

'I trust you and yours are well?' he asked.

The way his dark brown eyes stared warmly into hers made her heart miss a beat and she felt her colour rise. She quickly averted her eyes.

'All's well with us, thank you,' she quietly replied, hoping he hadn't noticed.

He flashed a smile. 'I'm glad to hear it.'

She returned his smile. Then, much to her dismay, his mood changed.

'I hope the addition to your workforce is not going to affect the price of your plait,' he said curtly. 'I don't know if you've heard but there's talk of new suppliers coming from abroad. Rumours are that their plait will be much cheaper and—'

'I've heard the rumours,' Kate interrupted in the same curt tone. 'It wouldn't surprise me to hear that your buyers started them, in an attempt to lower the price of plait.' She didn't mean to goad him, but he'd always had the knack of making her blood boil. 'All we ever ask is a fair price for a quality product. We're not afraid of competition from foreigners and the like. And I gather the "addition" you refer to will be my uncle, Joseph Devlin.'

'Yes, I have to say I was somewhat surprised when the plait school cancelled the collection of our weekly order – an arrange-ment that has worked perfectly well up to now.'

'An arrangement we paid for out of the cost of our plait – a cost we can now save by using my uncle to deliver it.'

'I'm pleased your uncle is proving his worth. For my part, I don't like the man – he's far too full of himself. And from what I hear, he doesn't have the best reputation. I don't think he's someone you should put your trust in.'

To hear Luke Stratton voice her very same thoughts felt strange and she wondered on what grounds. 'Why? What has he done? He's not been late with the order or—'

'No, it's nothing like that. I simply pride myself for having a nose for when things are not quite right. I intend to keep a close eye on your Uncle Joseph and I think you should do the same.'

Kate beamed a smile.

'I don't think my warning is anything to smile about,' Luke Stratton snapped.

'N-no … I'm sorry. I wasn't smiling at you, but at the sight of my friend Daniel Groves.'

'Your *friend*, you say. The other day, when I saw the two of you canoodling atop his trap, you looked to be much more than friends. To be honest, Miss Devlin, I thought better of you.'

Kate felt the colour return to her cheek, this time in anger. She flared back at him. 'Oh you did, did you? And I thought better of you than to add two and two to make five. It's no business of yours, Mr Stratton, and I'll thank you not to spread false rumours. I dread to think …'

'Calm down, I didn't mean to upset you so.' His dark eyes studied her regretfully. 'I think it best if I bid you good day.' And with that he turned and left.

'What did you say to Luke Stratton? He walked past with a face like thunder,' Daniel said.

'I just gave him a piece of my mind, that's all. He might be my ma's main customer, but he's no better than you or me. In fact, you have better manners.'

'My my, remind me never to upset you. I'd not relish a tongue lashing from you and that's for sure,' he said, laughing.

Kate chuckled self-consciously. 'I must say, I did send him away with a flea in his ear. And come to think of it … you have upset me. It's been weeks since I've seen hide or hair of either you or that brother of mine. How is he? And how's your new venture coming along? You made many friends in the town when you kept the workforce.'

'Liam is fine. He sends his love.' He paused, and she was aware of something just below the surface that she couldn't quite fathom. 'And yes, keeping the workforce made perfect sense and, if all goes well, my plan is to extend the number – I aim to offer the women of this town a different trade from the usual hat-making … but more of that another time.' He tucked her arm through his. 'I have been working Liam so hard that I'm afraid there's been no time for days off … until now, that is. With the refurbishment of the farmhouse almost completed, starting tomorrow, Liam can return to having his Sundays off.'

'That's great news.' She was aware of the strength of his arm next to hers. 'And what about you, will you be calling to pick him up?'

'No. I'm afraid not. Now that he's learned to take the reins, he can drive himself there and back in the company transport.' He smiled as he motioned to his horse and trap, but his eyes were serious. 'I've come today instead – I'm glad I caught you. I thought to give you a lift home. I know you have to get back for plait school, but there's something I need to tell you about your Uncle Joe.'

During the ride home, Daniel told her everything he'd found out about her uncle.

'In my opinion, he's not to be trusted,' he warned Kate. 'No one had a good word to say about him in and around Clophill, where he's known as a drunkard with a vile temper and far too eager to use his fists to prove a point. I don't like the way he's hanging around your house. He used to be a man of means, by all accounts, until his drunken, gambling ways made him unreliable as a carter.'

Kate shook her head in disbelief. 'I can't believe we're talking about the same man. Is it possible that Joseph Devlin *has*, as my mother would have us believe, changed his ways? Or, as I've always suspected, is he simply putting on an act to get … what exactly? Is it the plait school he wants?'

'I hardly think so. I'm sure there's more to it than that. The next time I go into Clophill, I shall pay a visit to one of his ex-landladies. He's moved digs that many times, it got me to thinking there has to be a reason.'

'You be careful, Daniel. I'm sure he'll not think kindly to you snooping around. I don't want you to get hurt.'

They were just about to turn into Plaiters Way when Daniel called out, 'Whoa, boy,' pulling the horse to a halt. 'If you don't mind, Kate, I'll drop you off here. I think it wise if you don't mention seeing me today. I don't want you getting into trouble. The last time I called at the house, your uncle warned me off seeing you and made it quite clear that I was no longer welcome at your house.'

'He did what? How dare he? He doesn't even live there! I'm sure my ma will have something to say about that.'

'I'd rather you didn't mention it to your mother, not just yet. If Joseph really is up to something, then it's my guess we'll not have to wait long before he shows his hand. We don't want to give him a reason to delay things, now do we?'

Kate nodded her head, heartened by his support. For weeks she'd had doubts concerning her uncle's intentions. It felt good to have Daniel on her side and he wasn't the only one. Luke Stratton had also advised her to be on her guard where Joseph Devlin was concerned.

'I also think it best if you don't mention anything to Liam,' Daniel advised. 'At the moment, he looks upon your uncle as something of a godsend. I don't want him to get caught in the middle.'

CHAPTER EIGHT

IT WAS LATE Sunday night. Kate had been glad to see Liam today – he was so excited, telling everyone about his new job and how Daniel had insisted he have his own room in the farmhouse – no more dossing down with the rest of the workforce in draughty barns for him. Kate had not mentioned the fact that she'd seen Daniel the previous day and couldn't bear to even look at her uncle across the dinner table. She'd been relieved when he'd left for his digs.

Kate sat at the kitchen table, busy working on one of her bonnets by the amber light of the oil-lamp. With her mother and Annie already in bed, she enjoyed this quiet time alone stitching hats. With needle deftly poised, she lovingly shaped and stitched the bonnet and allowed her mind to wander, to imagine what it would be like to be a full-time hat-maker. She was disturbed from her pipe-dream by the sound of the loud clip clop of a horse's hooves along the cobbled street, and was surprised to hear it halt outside her house. Was it her Uncle Joe? But why come at this late hour?

She quickly threw a shawl around her nightdress to help protect her from the cool night air and headed toward the front door, hoping to get there before her uncle had time to knock and possibly wake Ma and Annie. She just made it. As she opened the door she found a dishevelled Joe leaning against the door-jamb for support, fist poised ready to bang the door, obviously the worse for drink.

'Uncle Joe, what are you thinking, coming here at this late hour?' Kate asked. She tried to keep her voice calm.

'I've been kicked out of me digs. I need a place to sleep,' he slurred.

Kicked out of his digs, he'd said. No doubt yet another landlady who'd had enough. 'Well, you can't stay here,' Kate said firmly.

'We'll see 'bout that,' he said, as he made to enter.

Kate attempted to bar his way, but the sheer strength of the man made it easy for him to push past her, stagger down the passageway and into the kitchen.

She followed him, annoyed at being so easily overpowered. 'You wouldn't be doing this if my father was here.'

'Well, he's not, is he? And I say good riddance.'

'That's a wicked thing to say,' Kate reprimanded him.

He moved closer to her. 'I'll thank you to show some respect, girl.'

Kate stood her ground. 'My father always said that respect has to be earned.'

'How dare you speak to me like that?' He made to grab her but Kate managed to dodge him.

At that precise moment her mother entered the kitchen.

'Stop this, you two. Kate, come and stand by me. Joseph, I'll thank you to leave my house. I'll not have my girls subjected to your drunken ways, do you hear?'

'My dear – dear Rose, I'm so sorry,' Joseph slurred again. 'The thing is,' he began to sway, 'I need a bed.' He ground his teeth and clenched his fists, his eyes dark and frightening. 'I need a bed, now! Do you hear?'

'I—' Kate started to object, but stopped when her mother shook her head and flashed a look, warning her not to antagonize him.

'All right, Joseph, I can see you're in no fit state to take yourself back to Clophill. Follow me and I'll show you to Liam's room to sleep off the booze. But first thing tomorrow I want you gone.'

'Oh, first thing, is it? We'll see. Tomorrow I just might want to talk to you, 'bout me taking over this pious bloody family.' He chuckled to himself as he followed Rose up the stairs, a low sinister chuckle that sent a chill through Kate's whole being.

By the time her mother returned, she had made them both a hot drink.

'Thank you, Kate,' her mother said, as she wearily slumped into her chair.

'Ma, do you think he was serious about "taking over the family"? Is this what he's been planning all the while?'

'No, I'm sure it'll be just the drink talking, love. I'm so sorry, Kate. You warned me not to trust him. I really thought he'd changed.'

'Don't blame yourself, Ma. For a while there he even had me fooled.'

Her mother sighed. 'Well, there's nothing we can do about it tonight, so let's get ourselves back to bed.'

'All right, Ma, I'll just take Samson around to the backyard, where he can lie down.'

'I hadn't given the poor horse a thought. There's an old blanket on the clothes-line that you can put on the ground for him. Do make sure you tie him up well. The last thing we need is for him to run amuck through the streets.'

'I will, Ma. I'll not be long and then we can get to our beds, although I don't think I'll be able to sleep knowing that man is in the house.'

'I know what you mean. This is the last thing I wanted. And just for tonight, I shall sleep in with you and Annie.'

They entered the bedroom to find Annie still soundly asleep.

'Pa always said she could sleep through a storm,' Kate whispered.

'I'm glad she's asleep, Kate. Help me wedge this chair against the door, we can't be too careful.' Her mother's quiet voice sounded fearful.

'Surely you don't think we're in danger, Ma?'

'Let's just say ... it's better to be safe than sorry. Your uncle has been drinking. And I know from past experience, when there's ale in his belly, he cannot be trusted.'

Kate lay on the bed, staring into the darkness. Daniel said her uncle had a reputation as a drunken bully – and now here he was, sleeping it off in Liam's bed. Was this the start of him showing his hand, she wondered?

Kate and her mother spent a restless night, but were up at dawn and while her mother busied herself brewing tea and baking oatcakes,

Kate prepared the room for plait school and wondered what the morning would bring. She felt sick to her stomach, remembering her uncle's last words. Surely he didn't really intend taking over the family. She hoped her mother was right and it was the drink talking.

'Now, Kate, when your uncle gets up, leave the talking to me. He'll no doubt have a sore head ... drink does that to folk.'

'I just want him gone. Ma, he has no right ...' Kate's voice trailed away when she heard the loud sound of a bedroom door closing and the thud of Joseph's feet on the stairs. He was on his way down.

'Well now, there's a sight for sore eyes ... and a sore head.' He rubbed his forehead. 'I've always wanted to have two women at my beck and call. Rose, I'm off to check on Samson – the poor devil must have thought I'd deserted him.'

'You'll find your horse around back. Fancy leaving him tied up outside with no room to lie down. The state you were in last night, I don't know how you managed to even get on his back,' Rose admonished.

'Samson and I understand one another. I'll go see to him and, when that's done, for my breakfast I'll have a brew of tea and a few oatcakes. And Kate, I'll need a bowl of hot water if I'm to shave. See to it.'

'See to it yourself. I've a plait school to prepare.' Kate hoped her voice sounded much steadier than she felt.

'What harsh words. And there was I thinking you were beginning to believe you'd misjudged me.' He gave his low sinister chuckle.

'You didn't have me fooled ... not really. I think it's time you got yourself back to Clophill and left us alone.' Kate struggled to control her temper.

'Oh you do, do you? And I think it's about time you learned some manners, and I'm just the man to teach you.' He moved closer to Kate, so close she could smell the stale ale on his breath.

'Joseph, leave her be. You broke your promise. You said you'd given up the drink. Now, last night you said you had something to talk to us about, so I'll ask you to say your piece and then leave us be.' She failed to hide the tremble in her voice.

'Well now, Rose, surely that's no way to talk to your new ...

landlord.' The look on his face was one of utter pleasure.

'Landlord? What are you talking about? I pay my rent to old Mr Fitzpatrick of Dunstable. His man calls, as he did to my parents before me, every fortnight as regular as clockwork, so how—'

'For your information, "old" Mr Fitzpatrick as you rightly called him, upped and popped his clogs more than a year ago. It fell at just the right time for me – a time when I found myself playing cards with his solicitor and, thanks to a great poker hand, I was able to make a deal there and then for this very dwelling, number 10 Plaiters Way.' He opened his arms and turned full circle, his eyes taking in all he surveyed.

'So, not only a drunkard but a gambler ... and do you also tell lies? Why should I believe you?' Rose demanded, as she struggled to control her emotions.

Kate went to her side. 'That's right, Ma, why should we take his word for it? What proof do you have?' Kate challenged him.

Joseph's hand went to the inside pocket of his long coat. 'If you're looking for proof, here are the papers to prove that I own this house, lock, stock and barrel.'

Kate heard her mother take a sharp intake of breath and saw her knees buckle beneath her, as she slumped into her chair.

'I don't understand. If this is the case, then why haven't I been informed?' Her mother's voice was weak.

He shook his head. 'As long as you kept paying the rent, which you have without fail, there was no need. I simply continued to use the same rent-man as Fitzpatrick ... I requested no mention of the change of ownership.'

'I remember now, the last time the rent-man called, you were here. You took him outside on the pretence of sending a message to your landlady back in Clophill.' How could she have been so naïve?

'Yes, I think my being here surprised him. I was afraid he'd reveal all.'

'If you went to such lengths to hide it from us, why tell us now?' Rose asked.

'The truth is, I've been biding my time. It felt so good knowing that I had the power to throw my brother out on the street anytime

I chose. I intended to keep it as an investment until such time that I chose to sell. I was so relishing kicking the lot of you out. And then fate dealt me a blow I didn't expect.'

'I can't believe it was in your mind to throw your own brother and his family out on the street. Do you hate us that much?' Rose shook her head, as if unable to take it all in.

'Revenge is sweet, my dear Rose.'

From the look that passed from her mother to Joseph, Kate knew that this decision of her uncle's had something to do with the family rift. It made her wonder what could have caused it.

'So what stopped you throwing us out?' Kate demanded.

'My brother's untimely death robbed me of seeing him squirm, to have him plead with me to—'

Kate forced a wry smile. 'That just proves how little you knew your own brother. My father would never have pleaded with you – he was made of much sterner stuff. He was a proud, well thought of man, a good husband and father. Why, you're not fit to lick his boots—'

The next thing she felt was the back of Joseph's hand as it landed with force across her cheek, almost sending her reeling. Kate grabbed the back of her mother's chair to steady herself.

'Kate, love,' her mother called out. 'I'm so sorry, this is all of my doing, I should never have trusted him. Now God knows what's to become of us.'

'Well, from where I'm standing, I'd say you have two options,' Joseph said, his voice calm and calculating. 'The first is to accept that, as the new owner, I deem it my right to move in as head of the family. I know how much work you've put in to establish your plait school. I'm sure that with my vision and your expertise, the business can move on to great things.'

'And there was I believing that all you wanted to do was to help us.' Rose shook her head. 'I can't believe I fell for your scheming lies.'

'It was my intention to ease myself in gently, learn all about the plait school before showing my hand. But I'm afraid recent developments changed that.'

'Because you were thrown out of your digs, you mean?' Kate demanded, still holding the side of her face.

'To be sure, while it's true that my landlady and I might have had a difference of opinion, it only speeded things up. Anyways, I don't need to explain myself to you, girl.'

'You said we had two options,' Rose reminded him.

'You've heard the first; if you want to stay on here you have to accept things as they are now, and continue running the plait school – a job you and Kate do so well. But, if you feel you can't – or won't take up this offer, then you can all pack your bags and leave. Just take heed, if this *is* the path you decide, I want you and yours packed up and off the premises within the hour.'

'Packed up to go where exactly?' Rose asked, her voice trembling with the shock of it. 'Why, it would be almost impossible to find suitable digs at such short notice.'

'That's not my concern.'

Kate moved to comfort her mother as Rose pondered her options … or lack of them, but at that moment, Annie entered the kitchen. Her eyes darted around the room first to her uncle, then to her mother and Kate. Feeling the obvious tension between them, she ran to her mother's side.

Joseph's eyes went to her. 'There's no need for a pretty little thing like you to be frightened.' He edged closer and bending down he took her chin in his large hand, his thumb gently brushing her cheek. 'Whatever happens, there'll always be a place for you in this house.' He made to place a kiss on Annie's cheek.

'You leave her be!' A frightened Rose ordered, instinctively pulling Annie away from him.

'You stay away from my sister!' Kate called out, ready to strike him if she had to.

'Rose Devlin, your children need to understand that I am now the master of this house. Is that clear?' He banged his fist down on the table.

Then, as if saved by the bell, there was a knock on the front door.

'Joseph, that'll be the children arriving for plait school. It wouldn't do to frighten them. Their parents trust me with their care and safety in their workplace. Any unfavourable reports could lead to gossip – we need to protect our livelihood.'

'I quite agree. Does this mean that you've decided to stay?'

'Joseph, you moving in can't be right. But, under the circumstances ... and for the sake of all concerned, I feel I have little option.'

'Ma, what are you thinking? Let's go, let him have the house. I'm sure we'll soon find digs. Anyway, I'd rather sleep on the streets than be beholden to this drunkard,' Kate urged.

'Well, Rose, are you going to silence your insolent daughter or shall I?'

'Hush, Kate. Please, child, if not for me, then for the families that depend on us – on the plait school. I'm sure everything will work itself out,' Rose attempted to reassure her.

Kate felt betrayed. Was she the only one willing to stand up to this man? She started to protest, but the look of desperation in her mother's eyes stopped her. Kate felt so helpless and ... alone. No, she wasn't alone, she had Daniel, she'd speak to him – he'd know what to do. If there was a way to rid this man from their lives then she intended to find it.

As Joseph headed down the passage, Kate followed him. It was time to let the pupils in. As he opened the front door he came face to face with Dilly Proctor and the other girls.

'Hell's bells, not you again?' Dilly exclaimed.

'Get out of my way, you scruffy young wench,' he mumbled under his breath as he brushed past her.

'Charming!' she said, as she and the girls followed Kate down the passageway.

As they took their places for plait school Rose slowly stood up to welcome them, but immediately slumped back into the chair.

Kate rushed over to her. 'Ma, are you all right?' she asked, gently taking her mother's hands in hers. 'Why, your hands feel as cold as ice.'

'Kate, she has no colour in her face. I think we should send for the doctor,' Annie urged.

'I'll go fetch him if you like,' Dilly offered.

'Now, now, there'll be no need of a doctor. I'm thinking I may have caught a chill. Kate, love, if you can manage this morning's plait school, I'll just take myself to my bed.' Rose made to stand up but, once again, her legs buckled beneath her.

'Ma, take my arm, I'll help you up the stairs,' Kate insisted.

'But—'

'There'll be no buts, Ma. I'm sure you'll be as right as rain after a lie down.' Kate forced a smile, hoping this was indeed the case. She looked across at Dilly and the other pupils who looked lost and confused, unsure of what they should do. 'Dilly, while I see to my ma, I'd like you to begin plait school. I'll not be long.'

As Kate helped her mother onto the bed, she attempted to raise her spirits. 'You were right, Ma, why should we move out and give up all we have worked for? It's much better we stay put and play a waiting game. He may have big ideas now, but I can't wait to see him fall flat on his face.'

Her mother gave a heavy sigh. 'What worries me is that he may take us down with him. I'm sorry, Kate. I should have listened to you. You—'

'Just you rest, Ma. He may have won this argument but we will win the war ... I promise. Now get some rest.'

'Thank you, child, just promise me you'll stay clear of him. He cannot be trusted, especially when he's drinking.' As she said the words, her heavy-lidded eyes began to close, and within minutes she was fast asleep.

Kate returned to the kitchen to the sound of the girls singing 'Over one, under two' as cheerily as ever, as if nothing had changed – but it had, and Kate had to wonder if things would ever be the same again. She took her place at her workstation and, picking up the song, began plaiting, determined to stay focused on the job in hand – her mother had spoken the truth, too many families depended on the plait school. There had to be a way to make her uncle go away – but how?

'Kate, is everything all right? What's that red mark down the side of your face?' Dilly asked.

Kate's hand touched her cheek. 'It's nought to concern yourself with. I had a bit of a run in with some cut straw ... and the straw won,' she lied.

'Is that so? Looks more like someone's given you a back-hander,' Dilly observed.

'And when was the last time you had one of them then, Dilly? Does your pa often crack you across the face?' Mary Parsons, Dilly's best friend, teased.

''Course he doesn't. You've been to our house often enough to know better than that. Despite his reputation, in our house my pa's as gentle as a lamb. He knows that if he ever laid a hand on any one of us he'd have me ma to deal with.'

Just then they heard the front door open and minutes later, Joe Devlin entered the kitchen.

'Believe me,' Dilly continued, 'my ma would put fear in any man.' She flashed a look at the man standing over her. 'Even this one.'

The girls giggled. Joe came up behind them and with a flick of his hand, gave Dilly a swift clip around the ear.

'Ouch!' Dilly cried. 'What you do that for, mister?'

He stood over her. 'There's to be less chatting – you've come here to work, there's no time for idle gossiping. And I'll thank you to address me as Mr Devlin. Take heed. There are plenty of other girls waiting to take your place, and as the new landlord of these premises, I only need to say the word and each and every one of you will be out of a job.'

They all looked at Kate, who was fighting to keep control of her temper.

'Girls, let's just settle down to the job in hand and not give Mr Devlin any cause to take any such action. Now – under one and over two ...' Kate prompted, then after flashing a defiant look in the direction of her uncle, she smiled at Annie and the girls by way of encouragement. They all looked scared to death. She wished her mother was there to support her. She wanted to stand up to him, but instinctively knew that now was not the time.

His eyes then went to the empty chair by the fireplace. 'Where's your mother?'

'She wasn't feeling well. She's gone for a lie down. She's had a very upsetting morning.' Kate stared into his cold, unfeeling eyes.

He stared back at her. 'Well, if that's the case, my *dear* niece, I shall take her place as overseer this morning. I'm sure my sister-in-law would approve. She knows how interested I am to learn the workings of the plait school.' He made his way to the empty chair and fell into it with a thud.

Kate felt her colour rise. She had the urge to scream out. How dare this man sit in what had been her father's favourite chair? But she knew she couldn't – once again she must hold her tongue. For the next four hours the girls got on with their work, singing and busily plaiting, all the while under the watchful gaze of Joe Devlin.

Kate inwardly seethed. This man had no right to be here. He may own the house but he was nothing to do with the plait school. The question that played on her mind was why her uncle was so keen to be involved with a business that barely scratched a living. She remembered how Luke Stratton had warned her not to trust him. Did he know something she didn't? Was Luke Stratton the one to help her remove her uncle or if need be, her mother and Annie from the house? Convinced her uncle had a hidden motive, Kate knew she wouldn't rest until she found out what it was and the effect it would have on her family.

At 12.30, Kate gave the signal for the girls to stop plaiting.

'What's this? Why have they stopped work?' her uncle demanded.

'It's the law. We have to comply with the rules laid down by the Board regarding the employment of children. They have to be given a break at midday, that's when we teach them their reading, writing and sums,' Kate informed him.

'Tell me ... how does this work, exactly?' he asked, with more than a hint of sarcasm in his voice.

'Well, after they've had a bite to eat and a drink, Ma usually goes through some scriptures from the Bible and then afterwards I teach them some simple additions and their letters. Most of the girls can already write their names,' Kate said, with pride.

'And how long does all this schooling take?'

'No more than an hour.'

'Surely half an hour is long enough. What are we running here, a business or a charity?'

'But—' Kate started to object.

'I'll have no buts from you, girl. Is that understood?' He didn't wait for an answer, but continued, 'I'm going out. I trust that on my return there'll be a pile of plait to show for your day's efforts.'

At that precise moment Rose Devlin entered the kitchen. Kate took a sharp intake of breath; her mother had suddenly taken on the appearance of a woman she did not recognize – a woman of purpose.

'Ma, what are you doing out of bed?'

'While I lay in my bed listening to the goings on between you all, I gave a thought to what your dear father would have done. I soon realized that my place is here.' She looked directly at Joseph and took a deep breath, as if summoning all her strength. 'Let's not forget that *I* am the overseer of this plait school. Joseph, if you don't mind, I'd like to sit in *my* chair.'

For a moment or two, you could have cut the atmosphere with a knife. Everyone was waiting for Joseph's reaction, and in anticipation both Kate and Annie went to stand at their mother's side – as a show of solidarity.

Joseph looked around the room as if weighing up his options. And to everyone's surprise he stood up from the chair and walked over to his sister-in-law with his arms open wide. 'My dear Rose, please let me help you to your chair.' He offered his hand.

She hesitated, but forced a smile for the sake of the onlookers and took his hand.

'I so hope you feel refreshed after your lie down,' he said, as he walked her to her chair, continuing with, 'I can assure you, my dear, that during your short absence away your pupils have worked well. I'm very impressed. But I'm glad you feel recovered enough to take your place as overseer.'

'I'm pleased you feel that way, Joseph.' Rose's voice sounded stronger.

'Indeed, I believe my talents would be better spent trying to find ways to increase our earnings. And to this end I shall leave you be, and head for Clophill and pick up my belongings.' And with that he turned and left.

Kate was lost for words, shocked by the sudden change in her uncle's demeanour. He was clever, she'd give him that. But having shown his hand, she now knew what she was up against.

'Well, I for one don't like him,' Dilly announced. 'I think he's a brute of a man and you just wait till I tell my father how he clipped me round the ear.'

Everyone knew how big and strong Dilly's father was. Once a year, when the fair visited Luton, he always entered the bare-knuckle fighting competition – he seldom lost.

Rose shook her head and looked first to Kate and then to Dilly. 'Dilly, love, if I were you I wouldn't mention it to your father,' Rose advised. 'I heard what happened. I'm so sorry Mr Devlin took his hand to you, but I'm sure it was no idle threat when he said he'd replace anyone who goes against him. You know how much your parents depend on the income you bring in.'

'Ma, that's not fair to Dilly,' Kate insisted. 'The way he was before he left for Clophill was an act. Surely you can see what a bully the man is and I for one would love Dilly's father to give him what for. Joseph Devlin's brave when it comes to women and children. Let's see how he'd fare against a real man.'

'And are you prepared for the consequences, not just to Dilly and her family but to the future of our school? As you well know, the do-gooders at the Board are always looking for an excuse to shut us down. They want you all to attend the new council-run schools opening up in the villages,' Rose argued.

'My parents need the money, Kate,' one of the girls called out.

'And mine,' another echoed.

'And think of the under fives who come every Sunday morning to the pre-school class. If we close down, where would they go?' Her mother's voice sounded distressed.

Kate shook her head. She loved Sunday mornings when the little ones arrived eager to learn how to plait. It cost each parent tuppence for a child to be taught 'widdle-waddle' – unsellable plait work made from old pieces of string. Although this was money the family could ill afford, in the parent's mind it was money well spent. It meant the children were well practised by the time they were old enough to attend plait school.

'What do you think I should do, Kate?' Dilly asked. 'Just say the word and I'll have my father show your uncle what for.'

Kate knew she'd lost the argument. So many people depended on their plaiting school staying open. If they closed, then others may follow and with it the art of plaiting might be lost forever.

'As much as it pains me to say it, I think we should listen to my mother and do nothing, at least for the time being.'

If it had been her uncle's intention to put the fear of God into the young plaiters, it had worked. They all knew how much their families depended on what they earned at the plaiting school. By the end of the day the pupils had produced more plait than ever before.

In contrast Kate, who usually loved working the plait, found her normally nimble fingers reluctant to complete even the simplest of tasks. She hated her uncle being there. His presence created a dark cloud of doom and despair over a previously happy workplace.

During the week that followed, Joseph was on his best behaviour and although he had taken to occasionally calling in during the hours of plait school – his presence sending gloom over everyone in the room, strangely, he no longer tried to interfere with the running of it. Could the fact that her mother had stood up to him that first morning have made him stop and think? Whatever the reason, it more than suited Kate. One day he even returned from town with a few gifts for the plait school; a new measuring stick for the plait, a hard broom and pan for Annie to sweep the floor, and a mantle-clock that chimed on the hour.

'A small contribution to ease your working day,' he'd said with a wry smile, one of those smiles that Kate had learned not to trust.

CHAPTER NINE

IT WAS SUNDAY and Liam was due to arrive. Kate, her mother and Annie waited at the front door and greeted him when he drove up in Daniel's horse and trap. Kate thought how grown up he looked – her little brother was quickly turning into a young man. Rose Devlin had suggested she be the one to tell Liam of the family's change of circumstance, but her brother-in-law was having none of it.

'It'll be best coming from me,' Joe insisted. 'The lad doesn't need to know the full story. I'll simply explain that when it came to my notice that Fitzpatrick had died and the house was up for sale, out of the goodness of my heart and for the sake of the family, I put up all my hard earned savings to purchase it to save you from eviction.' He puffed out his chest – obviously pleased with himself.

Kate couldn't believe how easily the lies poured from him, proof to her that this man had no conscience.

'And you expect him to believe this version of events without question?' she asked. 'No mention of your own devious intentions, then?'

He gave a wry smile. 'Well now, that's up to you. Your brother has recently entered into a new venture, and while I might not approve of the Groves lad, he has given Liam a chance to make something of himself. Are you prepared to jeopardize that?'

Once again Joseph Devlin had them over a barrel.

'So let me get this straight, Uncle. You now own this house?' Liam asked, with obvious surprise. 'I can't believe I never heard anything concerning Mr Fitzpatrick's death or the sale of this house. And I'm sure if Daniel had, he'd have told me.'

'It was all a bit hush-hush, as they say,' Joseph said, tapping the side of his nose. 'I was in a little business with his solicitor at the time, so I managed to make the first offer. After all the hard work this family has put into the plait school, I couldn't see them out on the street so, I decided to buy it.'

'That's great news. I'd have thought you'd all be jumping for joy, Ma. So what's with the long faces?'

'That's probably my fault. You see, with having put all my money into buying this house, I needed a place to live ... and work. For some weeks now I've been helping your ma and Kate, so it made perfect sense for me to move in, too.'

'So where's the problem?' Liam asked.

'The thing is, lad, I've moved my things into your old room. And I think your mother and sisters think it might upset you.' His beady eyes looked to Rose, Kate and Annie. 'You know how women worry about such things.'

The obvious smirk on his face made Kate's blood boil. She hoped that Liam would see through his lies.

'Well, they're just being daft,' Liam said. 'I live and work up at the lavender farm now, and that's where my future lies. Please, Ma. Don't give it another thought. I'm happy to have Uncle Joe move in with you.'

'Glad to hear it, lad,' Joe gushed. 'Now, if you're ready to head back to the farm, I'll go prepare Samson. You're doing so well at the reins.' He flashed a broad smile.

Kate saw it as a smile of self-satisfaction for having successfully pulled the wool over her brother's eyes.

With Joseph still not back from accompanying Liam, the Devlin women readied themselves for bed.

'Annie, you take yourself up to bed. Kate and I will follow shortly.'

'Kate, will you finish the story from *The Penny Illustrator* when you come up?'

Kate nodded and smiled. 'If you can stay awake long enough.'

'I do try, honest. But it's so cosy in bed,' she called as she headed upstairs.

'Ma, do you think it right that we lied to Liam?' Kate whispered when Annie was out of earshot.

'A little white lie never hurt no one. The lad has enough on his plate. The last thing he needs is to be worried about us. It's for the best.'

'I'm not so sure, Ma. I hate the thought of having to share this house with that man.' Kate shuddered. 'Pa must be turning in his grave.'

'Now stop that, do you hear? Your uncle is now our new land-lord and there's nothing we can do about it. The best we can do is to keep our heads down and carry on with the plait school. It's our livelihood.'

'Uncle Joseph thinks he's being so clever. But even the cleverest of men make mistakes and when he does, I'll be there to show him for the liar he is.'

'It does you no good to carry such a grudge. Your father and Joseph did and this is the outcome.'

'I wish you'd tell me what happened between them, I—'

'I'll tell you one day, I promise. But not tonight – tonight I'm just ready for my bed.'

Hours passed and the weather outside had taken a change for the worse – the wind and rain against her window made it hard for Kate to get to sleep. It must have been well after midnight when she heard the distinctive sound of her uncle's horse cart stop outside the house. As he entered the kitchen she heard him fall over a chair. He was obviously the worse for drink. It crossed her mind that poor Samson would have to stay outside tonight.

'Where's everyone then? All hiding, eh?' he mumbled. 'It's a ter-rible night and I need warming up, do you hear?'

As he slowly began to climb the stairs she held her breath. It took him a while to reach the landing; she counted his heavy footsteps as he trod the uneven floorboards, one – two – three – four, coming to a stop outside her bedroom door. She heard the doorknob turn and her heart was banging against her ribs, but thankfully, following her mother's lead, she'd had the foresight to wedge a chair against the door. It did the job of keeping him out.

'Think they're being clever, don't they?'

She heard him step away from her door and move down the landing, this time stopping outside her mother's room. She crept to her door and listened hard.

'Rose, open this door,' he ordered.

'Joseph, you're drunk. Please take yourself off to bed.' Her mother's voice quivered.

'So that's your game, is it? If I'm taking over providing for my brother's womenfolk, I intend to have the pleasures that go with it.' He gave a deep, sinister laugh. 'With three of you to choose from, I'll be spoiled for choice.'

Kate felt a chill run down her spine. She knew what he was referring to and the thought of it made her feel sick to her stomach.

Then her uncle spoke in a whisper so quiet Kate failed to hear what he said. What she did hear was Liam's bedroom door opening and closing, and she breathed a sigh of relief. It appeared the Devlin women were safe – at least for tonight. First thing tomorrow, she would speak to her mother and suggest that for the foreseeable future, the three of them should share a bedroom – safety in numbers. Before getting into bed Kate decided to go down to Samson, the poor horse was probably soaked through.

Half an hour later when Kate finally crept into bed, Annie was sound asleep. As tired as Kate was she couldn't doze off, the usual silence marred by the sound of her uncle's heavy breathing. It sounded close – too close to be coming from Liam's room at the end of the landing. Then as realization dawned on her, she gave a sharp intake of breath. Her uncle's heavy breathing was coming from her mother's bedroom along with the distinctive noise of bedsprings repeatedly squeaking, slowly at first, then faster and faster followed by a loud groan from her uncle and a muffled cry from her mother. Kate could be in no doubt what had just happened. She'd heard similar sounds when her pa was alive, but then there had been soft words and muffled giggles ... this was different and she felt shocked to the core, at a loss to know what to do. She was sure she'd heard him retire to Liam's room. How could she have got it so wrong? He must have doubled back and forced her mother to lie with him ... but if that was the case, then why hadn't her mother cried out for help?

It was 5 a.m. and Kate hadn't slept a wink all night. Ten minutes ago she'd heard her mother creep downstairs. Kate quietly slid from the bed; the last thing she wanted was to disturb Annie. She crept from the room, eager to confront her mother. What she had heard her uncle and mother doing last night had disgusted her.

She found her mother naked but for a towel around her shoulders, standing over the earthenware sink, a block of carbolic soap in one hand and a scrubbing brush in the other, vigorously scrubbing her body, her arms and legs already red raw.

'Ma, stop!' Kate cried out.

Her mother turned around, her eyes full of anger and rage. 'Oh, Kate, this is all my fault.' She shook her head. 'I should never have allowed him back into our lives. But I swear I'll swing for him if he tries ...'

Kate rushed to her mother's side and reached for her warm coat behind the door. She helped her into it before holding her close. She had never seen her mother so vengeful and ... obviously scared. 'It's all right, Ma, you're safe now.'

Kate was suddenly overcome by a feeling of deep remorse. How could she, knowing her mother as she did, ever think for one minute that she had given herself willingly to Joseph?

'Ma, I know what that lecherous pig did to you. I've been awake all night listening to—'

Her mother looked mortified.

'Oh. Kate, you have to believe that I had no choice. It was the only way to—'

'To what? I don't understand. Why didn't you call out? If you had, I'd have come to you and helped—'

'No one could have helped me. I did what I had to do.'

'I don't understand. Ma, you have to tell me why you did it. For my own sanity I need you to tell me the truth.'

Rose looked up at Kate, tears now streaming down her face. 'I did it to save Annie ... and that's the truth.'

'Annie? What's she got to do with all this?'

'He threatened me last night. He said if I didn't give myself willingly to him then he would take what he wanted from Annie and I knew he meant it.'

Kate realized her uncle must have whispered this threat to her mother when Kate went downstairs to see to Samson.

'Kate, love, Annie was alone in your bedroom. He could have easily gone to her, barred the door behind him to stop me helping her. I couldn't risk him hurting her the way he had me all those years ago.'

'Mother, if I'm to understand, you have to tell me everything. But not out here in the cold, let's go into the kitchen and I'll light the fire.'

Rose nodded.

With the kitchen fire lit and her mother now sitting in her dad's chair, Kate pulled a stool close to her and, taking her mother's hand, prompted her to begin.

'I don't know where to start.' Rose shook her head. Then after taking a deep breath she began. 'It all seems so long ago ... almost a lifetime. And if I'm honest, back then the blame did not fall just on Joseph's shoulders. Your pa and I frequently looked to ourselves for the spark that lit the flame.'

'Well, it must have been some spark to have caused the rift to last for so many years. As brothers, surely he and Pa must have got on at some time in their lives.'

'Oh yes, they were close once. We all were. The three of us used to go everywhere together.' She forced a smile.

'So what happened?'

'Well, child, it might surprise you to know that it was Joseph I first took a shine to. He and I had been courting for about three months when—'

'What? You and Uncle Joseph? I don't believe it.'

'It's true. I was very young and mixed up. I was happy to walk out with him as a friend, I so enjoyed being with him and William.

And then Joseph began to get serious, he said he loved me and if I loved him then I should—'

'He wanted you to go to his bed,' Kate said, sensing her mother's reluctance to talk about such a sensitive subject with her, especially in the light of what happened last night.

'Yes, and I refused. It was then I realized that I had only been playing at being his sweetheart, we were just friends and I couldn't think of him in any other way. So one day I sat him down and told him how I felt.'

'How did he take it?' Kate asked.

'Not good. In fact, he left Luton. We found out later that he had joined the merchant navy.'

Kate moved closer to her mother. 'So is that why Pa fell out with him?'

'No, during the time that Joseph was gone, your father and I became much closer. In fact, we fell in love and I was so happy. Our wedding day was planned for the spring.'

'That's so romantic, Ma.'

Her mother nodded. 'Then toward the end of February, I was walking home from the market along the back lane to this house when I came face to face with Joseph. He had grown taller and was thicker set, but I instantly recognized him. And then without saying a word, he lunged towards me, throwing his arms around me and trying to kiss me – he reeked of beer.'

'Oh my God, how awful. Did you manage to push him away?' Kate's stomach churned at the thought of what might have happened.

'No. He was too strong. I pleaded with him to stop, but he just laughed in my face. He pulled me down to the ground and ... well it was obvious what he intended to do – and even more obvious that I, a mere slip of a girl, was powerless to stop him.'

Kate put her hand to her mouth to muffle her cry. 'And did he—'

'No, child. William, your father, had thought to call and see me and, as luck would have it, he decided to take the same route to my house. It was he who pulled Joseph off me, he who stopped the attack.'

'Good old Pa!' Kate pulled her mother to her and kissed her forehead.

'Please let me finish, child.'

Kate released her, although unsure she wanted to hear more.

'No one will ever know how frightened I was for your father. I had never seen him so angry ... he saw red and couldn't stop lashing out at Joseph. It coincided with closing time at the Golden Lion and the commotion soon drew a crowd. I truly thought your father was going to kill his own brother. It took seven strong men to pull him off Joseph, who suffered a broken cheek and collar bone and his body had taken a beating that might have killed a weaker man. They never spoke again.'

Suddenly, all those years of wondering about the family rift now became crystal clear but one thing still bothered Kate.

'I can understand now why Pa never wanted anything to do with him. But, Ma, knowing all that happened, why did you let him back into our lives?'

Her mother gave a deep sigh and shook her head. 'You don't know the struggle your father had to come to terms with what he did. Oh yes, everyone agreed he acted with good intention to stop Joseph's attack on me. It played on his mind that he had almost killed a drunken man and, not just any drunk, but his brother. Neither of us was blameless. In Joseph's eyes, I'd walked out on him only to take up with his brother and, when he heard of our forthcoming marriage, he got drunk and just snapped.'

'So that's why you wanted to give him another chance – eager to believe he'd changed. But Ma, what he did last night proves he's still the same vile drunk.' While desperate to understand, Kate doubted she would have been so benevolent.

'I know. And that's why I intend to confront him today and tell him that if he ever lays a finger on any one of us, or tries to blackmail me again, I'll have the law on to him.' Rose began shaking her fist. 'And as God is my witness ...'

Kate vowed that from then on she would take the coal shovel upstairs every night, to use as a weapon – a weapon she would readily use to defend her mother, sister ... and herself.

'I'm sure it won't come to that, Ma,' she said. 'Joseph Devlin is a dishonourable man, but he'd not risk the law. He believes he's too clever for that. Men like him eventually make a mistake – I've an idea he already has. And I can't wait to see him get his just desserts. But in the meantime I think that from now on, you should sleep in with me and Annie.'

Her mother nodded. 'I think that's wise – safety in numbers, eh? With Joseph back on the demon drink, he may disregard my threat to go to the police. Kate, love, it's time to prepare for plait school. We shall carry on as normal. I intend to show him I'm made of stronger stuff than to be beaten into submission by a drunken bully.'

Kate marvelled at her mother's sudden inner strength. Earlier this morning she had found a sobbing wreck, yet what she saw now was the same woman who'd stood up to Joseph Devlin that first morning when he tried to take over her workshop – a strong woman determined to fight for what was hers.

'By the way, Kate, I'm asking you never to mention to anyone what went on last night or our chat this morning. It'll be our secret, eh?'

Kate placed a kiss on her mother's cheek. 'I love you, Ma.'

The plait school was already up and running before Joe Devlin deigned to grace them with his presence. As he made his way to the scullery where Rose had taken to leaving his breakfast – a slice of bread and dripping and a mug of ginger beer, he mumbled under his breath. Kate couldn't even bring herself to look at him. Her mother, on the other hand, sat in her chair and glared defiantly at him. He turned his head away.

'Why do you lot have to sing so bloody loudly of a morning?' he growled.

The girls all stifled a giggle. Kate put her fingers to her lips. It was best not to antagonize him.

For the rest of the morning, Joseph kept himself to himself, either in the yard working with the bleached straw or seeing to Samson. He made no mention of his drunken behaviour of the night before.

And it was only when he announced that he was going into town that Kate's mother asked to have a private word with him in the yard. Kate wished she could have been a fly on the wall.

CHAPTER TEN

WHEN DANIEL HEARD the news from Liam about Joe Devlin's recent purchase of 10 Plaiters Way, he was instantly suspicious – a fact he hid from the lad. He seemed to accept the new arrangement and only had good words to say about his uncle. But Daniel couldn't believe there'd been no talk of this house sale in and around Luton. He suspected him of shady practice.

In contrast, by the following Saturday, the news that Joe Devlin had not only bought the house but had moved in to live with the family was the talk of the town. Luke Stratton very soon heard what the gossips were saying. They suggested that with his brother's wife not long widowed there must be more to it than meets the eye – a rumour Luke found hard to believe. His dealings with Rose Devlin had shown her to be an honest, upstanding person who was beyond reproach. He doubted the lovely Kate Devlin would welcome having to share her home with her uncle. A question he would indeed ask her the first chance he got. With his thoughts now turned to Kate, warmth penetrated his whole being – a feeling he recognized only too well.

Daniel arrived at the market, looking every bit the farmer; dressed in a green calico shirt, a tweed jacket with a matching waistcoat, heavy britches tucked into his sturdy boots and a flat cap that struggled to cover his mop of blond hair. And having tied up his horse and cart outside the Red Lion, he was heading through the market when he saw Dilly Proctor coming toward him. She was wearing her usual serge grey tunic and well-worn boots with no shawl or hat to protect her against the cold, early October morning.

'Hello, Daniel – Mr Groves,' she said with a smile.

'Hello, Dilly, and please, Daniel is fine. I'm on my way to see Kate.'

'You'll find her working alongside Ma at the usual spot.' She seemed to hesitate before continuing. 'I 'spect you've heard the news about the new landlord at number 10?'

He nodded. This was the reason he was here. He needed to speak to Kate to find out how things really stood between her family and her uncle.

'Yes. Liam told me. And how do you feel about it?' he asked.

'I don't like him. He's too quick with his hands. About a week ago the brute only went and clipped me around the ear for no good reason. I'd have told my pa, but Mrs Devlin thought it best not to.'

Daniel was shocked by this. 'Dilly, are you sure you're not making this up? I doubt Mrs Devlin would stand by and let *anyone* hurt her pupils.'

'You'd think so. But it wasn't just me. He also slapped *your* Kate across the face … she said she'd had a run in with a bundle of straw … bundle of straw, my arse. It was him that did it, I'm sure of it. I thought you should know.'

Daniel's body went rigid with anger. 'Thank you, Dilly. One way or another, I promise I'll get to the truth of it.'

'Good luck with that. I think everyone's so afraid of him that he'll likely get away with murder. See you, Daniel,' she said, as she turned and headed in the other direction.

A chill ran down his spine as he hurried to find Kate. His mind was racing – had Dilly spoken the truth, were her fears about Kate well-founded or was she just being fanciful and trying to make trouble?

'Hello, Daniel, how nice to see you.'

Her greeting was warm and he took this as a good sign that all was well, but he had to be sure. 'Kate, can you take a break? I need to speak with you.'

Maude looked up from the market stall and smiled. 'And hello to you, too, Daniel.'

'I'm sorry, Mrs Proctor, good morning. Is it all right if I take Kate from the stall for a few minutes? I'll not keep her long, I promise.'

'No, lad, you two go. I can watch the stall.'

With her shawl tightly wrapped around her shoulders, Kate followed him as he headed away from the crowds to the settle on the corner of Castle Street, from where they could keep an eye on the market.

'Daniel, what's wrong? Your face is as red as beetroot and you look fit to burst. Are you unwell?'

'No, I'm fine. Well, I was until I spoke to Dilly Proctor a few minutes ago. Kate, is it true what she told me, that Joe not only clipped her around the ear but that he also slapped you?' He watched for her reaction and, much to his surprise, she laughed aloud.

'Oh, Daniel, of course it's not true. It's just Dilly being Dilly. Why, that girl should be on the stage, she's such a good actress. Now tell me, do you really think my mother would stand by and let anyone hurt her girls, be it a pupil or family?'

'No. That's exactly what I told Dilly, the trouble-making little madam! Kate, you would tell me if anything was amiss? It must have been quite a shock to find out he'd bought your house ... and now I hear he's moved in.'

'Yes, and Daniel, while I know you mean well – I think it best if you let sleeping dogs lie. No more snooping around. What's done is done, and it's up to Ma and me to make the best of things. We still have the plait school to run.'

'But last week—'

'I know what we said last week, and what were we thinking of? I've come to realize that my uncle is no different from the rest of us; we all have skeletons in the cupboard. So let's just forget about him.'

Daniel stared into her eyes. He was sure he'd be able to tell if she was speaking the truth, but her eyes gave nothing away. Perhaps Dilly Proctor wasn't the only good actress here about.

'All right, I'll do as you ask. No more snooping around. But that won't stop me coming to see you at the market on Monday and giving you a lift home.'

'I'm glad. Now I'd better get back to the stall.'
'And I'll go about my business. I'll pick you up later.'

As Kate made her way back to the market, she hoped Daniel had accepted her account of things. She couldn't risk him facing up to her uncle. Not when things were so fragile at home – she didn't want to risk Joe getting wind of her plan. Thankfully, up to now her uncle had not bothered them at night.

CHAPTER ELEVEN

IT WAS SATURDAY afternoon and Joe had taken himself off to Luton for a porter of ale.

'It's what I deserve, especially after looking at your sour faces,' he'd said. 'And providing the blustery winds outside don't blow me knackers off, I'll be back in good time to make the weekly delivery to the Stratton factory. I do so enjoy watching those pompous bastards spew up money!'

'Joseph Devlin, I'll thank you not to use such coarse language in front of my pupils,' Rose reproached him.

Joe's nostrils flared as he stared at her in disbelief. 'And I'll thank *you* to remember whose house this is. I shall speak as I bloody well like.'

The girls had all stopped what they were doing and held his gaze.

'Get back to work! This order had better be ready when I return … or I'll have your guts for garters!' And with that he left, slamming the door behind him.

The order was almost boxed and ready for delivery when there was a knock on the door. Kate and the pupils were busy finishing the order, so her mother went to the door. From the kitchen, Kate heard Luke Stratton's voice and felt suddenly uneasy.

'Mrs Devlin, may I come in out of these high winds? October might have come in like a lamb but it's leaving like a lion.'

'Quite,' Rose agreed as she stood aside to let him enter.

Once inside and with the door firmly closed against the elements, he turned to Rose.

'Mrs Devlin, I do believe we have a problem.'

'A problem, Mr Stratton, and what might that be? It can't be the plaiting. I know how rigorously my Kate checks it before passing it for sale,' Kate heard her mother say as she entered the kitchen, closely followed by Luke Stratton.

Kate's eyes met his and he gave her a quick smile. She felt her colour rise and hoped no one else noticed.

'Mrs Devlin, please be assured, it's not the quality of the plait in question; that is up to your usual standard ... it's the lengths.'

'The lengths? Surely not, we've been using the same measuring stick—' She stopped in her tracks. 'Now come to think of it, when Joseph moved in, he treated us to a new one.'

'Well, that could be the answer we're looking for, because all the lengths are an inch short.'

'Are you sure? Kate, please get the measuring stick for Mr Stratton to see.'

'I'm afraid I can't do that, Ma. Uncle Joseph has taken to locking it away in the tool chest and only brings it out at the end of the day.'

'Then pray, tell me how you know what length to work to?' Luke enquired.

'With these.' Kate held up eight lengths of cord. 'We each have one of these at our side while we work.'

'May I?' Luke held out his hand.

As Kate handed him the lengths of cord, she couldn't help but be impressed by his businesslike manner.

'If it's all right with you, I'll take one of these lengths back to the factory with me to check it against one of our measuring sticks. When do you expect your brother-in-law to return?'

'He's usually back from the Red Lion by four o'clock,' Rose said.

'Right, I shall take my leave now and return later. I'd prefer it if you didn't tell him of my visit or of my concerns about the plait. If my suspicions are correct, it'll be up to the constable to deal with him.' And with that he turned and left.

Kate pulled her mother to one side. 'Ma, I think we ought to warn the children not to breathe a word of what they may or may not have overheard. We don't want Joseph to get wind of what might be coming to him.'

'Oh, Kate, do you think it's true? Has Joseph been up to no good and selling short lengths of plait?' Her mother spoke quietly.

'I'd not put it past him. Why else would he have taken over the actual measuring of the plait and why keep the measuring stick locked away?' Kate whispered, not wanting the children to hear her suspicions.

'If that's true then it would mean that we played our part in the crime, however innocently. It would still fall on us to explain ourselves to the law. What must Luke Stratton think of us? Oh, Kate, we could lose everything ... even our liberty.'

'Ma, try not to worry. I'm sure your long-standing good name will count for something.' Kate wanted to say more but knew she couldn't. She had to wait and trust Luke Stratton on this.

They waited in silence for Joe's return. Time dragged so slowly, they felt he was never going to show. Then not long after four o'clock, they heard the front door open and Joseph burst into the room.

'Well, what have we here? You look like a coven of witches.' He began to remove his leather belt. 'If I find that any of you have been slacking your workload, then it'll mean a good beating,' he bellowed as he inspected the plait in each box.

The children looked to Kate, fear written over their tiny faces. Kate forced a smile, hoping to reassure them that all was well – although she herself was filled with apprehension. It was obvious he'd been drinking; the smell of stale beer and tobacco hung about him.

There was a loud knock on the door, followed by the sound of the latch being lifted and heavy footsteps heading down the passage. The kitchen door opened and in marched a sergeant and two burly police officers, closely followed by Luke Stratton and the bailiff. Kate, Rose and the pupils were shocked into silence.

'What the hell?' Joseph shouted.

'Mr Joseph Devlin, I'm arresting you for the fraudulent act of selling short measure plait.' The officers stood either side of him and began to handcuff his hands behind his back.

'Get off me. There's been some mistake. I ...' He stumbled drunkenly.

'There's no mistake,' Luke Stratton assured him. 'I called here earlier today and removed the evidence to prove what you've been up to. So you can't bluff your way out of this one.'

'It was her! Not me,' Joseph pleaded, his eyes fixed on Kate. 'She's the one who did it. It was all her idea.'

'Stop your blabbing, man. I can't believe you're trying to pin this on your niece. What are you, a man or a mouse?' the sergeant snapped.

Kate couldn't believe what she was hearing. She hoped with all her heart that Luke Stratton had explained her part in bringing the law to their door.

As the police officer escorted Joseph from the kitchen, she couldn't resist telling him, 'You were right about one thing, Uncle. It *was* my idea – my idea to go to Mr Stratton with my suspicions. Ever since you treated us to a new measuring stick, I was sure the lengths felt different. When you've been dealing with plait as long as I have, you get to know when things are not right.'

He glared at her. 'You mark my words, I'll get you back for this,' he spat, before being escorted down the passage and out to the waiting police cart.

'Oh my lord!' Rose exclaimed. 'Mr Stratton, I promise you, I had no idea.'

'Mrs Devlin, I already know that. Your daughter here explained everything to me.' He looked across at Kate and flashed a warm smile – a smile she willingly returned.

'Kate, why ever didn't you tell me what you suspected?' her mother asked.

'That was my fault, I'm afraid. I swore her to secrecy. I always believed your brother-in-law was up to something. I just couldn't pinpoint what it was.'

'So you, like my Kate, never really trusted him, while *I* foolishly let him back into our lives and have since lived to regret it.' Rose dropped her head in shame.

'My dear lady, I am in no doubt that Joseph Devlin played on your good nature. The man is a bad lot. Now, thanks to your daughter's initiative, he'll soon be up before the magistrate.'

'But what if they let him go? You heard the way he threatened me.' Kate's concern was obvious.

Luke walked across and took Kate's hand gently in his. 'Don't worry, Kate. Take no heed of hollow threats of a scared man afraid of the justice he must now face. I know for a fact that the law here takes a dim view of this particular fraud. It's a given between hat-maker and the supplier that there must always be trust and if I'm not mistaken, he'll be sent down for a long spell.'

Was it her imagination or did he hold onto her hand longer than necessary?

While Joseph was held in custody awaiting magistrates' court, word got round about his arrest and three of his ex-landladies came forward and made accusations against him – of both physical and sexual violence. And just a week later, he was duly charged with fraud and three accounts of assault and attempted rape, and later sentenced to seven years in prison.

With Joseph Devlin safely locked up, Kate, her mother and Annie could sleep soundly in their beds. The testimony of his previous landladies had shocked and disgusted them. To think they had given shelter to someone that evil gave them food for thought. Kate hoped her family could put this episode behind them and things could now get back to normal – but of course there was still the fact that her uncle owned the house, and could at any time instruct his solicitor to throw them out. So Kate set her mind on finding new premises; her goal was to have them safely relocated before the winter set in.

It had been a whole week since her uncle's imprisonment and every day the threat of being thrown out of the house hung over them like a shroud.

'Ma, I've heard where there's a house for rent. I think I might take a look on my way home from the market.'

'All right, love. I'll have a nice fire in the grate for when you get back.'

'Mrs Proctor, would it be all right if I leave the market a little earlier today? I've heard there's a house for rent in Adelaide Street.'

'Of course you can. Adelaide Street, you say? Are you sure, ducks? It's very rough down there.'

'So I've heard, but I have to take a look. Every day I expect the family to get notice from my uncle's solicitor to quit number 10. I need to find somewhere before that happens.'

'It's such a shame – Plaiters Way just won't be the same without you as neighbours. That miserable Joseph Devlin has a lot to answer for. How two brothers could be so different is a mystery to me.'

Kate nodded in agreement. 'You're not the first I've heard say that.'

'Anyways, you go when you're ready, ducks, and good luck. What'll I tell young Daniel if he comes to pick you up?'

'Just tell him I'll see him back at number 10.' Kate smiled.

With Joe gone, Daniel had again become a regular visitor to the house. Last Sunday he'd even arrived with Liam to spend the after-noon with them. When Liam heard the truth about what his uncle had been up to, he was shocked and felt embarrassed for having so easily been taken in by him. Kate was sure it helped him to have Daniel there for support.

After dinner they talked about Kate's plan to seek alternative accommodation.

'Kate, do you really think Uncle Joe would be vicious enough to kick you out?'

'Yes, Liam, I do. If only to get back at me for telling the Strattons of my suspicions,' Kate answered. 'The thing is, I so wanted him gone from the house – I forgot it was *his* house. If I'd have given it more thought then I—'

'You did the right thing,' Daniel assured her.

'And I'll second that,' Rose Devlin said. 'Joseph got what he deserved. When I think how he wormed his way into this house and then – to hear what he did to those other women who gave him accommodation, I can only give thanks to God to be rid of him.' She exchanged a look with Kate to acknowledge their shared secret.

'I just wish you'd all told me the truth, instead of hiding every-thing from me,' Liam said.

'Liam, lad, it was done with the best of intentions.'

'I miss Samson,' Annie piped up. 'But I am glad you took charge of him, Liam. I'm sure he'll enjoy living with you up at the lavender farm.'

'As would you, Annie,' Daniel said before turning to her mother. 'Mrs Devlin, I have a suggestion. Why don't you *all* come and live with me and Liam at the farm?'

'Daniel, that's a great idea,' Liam enthused. 'Ma, you'd love it there. The farmhouse is that big and there are plenty of spare rooms.'

Kate's eyes darted to her mother, who seemed to be actually con-sidering it as an option.

'I'm sorry, Daniel, there's just no way we could do that,' Kate was quick to respond. 'As tempting as it sounds, the last thing we need right now is to fuel the gossips … what with you being a single man and all.' Kate knew she was blushing, but it had to be said.

'Blow the gossip, that's what I say. I'll not stand by and see you out on the street.'

'I'm sure it won't come to that. Anyway, your farmhouse is too far out of town. We need somewhere close by, where the pupils can easily walk to plait school.'

'Kate's right, the school is our livelihood,' her mother agreed.

Thankfully Daniel didn't pursue it and, though both Liam and Annie looked despondent, they seemed to understand the sense it made.

It was just after 11.30 when Kate left the market, her shawl wrapped tightly around her shoulders to shield her from the cold winds of early winter and made her way across George Street, expertly side stepping the horse-drawn delivery wagons, hawkers, tradesmen and townsfolk all going about their business, oblivious to her and her eagerness to get to Adelaide Street.

The walk took longer than she'd expected, which gave her doubts about its closeness for the pupils. As she made her way through the narrow arched alley leading to Adelaide Street – a small hamlet in the heart of Luton town – she was instantly overcome by the acrid stench of excrement, both human and animal, that filled the air and dirty water that ran down the street and she watched in horror as shabbily dressed, barefoot young children played dangerously close to it. She remembered reading in the local newspaper how this particular hamlet had not benefited from the new drainage system recently put in place by the water company. The old houses were in such disrepair, most with windows missing, some without roofs and open to the elements. They were overcrowded with what appeared to be two or three families to each dwelling, while dishevelled men and women stood outside their houses on the dirty road – all had a look of desperation, as if all hope was lost.

Kate instantly realized that this place was definitely not some-where she could bring her family or, for that matter, the pupils of the plait school. Her heart went out to these neglected street-urchins and she gave two thin little sisters some coins from her purse before she turned on her heels and headed for home and afternoon plait school.

She was only a ten minute walk from Plaiters Way when she heard a fine jet black horse and gig pull up alongside her. She glanced up, pushing back her bonnet, and saw it was Luke Stratton.

'I'm so glad I caught up with you,' he said, pulling the horse to a stop. 'Mrs Proctor at the market told me you went to see a house in Adelaide Street. Please don't tell me you're seriously thinking of moving there?'

'No. Not now. Mr Stratton, I had no idea there were still hamlets in the town as bad as that. Our house is a palace in comparison and—' She stopped in mid-sentence, alerted by the sound of the long, wooden fire truck loaded with tin buckets, being pushed along the cobbles over Bridge Street, its large bell clanging with urgency, sending fear and dread into her. 'Oh my God, I hate that sound. There have been so many lives lost to house fires recently, most caused by embers falling from the grate.'

'Yes, with so many townsfolk working the straw-plait, the small-est spark can quickly turn to a blazing inferno,' he agreed.

The fire truck looked to be heading in the direction of Plaiters Way.

'I can see the smoke in the distance but I can't make out where it's coming from.' Kate strained her eyes, but there was too much smoke.

'Miss Devlin, let me give you a lift home. I can have you there in minutes.' Luke offered his hand to help her up onto the gig.

'Thank you. The sooner I get back the better.'

Kate felt uncomfortable sitting in such close proximity but told herself it was a means to an end. As they approached the entrance to Plaiters Way, she could plainly see the orange glow as flames billowed out of her and Annie's top bedroom window and she let out a painful cry. 'That's our house. The fire is at number 10! Oh God, please let Ma and Annie be safe.'

'Come on, boy,' Luke said, shaking the reins and sending the horse into a canter. 'We'll soon be there. Look, the fire truck is positioned close to the alley leading to the backyard and the draw-well. We'd better stop here in the lane,' he said, pulling the horse to a halt. 'Miss Devlin, you wait here for me,' he called out, as he leapt down from the gig.

But Kate had already jumped down and, with her skirt hitched above her ankles, she ran across the lane and entered Plaiters Way, only to see her house engulfed in flames. Swirling smoke and ash stung her eyes, her throat was dry and her chest tightened with the dread. She watched as the firemen offloaded their buckets and formed a line from the draw-well to the house, urgently passing buckets of water and struggling to douse the flames. But it was obviously a lost cause.

A sea of milling faces; women and children were gathered in the street, watching their menfolk's brave efforts to help. Kate ran frantically among them, calling out for her mother and Annie, but there was no sign of them. She fell to her knees in floods of tears.

'Ma! Annie! Where are you?' she cried.

'Kate!' She heard Daniel's voice call out and within seconds he was beside her. She felt his arms go around her waist to help her to her feet and as he did so, she gripped his arm.

'Oh, Daniel, I'm so glad you're here. I can't find Ma or Annie!'

'Kate, let's go see Dilly Proctor, she's over there behind the fire truck with ... Kate, she's with your Annie!'

'Oh, thank God. I must go to her.'

Taking her hand, he led her toward the fire truck, but a fireman barred their way. 'I'm sorry, you can't come any closer,' he informed them.

'Annie, Dilly, it's me!' Kate called out.

'I really can't let you any closer,' the fireman repeated.

'But it's my house on fire ... and that's my sister and my neighbour over there. I need to know what's happened to my mother.... Daniel, please tell him.'

'Look, man, under the circumstance I think this young lady should be allowed past,' Luke Stratton said, the authority in his voice obvious to all.

'I'm sorry, miss, I didn't realize. If you'd like to follow me, I'll take you to your sister and then you can have a chat with my boss – he's the one to ask for news of your mother.'

Kate turned to Luke Stratton; the concern in his eyes touched her. 'Thank you for speaking up for me, Mr Stratton,' she whispered.

'Don't mention it. Now you go. I can see you're in good hands.' He looked to Daniel. 'I'll stay here for a while and if there's anything I can do, just ask.'

'Thank you. I'll remember that,' Daniel said, before leading Kate toward Dilly and Annie.

Minutes later, she swept Annie into her arms. The child was sobbing and looked dazed, her face and hair black with smoke.

'Oh, Kate, it's my fault. I shouldn't – have – left – her,' Annie sobbed.

'What happened? Where's Ma?' Kate asked, fearing the worst.

Annie's sobs became louder. She shook her head, unable to speak.

'Your ma told her to come and visit me before start of plait school. We were in the backyard when we saw smoke billowing from your ma's scullery. Annie wanted to go to her, she almost made it, too, but I pulled her back ... maybe if I hadn't—' Dilly tried to say.

'No, you did the right thing. And Ma?'

Dilly simply shook her head and Kate felt a sudden tightening in her chest. She looked to Daniel. He put his arms around her and Annie, taking Annie's weight on his arms.

'Miss Devlin,' the head fireman spoke softly, 'I'm so sorry, we tried our best to save your mother, but thick smoke and the ensuing fire stopped us getting any further than the end of the passage – it was all we could do stop it spreading to the neighbouring properties.'

'No, no,' Kate moaned, struggling to breathe. 'Not my lovely ma, please!'

The fireman gently touched her arm. 'Miss, the smoke was that thick, your dear mother would have quickly passed out ... I'm sure she wouldn't have known a thing.'

'My good lord, whatever's been happening here?' Maude Proctor exclaimed as she arrived home from market.

Dilly quickly pulled her to one side to explain.

Maude Proctor shook her head in disbelief. 'I can't believe such a good woman has been taken from us, and one I was only speaking to this morning.'

'It was my fault,' Annie cried.

'No, Annie, if it's anyone's fault it was mine,' Kate insisted. 'I keep hearing Ma's last words in my head ... she said that the two of you would make sure to have a big fire in the grate for when I came home. I bet that's what caused the fire.'

'The truth is none of us know what really happened,' Daniel said. 'And there's nothing to be gained in blaming yourselves. It's getting late and we need to find you somewhere to stay. I suggest you both come home with me—'

'Daniel, I – we can't. It just wouldn't be right and proper, and anyway I need to stay close to Ma. I'll not leave her.... Mrs Proctor, where will they take her?'

'Don't you worry, child. They can take her to my place. And the same goes for the two of you.'

'Thank you, Mrs Proctor.'

'It'll be an honour to have your dear ma lie in my parlour. And if you and Annie don't mind bunking in with Dilly, then we'll manage fine.'

With an arm around both Kate and Annie, Dilly headed for her house. The Devlin girls didn't object, they were too shocked and dazed.

When Daniel made to follow, Maude Proctor pulled him back. 'Daniel, love, I think you should get yourself back to the farm – Liam needs to be told about what's happened and the tragic loss of his mother.'

'Yes, you're right. Although I don't relish giving him the news, he's only just come to terms with losing his father and now ...' He shook his head. 'I'm sure he'll want to come straight back to be with his sisters.'

'Then you mustn't let him. Tomorrow will be soon enough. There'll be the funeral to arrange.'

'Very well, Mrs Proctor. And please tell Kate and Annie that I'll be here with Liam first thing in the morning.'

'That I will, son.'

Luke Stratton could only look on from a distance. The acrid smell burned his throat. He had heard from the fire crew of Rose Devlin's tragic death. His heart went out to the Devlin girls, especially Kate. He so wanted to be the one to comfort her and envied Daniel Groves's closeness with her. If only it could have been his shoulder she cried on, his arms around her ... his ... He stopped himself and, not for the first time, questioned his feelings for the girl. There could be no denying his admiration for her but he was also attracted to her innocence and beauty and relished the prospect of having her fall for him.

CHAPTER TWELVE

IN THE AFTERMATH of the fire, Kate went through a dark time – the loss of her mother was almost too much to bear. She questioned God's wisdom. How could He let an evil man like Joseph Devlin live – albeit locked up in prison, and yet take her mother – a kind, caring woman, who had spent her life working for the good of her family, friends and neighbours? It just didn't seem right. *His* only saving grace had been in saving Annie and for that at least, she would be eternally grateful.

Her mother's funeral took place just two days after her death. Kate and Liam made all the arrangements. Liam, while obviously in deep shock, showed an inner strength she never thought he had.

'Kate, Annie, as upset as we all are, we need to stay strong for Ma, we need to do right by her. She's with Pa now and we three have to carry on as best we can,' Liam said, as he struggled to control his emotions.

It was then that Kate realized what a capable and dependable young man her brother had become.

The funeral, like her father's a few months before, was well attended. The minister said such lovely words about their mother – words echoed by everyone as they filed past the grave.

'I'm so sorry for your loss,' Luke Stratton said, looking straight at Kate. 'Your mother was an honest, hard-working woman and one I greatly admired.'

'Thank you, Mr Stratton. And thank you for your assistance the night of the fire. Ma always spoke highly of you and enjoyed doing business with you. A business I can no longer—' Kate stopped mid-sentence, as she fought against the emotions that welled up within her.

'Miss Devlin, some weeks ago, I remember making you an offer to come and work for me. When you're feeling up to it, you might like to call in at my office. There's no rush ... I'm not planning on going anywhere. So—'

'I don't think today is the best day to discuss such matters, do you?' Daniel interrupted brusquely. 'At present, Kate – Miss Devlin – has more pressing things to deal with, like finding somewhere to live.' Daniel's manner was curt.

'Quite. And it's good to see, Miss Devlin, that you have someone like Mr Groves to look out for you,' Luke Stratton said, his dark gaze intent on Kate, the sarcasm in his voice not lost on her. 'My deep condolences,' he softly repeated, as he walked past her.

Kate was puzzled. Why had Daniel felt the need to intervene on her behalf? And why had Luke Stratton been so obviously irritated? But right now she had to take care of Liam and Annie. Holding tight to their hands, she took a deep breath and continued to thank each mourner for their attendance and warm condolences.

As Luke Stratton strode briskly from the graveyard, he felt annoyed. How dare that upstart Daniel Groves tell him how to behave – what to say and when? Who the hell did he think was? He mumbled under his breath. And what right did he have to stand alongside the family of the bereaved? Had Luke's first thoughts been right – was there more between Kate and the Groves lad than she wanted to admit? He shrugged away such thoughts. The last time he saw her at the market, she had been so quick to deny this.

The memory of the feelings she had aroused in him that day and also the night of the fire were still with him and however much he tried, they would not go away. His dalliances with women like Ruby Cooper were just a means to an end. There were, of course, other more gentile women he mixed with. Society women whom he found to be pampered, spoilt and shallow – the type of women his father expected him to one day marry. He checked himself and remembering his father's warning, wondered if offering Kate Devlin employment was such a good idea.

Back at the Proctors' house, Maude Proctor had kindly laid on sandwiches and a few jugs of ale for the mourners. The house was crowded. Taking Kate's hand, Daniel led her outside to the yard.

'You did well today,' he said. 'Your ma would have been very proud of you.'

'I do hope so. I can't believe how much my life has changed in just a few short months ... losing Pa, the whole episode with my uncle and now Ma. All of a sudden I find myself head of the family and—'

'Don't let your Liam hear you say that. I'm sure he thinks that job now falls to him. In fact, I think it's one he secretly relishes. He wants to do right by you and Annie.'

'I know. He's been so strong since ... anyway I'm glad he's settled and, thanks to you, has a good job and somewhere to live.' She took a deep breath. 'Annie and I need to do the same. It's time for me to think to the future. There's nothing to be gained from dwelling on the past.'

Daniel took her hands in his. 'Kate, I know this is probably not the best time or place but I hate to see you so worried about the future. Like Liam, I want to take care of you and Annie, to give you both the security you deserve.'

'But Daniel, you know—'

'Marry me, Kate!' he said, before she could say another word.

She pulled her hands away from him. 'Daniel!'

'I'm sorry, Kate, I shouldn't have blurted it out like that. What I meant to say was ... Kate Devlin, will you do me the honour of becoming my wife?'

'Oh, Daniel, I'm so touched. You are probably the kindest, loveliest and most thoughtful man I know. And if I had any sense at all, I'd be screaming out "yes, yes," but—'

'But you're not going to, are you?'

She shook her head. 'It just wouldn't be right. I'd be saying yes for all the wrong reasons and it wouldn't be fair on you.'

'Let *me* be the judge of that. Kate, I love you and I know you love me too.'

'I do but not in the way you want. I love you as my best friend.'

'And there's nothing I can say or do to change your mind?'

Again she shook her head. He jolted back, as if she'd slapped him across the face.

'Well then, that's it. I might as well clear off and let you be.' He turned to leave, his broad back tense and ramrod straight.

She caught his arm. 'Daniel, please don't go, I …'

He pulled his arm away. 'I'll leave the trap for Liam. Tell him I'll see him back at the farm. I shall walk back – I need to clear my head. It's not every day a man makes such a fool of himself now, is it?' And with that he was gone.

'Oh, Daniel, I'm so sorry,' she whispered to herself.

CHAPTER THIRTEEN

IT HAD BEEN three weeks since the house fire and the tragic death of Rose Devlin – a time that both Kate and Annie spent under a dark cloud of uncertainty. With Liam paying for their keep and Maude Proctor happy for them to stay 'until they get sorted out', they spent their days quietly plaiting straw in the hope of selling it at the market.

While ever grateful to have a roof over their heads, bunking in with Dilly and more often than not, one or two of her siblings, was not the best arrangement. Kate knew it would be up to her to improve the situation and find a way to support them.

'Mrs Proctor, I thought I'd take myself down to the hat factory to see Mr Stratton. At Ma's funeral he said that he might be able to find me a position.'

'That sounds promising, dear. It'll be good for you to find work.'

'Well, if Dilly can do it, then so can I.'

'Yes, my Dilly's a good girl. I only wish she didn't have to go to work for Ada Tucker. The sly bitch didn't waste much time jumping into your ma's shoes and opening a new daytime plait school to replace yours at number 10. Still, I suppose we should be thankful that Dilly and the other girls have somewhere to go to earn a few bob.'

Kate entered the stark grey building at the end of George Street where the Stratton hat factory was housed. Once inside, the large entrance hall with its ornate high ceilings took her by surprise – it was much bigger than it looked from outside. She stared up at the tall wooden staircase that reached almost to the ceiling and, in particular, the door at the top marked 'Main Office'. There was also a large double door situated under the staircase and a sign pointing to 'The Factory Floor'. She decided to head for the Main Office.

As she gingerly made her way up the staircase, the butterflies in her stomach were doing somersaults and her mouth was so dry she could hardly swallow. On reaching the top, she took a deep breath before opening the door. This was the chance she'd been waiting for – a chance to become a real hat-maker.

'Good morning. I'm here to see Mr Luke Stratton,' she announced to the stern-looking woman seated behind a desk. Kate's voice sounded a lot more confident than she felt.

'And is he expecting you?' the woman asked.

'I'm not sure. I ...' Kate was suddenly lost for words but thankfully, at that very moment, a door leading to an inner office opened and out walked Luke Stratton. On seeing her he beamed a smile – a smile that made him look years younger and ... not half as intimidating. The fact that he seemed genuinely pleased to see her prompted her to return his smile.

'Miss Devlin. How very nice to see you. I hear that you've moved in with neighbours. The tragedy of the fire and your mother's ...' He stopped as if unable to find the right words then shook his head before saying, 'Please, come on through to my office.'

'Thank you,' she said, glad he'd not finished his sentence. It had taken all her strength to come here today; the last thing she needed was to be reminded of the tragic events that brought her here.

'Please take a seat. Am I right in thinking that you're here looking for a position with us?'

'Yes, you said I should call if I needed a job.'

'Indeed I did. I'm delighted you've come. Now, tell me where you think your talents lie.'

While his voice sounded every bit that of a prospective employer, there was something about the way he was looking at her that brought colour to her cheeks. She hoped he hadn't noticed.

'Mr Stratton, for as long as I can remember, I've longed to be a hat-maker. As you know, I already make and sell my own bonnets.

I'm afraid I only have the bonnet I'm wearing to show off my work.' She proceeded to remove her bonnet. 'The few I had in stock were lost in the fire and since then ... well, I've not had the heart.' She handed the bonnet to him.

He examined it, inspecting the hand-stitching under the brim and inside the crown. 'As I said that day at the market, your work is indeed excellent but if I were to take you on as an apprentice, you would need to learn to do things our way.'

'I understand,' she said, although she didn't really.

'Are you sure? If, after a few weeks of training, I were to put you to work on say, our Luton straw boater, would you not get bored?'

'Bored? I hardly think so. Why would I?'

He continued to examine her bonnet, before giving it a nod of approval. 'This bonnet shows flair. The way it's shaped and stitched tells me it's a labour of love. Am I right?'

'Yes. And I never make the same design twice,' she said with pride.

'And that's my main worry. You see, where the Luton straw boater is concerned, every hat has to be exactly the same. Each made to the same standard and proportion as the one before. In this factory, what we require is excellence and not flair.'

For a few minutes she was a little taken aback. 'All I know is how much I enjoy working with straw-plait – I know first-hand from working at my mother's plait school how much work goes in to produce it. To be able to take a few lengths of such plait and make something as beautiful as a straw boater would be a dream come true. I also believe that to know and understand and have a feel for the material, every hat-maker *does* require flair.'

'Wise words indeed ... and you may have a point. Miss Devlin, what age are you?'

'I've just turned eighteen.'

He rubbed his chin, as if pondering his decision.

Kate crossed her fingers.

'Well, the good news is, I'm willing to give you a chance.' His hand went to his watch in his waistcoat pocket. 'It's almost eleven o'clock,' he announced. 'With today being Saturday and almost the end of our working week, I think it best if you enjoy your weekend, then start work here first thing Monday morning.'

'Thank you, Mr Stratton, I promise I'll not let you down.'

'If you can be at the factory for seven o'clock on Monday morning, I'll instruct the forewoman to put you to work as an apprentice to one of our hat-makers. Your starting wage will be two shillings and six-pence a week. At the end of your training and, depending on which department you are assigned to, the amount you are paid will change accordingly. I trust you find this acceptable.'

'Oh yes, I most certainly do. Thank you.'

'I hope your coming to work here meets with Mr Daniel Groves's approval. He didn't seem keen on the idea the other day.'

She felt suddenly deflated, and annoyed with Daniel. 'I'm sorry, Mr Stratton, Daniel had no right to speak to you the way he did.'

He shrugged his shoulders. 'No harm done. And I'm sure he had your best interests at heart,' he said, his dark brown eyes fixed on hers.

'Sometimes he speaks up for me when he shouldn't.' She held his gaze and for a moment it felt as if time stood still. She quickly looked away.

Luke Stratton, still holding her bonnet, slowly stood up and walked from behind the desk. 'Daniel Groves is a lucky man to have you as a friend,' he said quietly, as he moved closer to her. 'I only wish—'

At that moment the door opened and an elderly man entered the office. 'Good morning and what have we here?'

'Good morning, Father. What brings you here at this hour?' Luke Stratton asked, quickly handing Kate back her bonnet.

She thought the younger man seemed a little put out by his father's presence and wondered why. She had heard a lot about old Mr Stratton but had never met him before.

'I was just passing. Tell me, who might this young lady be?' Mr Stratton Senior eyed her up and down.

Kate hastily replaced her bonnet and hoped she'd managed to tuck in her unruly curls. Out of the corner of her eye, she noticed

Luke Stratton was smiling at her – a smile that warmed her in a way she didn't understand.

'This is Miss Kate Devlin,' Luke answered. 'I've just taken her on as an apprentice.'

'Have you now? Kate Devlin, you say? And would this be the daughter of the late proprietor of the plait school?'

'Yes, Father, the very same.'

It annoyed Kate the way they were talking about her as if she were not in the room. She was about to say something when the old man turned to her and, pulling up a seat to sit next to her, took her hand in his.

'My dear, dear girl, my sincere condolences for your loss, I knew both your mother and father. They were good, hard-working and honest folk. I'm so glad you have decided to join us here at the factory. Your mother's plait was some of the best we used.'

'Thank you, sir. I'm that pleased to be given a chance of work. Now that the plait school is … no more, I need to bring in a wage.'

'What about your siblings, do they have work?'

'My brother Liam works at Daniel Groves's farm, it's also where he now lives. But my twelve-year-old sister, well, the truth is, sir, she was never any good at plaiting or sewing – she said her fingers weren't nimble enough.'

'How is she with horses?'

Kate thought it a strange question, but answered politely, 'Well, sir, I know she loves old Samson.'

'Old Samson?'

'He is … was my Uncle Joe's carthorse.'

'That blackguard who was sent to prison?'

The look of disgust on the old man's face made Kate wish she'd never mentioned her uncle. From the day he'd been put behind bars, Joe Devlin had ceased to exist for her. She prayed that the fact she was related to such a man wouldn't spoil her chance of employment.

'Don't look so worried, child. What that man did was purely down to him and you are in no way to blame for his misdeeds. Quite the contrary, you are to be applauded for your diligence in reporting him to my son.'

Kate breathed a sigh of relief.

'Tell me, where is this Samson now? I do hope he's being well cared for,' he continued.

'Samson is now with Liam, where I know he's well cared for.'

'Good. Now back to this sister of yours. My estate manager is looking for a general help with the horses and a menagerie of live-stock. Do you think she'd be interested? Of course, she'd need to live in. But rest assured, she would be well taken care of – my house-keeper is a kindly soul.'

'That's good to know, sir, and thank you. I'm sure my sister will jump at the chance to work up at Leagrove House.'

'Talk it over with her. If she is in agreement, bring her along with any personal items she might need, to see me up at the house on Sunday afternoon.'

As Kate walked from the factory heading back to Maude Proctor's, she had a spring in her step and for the first time in days, felt a glimmer of hope. Not only had she managed to secure a place as an apprentice hat-maker for herself, but also a position for Annie up at Leagrove House.

Luke Stratton was feeling good about himself. He had found what he believed to be a capable new apprentice. And deep down he was sure there was more to Kate Devlin than met the eye.

'So what's your interest in this girl?' his father asked when Kate left them.

'Interest? The girl needed a job. I've seen her work and she's good. I'm sure she'll prove an asset to us.'

'Don't misunderstand me. Taking on the Devlin girl was the right thing to do. Her mother's plait school stayed loyal to this company for years. And if, as you say, the girl has talent even better, but I can't help wonder if you might have a hidden motive.'

Although Luke shook his head in denial, he had to admit his father knew him too well. 'There isn't one.'

'Are you sure? I may be getting old but I can still appreciate an attractive and interesting young woman when I see one.'

'What are you suggesting, Father?'

'Do I really need to spell it out? I saw the way you looked at her ... and I warn you, if you are planning to add her to your list of dalliances, then think again.'

'You are wrong, Father. In fact, nothing could be further from the truth. I have far too much respect and admiration for Miss Devlin to ever play fast and loose with her.'

'I do hope so.'

Luke breathed an inward sigh of relief. He had managed to placate his father this time. Where Kate Devlin was concerned, he would need to tread very carefully.

'I don't want to go! Kate, why are you sending me away?' Annie's voice sounded desperate.

'Annie, love, you have to understand that with the plait school gone, we need to find work. I thought you'd jump at the chance to work with the horses ... and it's not just horses, there's other live-stock too.'

'It's not the job – I think I'd really like working with animals. It's the thought of being on my own. First I lost Pa, then Ma and now I'm to lose you and Liam.' She looked tearful.

'Don't be daft, you'll not lose us. Leagrove House is less than a mile from Daniel's farm. I'm sure both he and Liam will come to see you every chance they get. In fact, you'll probably see more of Liam than you do now. And, as for me, I'll be there as often as I can,' Kate assured her.

'You promise?'

'I promise. Now come here and give your sister a big hug.'

'I love you, sis,' Annie said, as she held Kate in a tight bear hug.

'And I love you and I want you to know that, as soon as I find a place to live, I shall make sure there's enough room for you to come and visit whenever you want.'

'I'd like that. Then we can swap stories about our new jobs.'

'I'm sure Ma would be proud of us both.' Kate gave a heavy sigh. 'Now, if we need to get to Leagrove House on Sunday, I'd best go and see Liam to arrange a lift. Look, I know it's a fair walk to Daniel's farm but you're welcome to come with me. Mind you, you'll have to wrap up warm, there's a frost in the air today.'

'Oh yes, I'd love to come. I've never been as far as the lavender fields. But everyone says they're a sight for sore eyes, with a sweet smell that's carried on the wind for miles.'

'There'll be no blooms at this time of year, the best time to see them is July and August.'

'I'd still like to come. I want to see Samson again.'

'Not to mention your brother and Daniel, eh?' Kate teased.

'Them, too,' Annie said as she chuckled to herself.

Kate smiled. It was so good to see her sister in good spirits.

'It's 12.30. If we take the bread and cheese Mrs Proctor left to eat on the way, we could head off now. I'll just leave a note for her.'

Kate had been right; there was a definite winter chill in the air and, as they left the house, they tightened their shawls and made their way out across Bridge Street and the direction of Daniel's lavender farm. On leaving the town and heading out into the countryside, they found the ground resembled a rust carpet, festooned as it was with dried leaves from the now bare trees. She loved the countryside at this time of year, when the air felt so clean and fresh, unlike the stench and grime of town, and she wished she had time to dawdle, but her plan was to get to the lavender farm, see Liam, then return to Luton before dark.

They walked briskly. It helped to keep them warm and, having made good progress, they approached the entrance to the lavender farm at around two o'clock. Kate stared at the new sign above the gate – 'Heaven Scent Lavender Farm'. She loved the new name and felt immensely proud of Daniel's achievement.

'What do you think?' Daniel's voice called from the field, where he was overseeing more than fifteen farmhands.

'I love the new name ... it's perfect,' Kate said.

'Thanks. You're the last person I expected to see ... there's nought wrong, is there?'

'No, Annie and I have a favour to ask Liam, that's all. I hope you don't mind us calling.'

'Why should I mind? This is your brother's home, and I'm sure he'll be eager to show you the farmhouse ... I'd have shown you around ages ago but then—'

'Kate, Annie, at last you've come to see us,' an out-of-breath Liam called as he ran towards them. 'I know you're going to love the farmhouse, it so big and so comfortable. Daniel, shall I lead the way?'

'Look, I've got work to do, so why don't *you* show the girls around? I'll catch up with you later.'

'Daniel, would it be all right if I went to see Samson? I'm not much for farmhouses and the like,' Annie pleaded.

'Of course you can. Liam, be a good lad and show Annie to Samson's stable.'

'Sure, in fact, why don't I take Annie to see Samson and you show Kate the farmhouse? Come on, you know you want to,' Liam joked.

'Didn't you hear me? I'm too busy,' Daniel snapped, before he turned and walked away.

'What's got in to him? He was in a fine mood earlier,' Liam said.

'I don't know, I'm sure,' Kate lied. She had hoped that they could get back to the easy way they'd always felt around each other before his proposal, but obviously it wasn't to be.

With Annie safely reunited with Samson, Liam said, 'Annie, love, the farmhouse is just across the yard. Come over and join us when you're ready.'

'Liam, you were right, I do love the place. I can't believe how big it is. This farmhouse is three times as big as our—' She stopped in mid-sentence and gave a heavy sigh.

'I know how you feel. I still find it hard to think of our home as an empty shell now. Sis, I keep thinking that if I had been there that day, then the tragedy might not have happened.'

'You mustn't think like that, it wasn't your fault. For a while I also blamed *myself* for the fire. I thought Joseph Devlin had put a curse on us – to get back at me for the trouble I caused him.'

'Now where did you get such a daft thought? Of course there's no curse. Thankfully our uncle is safely locked away. And are you forgetting it was his house? Not even he would be daft enough to damage his own property,' Liam pointed out.

'I know that now. I just wanted to prove to you what tricks the mind can play. Now come on, lead me to the kitchen, I'm parched.'

As they entered the kitchen, Kate was hit by the warmth of the open fire in the grate, a fire-guard strategically placed around it. If only number 10 had had one of them. She banished the thought, it was too painful. Instead she looked around at the well-equipped kitchen: various pots, pans, serving plates and utensils. The place was spotlessly clean – far too clean to be the work of two busy farmers, no, this definitely had the mark of a woman's touch. She walked over to the long oak table in the centre of the room, already set up for dinner with a freshly baked loaf of bread and a large meat and potato pie.

'This is really grand.' Kate thought how much her ma would have loved this kitchen, but she didn't say a word, not wanting to upset Liam.

'Sit yourself down and I'll pour you a mug of ginger ale. Will you and Annie be stopping for a bite to eat?'

'No, I don't want to be late back. Mind you, I have to say that the food does look good. So who's the cook, you or Daniel?'

He beamed a smile. 'Neither. Daniel's mother brings us something over every day and for breakfast and supper, there's always bread and dripping. She also does the cleaning. Daniel recently placed an advert in the *Penny-Bugle* for a housekeeper.'

'Is that so?'

'Yes, it is,' Daniel said curtly, as he entered the kitchen. 'I can't expect my mother to continue looking after us – she has enough to do looking after my father and brother.'

'Of course,' Kate said quietly.

There followed an awkward silence.

'What's wrong? Have you two had a row?' Liam demanded. 'It would certainly explain a lot. Since Ma's funeral, he's been like a bear with a sore head.'

'That's enough, Liam. Your sister doesn't need chapter and verse on my mood.'

'So what exactly did you two quarrel about?' Liam asked, not willing to let the subject go.

'It's nothing to concern you,' Daniel snapped.

Liam looked to his sister. 'Well?'

'It was a silly misunderstanding, that's all. Isn't that right, Daniel?' she prompted, hoping he'd agree, if only to stop her over-inquisitive brother. Daniel simply shrugged his shoulders.

'But I thought you two were—'

'You know what thought did? You really must stop seeing what's not there,' Kate scolded.

At that moment, Annie burst through the door. 'Samson was so happy to see me. I ... what's wrong? Why the long faces? I thought you'd be pleased with our news.'

'And what news would that be?' Daniel asked.

'The news that we've both got new jobs,' Annie blurted out.

'Yes, that's what we came to tell you.' Kate quickly told them about her job at the Stratton factory and Annie's at Leagrove House.

'Well, it didn't take you long to get yourself down to see Luke Stratton, did it?' The edge to his voice was not lost on Kate.

'I needed a job. And I'm grateful to Mr Stratton for taking me on. I thought you'd be pleased for me.'

'*I* am, sis. Although I'm not so sure about Annie working at Leagrove House, she's still a bit young to be away from us, don't you think?'

'She's to be looked after by Mr Stratton Senior's housekeeper, it's all very above board. I'll know more on Sunday.'

'What's happening on Sunday then?' Liam asked.

'That's when I have to take Annie to Leagrove House. I thought, if you weren't too busy, you might give us a lift there. We could walk but—'

'Of course I'll take you. Since Ma's ... well the truth is, although I've been coming to see you and Annie at the Proctors, it's not the same. It'll be good to have a ride with the pair of you on my day off.'

'You can come, too, if you like, Daniel,' Annie offered.

'I'm afraid I can't. I have too much to do here. But I'll call to see you soon, I promise.' He smiled – a warm friendly smile meant only for Annie. He didn't look at Kate.

'Daniel, if it's all right with you, I'll get the horse and trap and give the girls a lift back to Luton,' Liam said.

'Just don't be too long. We have to check on the bottom fields before supper. When you get back, that's where I'll be. See you soon, Annie.' And with that he turned and left without a word to Kate.

'My, I don't know what's happened between the two of you but I've never seen him this angry before.'

'If that's the way he wants to be, there's not much I can do about it. He always was stubborn,' Kate said, trying to sound as if she didn't care. But she did care.

'I'm sure he'll come round. Daniel likes us too much not to,' Annie pointed out.

'I truly hope so,' Kate whispered to herself.

CHAPTER FOURTEEN

O N SUNDAY MORNING, Liam arrived as promised to pick Kate and Annie up from the Proctors'.

'Well, Annie, me ducks, it's a big day for you today. But I have every faith in you and if your ma was here, she'd say the same.' Maude Proctor drew Annie close. 'I shall miss seeing your pretty face around the house. And I want you to know, child, my door is always open to you.'

'Thanks, Mrs Proctor, I'll remember that. I may be back sooner than you think … if I can't do the work.'

'Get away with you. You'll do fine, won't she, Kate?'

'If the way she dotes on Samson is anything to go by, yes. I some-times think she's happier with that horse than she is with us,' Kate teased. 'Now, come on, we'd best get a move on. Liam has the trap waiting for us in the yard.'

The morning was clear and crisp and the dew lay heavy on the hedgerows. Kate and Annie sat alongside Liam, and even with their thick woollen shawls wrapped tightly about their shoulders, they were grateful for the blanket Liam had brought with him to cover their legs.

'It was good of Daniel to let you take the horse and trap this morning,' Kate said. 'How is he?'

'He's busy getting the new barn ready for his next venture.'

'What venture is that, then?'

'Haven't you heard? He's taken on fifteen girls from the village to work at drying the lavender blossom.'

'I hadn't heard. Fifteen girls, you say? That'll please the towns-folk. How do the girls get to and from the farm – it's a fair walk there and back.'

'Daniel's pa has loaned him a hay-wagon and, when hitched up to Samson, it makes for comfortable transport. Daniel and me take turns ferrying the girls back and forth, to and from the edge of town.'

'I see. So does that mean the farm has moved away from produc-ing lavender oil?'

'No. We're doing both,' Liam said. 'Apparently there's a good market for dried lavender as there is for oil. It's a long process, but once dried and placed in little calico bags, it holds its scent for ages.'

'I'm impressed. Please send him my good wishes and—'

'Why don't I take you to see him later? I know he'd be pleased to see you.'

'I'm not sure, but ... I *will* think about it.'

'Good. Now we'd better get a move on, if we're to get Annie here to Leagrove House.'

Kate couldn't help but feel hurt, not to have known about Daniel's new venture. There was a time when she would have been the first person he would have told – he always trusted her to give an honest opinion. Sadly, those days were gone.

They travelled in silence for a while.

This was a big step for Annie. She was entering a strange and unfamiliar world. Kate noticed how her hands were clenched tightly on her lap. The poor lamb must be scared to death, she thought. She felt it was up to her to lighten her sister's mood.

'Look, Annie, can you see how the spiders' webs glisten in the hedgerows like a delicate string of shiny beads?'

'Is that what they are, spiders webs? What makes them look so pretty?'

'The crisp weather and the early morning dew. There'll be plenty more sights like this for you to see up at Leagrove House. Isn't that right, Liam?' Kate nudged her brother's arm, urging him to cheer Annie up.

Liam nodded. 'Look, Annie, there's a little brown creature

running ahead of us. Now there's a sight you'll not see in town.'

'Oh, he's lovely. I've never seen a live rabbit before. Only the ones hanging from a butcher's hook.'

'That's only the start. Once you're away from the dirt and grime of the town, you'll see a different world. I love living in the country with all the wonderful sights and smells … think of it as your own little adventure, eh?'

'I hadn't thought of it like that,' Annie said.

'Liam's right. I bet Dilly Proctor and the others will be so jealous of you. If I'm honest, I'm envious myself. I'd love to live in the country … and who knows, I might just do that one day,' Kate said.

'If you married Daniel you could do it straight away,' Liam was quick to point out.

'How many times do I have to tell you? Daniel and I are just good friends, and if you don't mind, I shall find a husband in my own good time, thank you.'

'Just don't wait too long. You could end up an old maid. What do you think, Annie?'

Kate turned to her sister, who was now smiling. 'So you find the prospect of me becoming an old maid funny, do you?' she said light-heartedly, trying not to laugh.

'It would serve you right, if you did. If I was old enough, I'd marry Daniel. I think you're mad not to beg him to wed you.' Annie rolled her eyes with impatience.

'First an old maid and now I'm mad! What am I to do with the pair of you?'

Liam began to laugh, an infectious laugh that soon had Annie and Kate joining in. It warmed Kate's heart to see her sister in good spirits once again.

It was late morning when they approached the entrance to the long driveway and caught their first glimpse of Leagrove House. A large imposing grey stone building stood in glorious splendour; fronted by a large courtyard with enough room for five or six carriages, and surrounded by lush green fields.

Annie put her hand in Kate's and squeezed hard.

Kate patted her hand and turned to her. 'Don't worry, sis. You'll be fine, and I promise we'll not leave you until we're sure you like it here. Isn't that right, Liam?'

Liam flashed a smile. 'Like it? I reckon she'll love it.'

He pulled on the reins and steered the horse through the ornate iron gates and up the long driveway. Minutes later, he turned into the courtyard and pulled the horse to a stop. Across the courtyard, a groom stood at the bottom of a flight of sandstone steps that led to the house, holding tight the bridle of a beautiful bay mare – its highly polished leather saddle and reins complimenting the sheen on its deep mahogany brown coat – the brasses and bit between his teeth gleamed in the autumn sun.

'Now there's a sight for sore eyes – it was worth the long trip out just to see it,' Liam enthused.

'Yes, it's as if one of those paintings that hang in the town hall has come to life,' Kate said.

'I've never seen a horse as pretty as that.' Annie's eyes lit up. 'Do you think this mare might be one of the horses I'm to help look after?'

'Could be, I suppose. You'll have to wait and see, won't you?' Liam said.

Just then a man strode out of the house and Kate instantly recognized Luke Stratton. Dressed in a smart riding outfit; tweed jacket, waistcoat, white knotted stock around his neck, jodhpurs, boots, riding crop and hat, he looked so handsome the sight of him caused Kate to catch her breath.

'Good morning, Monty,' Luke Stratton called to the groom, as he made his way down the steps. 'I must say the mare is looking in exceptionally good form today.'

'Thank you, sir. She does enjoy being groomed.'

'I think you must have a special touch and, like all women, she thoroughly enjoys it.' Luke Stratton chuckled to himself then, seeing the party in the trap, he checked himself. 'I hadn't noticed we had company,' he said.

Moving away from the horse, he made his way across the courtyard.

He greeted them with a friendly smile. 'Good morning, I wasn't expecting visitors.'

'We're here to see Mr Stratton Senior, sir,' Kate said. Then pointing to Annie she added, 'This is my sister, Annie. She's to be taken on as general help to the—'

'Of course … I remember now. I was there when my father mentioned the position to you. It had just slipped my mind.' Luke Stratton offered his hand to Annie. 'Here, let me help you down from the trap.'

Annie looked to Kate. The reassuring smile her sister gave was all she needed.

'I promise I don't bite, unlike my mare over there; she has a right temper,' Luke Stratton said.

Annie suppressed a giggle and, taking his hand, allowed him to help her. With her safely down, he reached out for Kate's hand – the touch of his leather gloved hand on hers made her colour rise. She tried to compose herself, telling herself she mustn't blush.

'The cold wind has reddened your face, Miss Devlin,' he said with a broad smile. 'My father will be along shortly, and a spell in the housekeeper's kitchen will no doubt warm you up.' For a while he held her gaze then, turning to Liam he said, 'You must be the brother of these delightful girls.'

'Yes, sir,' Liam said as he jumped down from the trap. 'Liam Devlin – I work at Heaven Scent Lavender Farm.' He touched his cap.

'So your sister informed me when she came to my office. Tell me, what's it like working for Daniel Groves?'

'He's a good master and an even better friend,' Liam boasted.

'Praise indeed. I shall have to remember that when next our paths cross.' He flashed a look in Kate's direction. 'Ha, here's my father. It's time for me to take my leave.' And with a light touch of his riding crop to his head in salute, he turned and headed back to his mare, only stopping briefly to exchange a polite 'good morning' with his father as they passed each other.

Mr Stratton Senior stopped and waited until his son had mounted his horse and had ridden through the gate leading to the open fields, before addressing his visitors.

'Good morning, Miss Devlin. It is a pleasure to see you.'

Kate, whose eyes had been fixed on the horse and rider, quickly turned to face him. 'Good morning, Mr Stratton,' she replied with a smile. She did like this kindly gentleman.

'I hope you are keeping well.'

'Yes, thank you, sir.'

'Good, now on to the business in hand.'

'Sir, this is my sister, Annie. You asked me to bring her to see you.' Kate put her arm around her sister's shoulder.

'That I did,' he said, then, looking past Kate he said pleasantly, 'So you're Annie? Your sister tells me you like horses. Is that right?'

'Yes, sir, I love all animals.'

'That's good to hear – Monty, the groomsman, is in need of a helper. And so is Mrs Montgomery, our housekeeper. I hope you'll be an asset to both of them.'

A moment's silence prompted Kate to give her sister a gentle nudge to encourage a response. Thankfully, Annie was quick to oblige.

'I shall do my best, sir. I want my brother and sister to be proud of me.'

'That is good to hear, child. Now, let me get Monty over here.' He looked across the courtyard to where the groomsman was standing and called to him. 'Monty, my man, we're in need of your services.'

The groomsman raised his hand in acknowledgment and headed toward them.

'What can I do for you, sir?'

'I need you to take Annie here to the kitchen to meet Mrs Montgomery. Her brother and sister escorted her here today.'

'Certainly, sir.'

'Good man.' He turned to Kate. 'I shall leave you all in the capable hands of Monty and bid you good day.' And with that he turned and headed up to the house.

'Right, miss, if you'd like to follow me.' Monty spoke directly to Annie.

Annie hesitated, and looked at Kate.

Seeing her reluctance, Monty quickly added, 'Your brother and sister are welcome to come with you, if they want.'

'Thank you, Mr—'

'Not Mr – just Monty,' he interrupted, flashing Kate a friendly smile.

'Thank you, Monty. I'd like to meet Mrs Montgomery.'

'Of course, and what about you, young man?' he said, turning to Liam.

'If you don't mind, Monty, I'll stay with the horse. I'd hate for him to be spooked.' He promptly handed Annie's small carpet bag to Kate.

'Good man. I'll get some refreshments sent out to you.'

Monty led the way across the courtyard and around the side of the building to the entrance to the kitchen. Kate and Annie followed.

Luke steered his horse through the gate leading to the open field and, with a small click of his heels on the mare's girth, she began a gentle trot and then with a little more encouragement, the mare pinned her black-tipped ears back and broke into a full gallop. Luke turned his head back to the house in the hope that Kate would be watching his display of horsemanship – only to be disappointed. His father had wasted no time in getting Monty to lead the visitors into the house. It was almost as if he deliberately set out to put distance between Luke and the Devlin girl.

Monty, closely followed by Kate and Annie, entered the large, well-equipped kitchen, and were immediately overcome by the smell of fresh baking. A young golden retriever bounded across the room and went straight to Annie's feet, and nestled against her legs.

Annie squealed with delight as she bent down to stroke him.

'Hello there, come on in, welcome.' A portly, ruddy-faced woman with grey hair tied into a neat bun greeted them.

'Mrs Montgomery,' Monty addressed his wife affectionately, 'this is Annie Devlin, your new charge and alongside, her sister, Miss Kate Devlin. They live in Luton.'

'Pleased to meet you, Miss Devlin ... and you, Annie.' The house-keeper beamed a smile. 'Looks to me as if you've already made a friend in Jasper there, he's not a year old yet and can be quite a handful.'

'He's lovely,' Annie said, crouching down to pet him. Jasper rewarded her with frantic licks to her neck and face. Annie giggled.

'So you've travelled from Luton? That's quite a distance on such a cold day as today. You must be frozen to the bone.'

'Right then, I shall leave you be,' Monty announced. 'Mrs Montgomery, the girls' brother is out in the courtyard, I promised him some refreshments.'

'Consider it done. I shall get Simon here to take him out a scone and some ginger ale.'

'Simon – will – take – it.' The young man standing by the fire-place said this with a smile.

Kate instantly recognized Simon Dobbs, the lad her mother had defended at the market a while back.

'There's a good lad,' Monty said warmly, before turning to Annie. 'And as for you, young lady, after you've settled you might want to head down to the stables to meet the livestock.'

'Thank you. I can't wait,' Annie said enthusiastically.

'Good. And you have a safe trip back, Miss Devlin.' He flashed a friendly smile before turning to leave.

'Here we are, Simon, me lad, take this to the girls' brother out in the courtyard.'

'Yes, Mrs Monty,' Simon said, and taking the small tray from her, limped out the door.

Mrs Monty watched him go. 'He's a good lad, with a heart of gold. I hope you and he can be friends, Annie.' She didn't wait for an answer. 'Right then, I think scones and a hot drink is the order of the day. Come on over to the table, Annie, and take a seat by the fire.'

Annie beamed a smile and, leaving Kate's side, made her way across the room to the seat by the fireplace, with Jasper the dog close at her heels.

It warmed Kate's heart to see her sister look so comfortable in her new surroundings.

'What about you, Kate, can I offer you a little refreshment before your journey home?'

'That's very kind of you, Mrs Montgomery, but I really should be getting back. I only came to see Annie settled and to make sure—'

'To make sure we weren't ogres, eh?' Mrs Montgomery gave an affectionate laugh. 'Are those Annie's things?' The housekeeper pointed to the carpet bag in Kate's hand.

'Yes, just a few items of clothing and a Bible.'

'Good. In a while I shall take her to her room. I've put her in the one across the hall from me and my husband. So rest assured we shall keep a good eye on her. Every Sunday morning we all attend the local church to give thanks to the Lord. Annie will also be allowed one Sunday afternoon off a fortnight.' The housekeeper motioned across to Annie, who was happily tucking in to a hot scone with Jasper at her side, his head nestled on her lap, looking adoringly up at her. 'Annie, as soon as you've finished eating I will show you to your room and, when you're settled, I'll have Simon take you to the stables. You can take Jasper with you, if you want.'

'Thank you, Mrs Montgomery, I'd like that.' Annie turned to Kate and smiled – a smile that said it was all right to leave her.

'I'll be on my way then,' Kate said. 'And if it's all right with you, Mrs Montgomery, I'll call to see my sister when it's her afternoon off. I'm sure my brother will provide my transport.'

'That's fine with me. As I said, every two weeks, preferably around two o'clock after we've eaten and all the chores are done.'

'That's very kind of you. I shall look forward to it. So-long, Annie, see you in two weeks,' Kate said.

'So-long, Kate,' Annie said, reluctantly raising one hand from Jasper to give her sister a wave.

As Kate made her way to the front courtyard, she felt pleased with the way things had gone. Mrs Montgomery seemed a good sort and she was sure Annie would be well cared for. She reached the courtyard to find her brother in deep conversation with Simon Dobbs. The lad was smiling and Liam was shaking his hand as if to seal a deal.

'Liam, I'm sorry I took so long. I needed to make sure that Annie was all right.'

'And by the smile on your face, I take it all went well?'

'Yes. I'm pleased to say it went better than I could have wished.... I see you've not been on your own.'

'No. Simon here kindly brought me a tasty scone and a hot drink. He's a good lad. Simon, this is my sister, Kate,' Liam said.

The lad beamed a smile and said, 'Hello, Kate, I've – seen – you – before.'

'Yes, at the market with my mother. I believe you also knew my pa.'

The lad nodded. The smile was gone from his face to be replaced by a look of sadness and without another word, he grabbed the tray from the trap and headed in the direction of the kitchen.

'Oh dear, I hope I haven't upset him. You two seemed to be getting on so well.'

'I shouldn't think so. The lad's been telling me how sorry he was to learn about Ma and Pa's death. They both seem to have had a soft spot for him.'

'I know, Ma told me.'

'Well, by way of repaying their kindness, he's promised to look after our Annie. We shook on it.'

'I did wonder what the handshake was all about.'

'I did it to make him feel useful. From what I've heard the lad's been dealt a raw deal.'

'I've seen first-hand the way Mr Stratton and Mrs Montgomery are with him. They both seem genuinely fond of the lad.'

'I'm glad. Now, climb aboard,' he said, offering his hand. 'Have you had any more thoughts about calling to see Daniel on the way back?'

'I'd rather not.'

'Sis, you really can't keep putting it off. I hate the thought of you two not speaking. The truth is, you're both as stubborn as each other.'

'I know, and I promise I will find a way to put things right between us ... but not today, eh?'

'All right, but I intend to keep you to your promise,' Liam said with a click of his tongue and a pull on the reins. The horse began to move off. 'Let's get you back to the Proctors', then.'

CHAPTER FIFTEEN

THE NEXT MORNING Kate was up at dawn. She had spent a restless night, trying to think of a way to make it up with Daniel to no avail. As she readied herself for her first day at her new job, she made a positive effort to put all thoughts of Daniel aside, at least for the time being. Today she had a chance to take a huge step forward to a better life. She wished her mother and father could have been here to share the moment with her. She stopped short, taking in a breath. She did that a lot now, always shaken by the realization that both her ma and pa were gone from her forever.

It was such a cold morning. Kate quickened her step in an effort to keep warm. As she approached the factory, much to her surprise, the workforce was already gathered outside, all huddled together. She had expected to be the first there and made a mental note to leave Mrs Proctor's much earlier tomorrow morning.

She arrived at the factory door and was greeted by a sea of faces – all staring at her. Most of the women were strangers to her but a few she could remember seeing at the market.

'Well, if I'm not mistaken, it's the little bonnet maker I met at the market.' One young young woman flashed a smile.

'Yes, the very same, my name's Kate Devlin,' Kate said, returning the smile. It felt good to see a friendly face.

'I'm Ruby Cooper.'

'I remember you – you came to Mrs Proctor's market stall.'

'Once seen, never forgotten,' one of her fellow workers called out. 'At least that's what most of your men-friends say, eh, Ruby?'

'Well, Peggy, I've never been one to hide my light under a bushel now, have I?'

'No. And that's a fact.' The woman laughed – an infectious laugh that had everyone joining in, including Ruby.

When the laughing had subsided, Ruby once again turned to Kate. 'So, how did you get a job here then? I see you didn't need me to put a word in for you.'

'Mr Stratton attended my mother's funeral and he offered me—'

'Offered you what, exactly? I hope you haven't been trading favours with our boss. Because if that's the case, then I'm sure our Ruby would have something to say about that,' the woman called Peggy sniggered.

'Now, I'm sure I don't know what you mean,' Ruby said, trying to look coy.

'Don't you try and act all innocent – you were seen in the Red Lion with Mr Luke last week.'

This was true, for even Kate remembered seeing Ruby and Luke Stratton entering the inn together once.

'I may have bumped into him, but that's all,' Ruby offered by way of explanation.

'Bumped into him, eh? Pull the other—'

At that moment the factory door opened and Peggy was stopped in her tracks.

'All right, you lot, let's have you inside,' an older woman's voice called out.

Kate looked across to see a tall, big-busted woman wearing a long black dress and a large white calico apron. 'Come on, it's time to give your mouths a rest and get your hands working,' she ordered in a loud voice.

As everyone piled in through the doors, Kate stayed put. She didn't know what she was supposed to do or where she should go.

'You must be Kate Devlin,' the woman said.

'Yes, that's right, miss.'

'*Mrs* Hobson, if you please. I'm the forewoman and *I* run the factory floor. Mr Stratton told me to expect you, and gave the instruction that you begin your apprenticeship under the supervision of one of our top girls. So, follow me.'

They entered the factory floor; a huge room with high ceilings divided into sections by wooden partitions.

'There are six departments on the factory floor; the small one at the end is my office. Take heed, workers only set foot in there at my request – usually to be reprimanded for some misdemeanour, a visit you should strive to avoid, do you hear?'

'Yes, Mrs Hobson.' Kate made a mental note never to get on the wrong side of this woman.

'Good. Now, next to my office is the design room, then the stock room, the cutting room, the packing department, the project room and finally, this one just here, is where you will be working.' Before entering the door marked 'Hat Department' the forewoman stopped. 'All the factory floor is overseen by Mr Stratton, who you will address while at work as Mr Luke. He watches our every move from up there in his ivory tower,' she said, raising her eyes to the roof of the building.

Kate looked up to the large glass fronted viewing platform which she imagined was off Mr Stratton's – Mr Luke's office. And as she did so, she saw him staring down at her. He smiled and gave a small salute. She felt her colour rise and looked away.

'I said Mr Luke watches *our* every move, it's not your place to watch *him*, do you understand, girl?'

'Yes, Mrs Hobson. Sorry, Mrs Hobson,' Kate felt she had not got off to a good start. And yet, it seemed almost worth it for a glimpse of Luke Stratton's smile.

'Well, come along, there's work to be done,' the forewoman ordered.

They entered a big room with four long tables; there were eight girls to a table, all busy working with straw-plait.

'As you can see, we have two tables working on the crowns which are then passed to the next two tables where the brims, ribbon trim and bands are added. The forewoman picked up one of the completed straw boaters and examined it. She gave a small nod of approval. 'Completed hats are passed on to the Packing Department at two hourly intervals. Sixteen to twenty a time is what we aim to achieve.'

She led the way to the head of the end table. 'Ruby, this is Kate Devlin, your new apprentice. Mr Luke has given strict instructions that you take her under your wing. He seems to think she has a natural talent and will be quick to learn ... we'll see. Let's hope she's more than just another pretty face, eh?' She then turned to Kate. 'I advise you to take heed of Miss Cooper's instruction. I will, of course, be keeping a close eye on you.' She turned to face her work-force. 'Good morning, ladies, I shall see you all later.' And with that she turned and left.

'Don't you go worrying yourself 'bout Hobson, her bark is worse than her bite,' Ruby said when the forewoman had gone. 'She's good at her job. Nothing gets past her. She examines every hat before it leaves the factory.'

Kate's first day at work had flown by. There was so much to take in. It was all so different from the work she did at Ma's plait school.

'See you tomorrow, Kate,' Ruby called as they left the factory.

'Aye, so-long, young 'un,' the woman called Peggy shouted, 'you'll soon get the hang of it.'

As she headed for the Proctors' house, Kate wished she was going home to her ma's to tell her all about her day. Instead, as she approached Plaiters Way, she caught sight of the burned out dwelling that was number 10. The time had come to look for new digs ... away from Plaiters Way.

The next morning, she left the Proctors' half an hour earlier and although the frost covering the ground meant she had to tread gingerly not to lose her footing, she was determined to get to the factory before the other workers. She needed to show how keen she was.

As she approached the crossroads leading to and from the town, she saw Samson, her uncle's cart-horse. He was hitched to a hay wagon. She remembered how Liam had told her he and Daniel took turns to pick up the workers from town. She held her breath, wondering whose turn it was today. It was then she caught sight of Daniel Groves standing on the top of the hay-wagon, helping girls and women of varying ages up into it.

He looked across and saw her. He smiled and called out a friendly, 'Good morning, fancy seeing you here.'

She returned his smile. 'What a nice surprise. Liam told me of your new venture. How's it going?'

'It's going well … I think. It's early days yet. Are you off to work?'

'Yes, and I'd best be on my way. It's only my second day and I wanted to get there early.'

'Do you think you're going to like it?'

'It's a lot different to the plait school but, as you said, it's early days yet.'

There was an awkward silence.

'Kate?'

'Daniel?'

They spoke in unison and both gave a nervous laugh.

'Kate, I'm sorry I said what I said,' Daniel said.

'Me too,' Kate said.

'Are we still friends?'

'I do hope so. Oh, Daniel, I've so missed our chats.'

'Me too. What time do you finish work? I drop the girls back around five o'clock. Perhaps we could meet and then I could walk you back to the Proctors'. It'll be good to catch up on what's been happening. What do you say?'

'I'd like that. Now I really have to go.'

'You're right. I'd better get a move on, too. If I don't get these girls to work soon, Liam will be sending out a search party. See you this evening.'

'Mr Groves, sir, it be cold enough to freeze the bits off a brass monkey in the back of this wagon. Can we please get a move on?'

Daniel chuckled. 'On my way, girls.'

Kate ran all the rest of the way to her workplace and only just managed to get to the doors as the forewoman was opening them to let the workforce in … so much for making an early start. But she didn't mind, she and Daniel were friends again, and that was far more important than trying to impress the factory girls.

*

With his workforce chatting away in the back of the truck, Daniel headed for his lavender farm. His heart felt lighter than it had for a long while. He had hated falling out with Kate. She was, and always would be his best friend. And if her friendship was all he could have, then that's what he had to settle for.

From day one Kate revelled in her work – Ruby taught her the skills needed to make a straw boater. It felt good to be working the plait and she proved to be a quick learner. Within just two weeks of stitching and shaping crowns, she'd moved on to adding the brims and ribbon trims. Every day she sat at her table next to Ruby and, having been chided by Mrs Hobson not to look up at Mr Luke's office above them, she struggled to heed her warning, but there was the odd occasion when she just couldn't help herself. To see him looking down on them – on her – gave her such a warm feeling, a feeling she couldn't explain. But in contrast she had to swallow the disappointment when she looked up and he was not there.

While Kate enjoyed being at the factory, lodging with the Proctors was proving difficult.

'You're very quiet today. What's up, ducks?' Ruby asked, as she deftly worked the treated straw around the crown of a helmet.

'It's nothing really. I didn't get much sleep again last night, that's all.'

'I'm not surprised. I don't know how you cope sharing a room with Dilly and her brood.'

'I admit it's difficult at times. Especially when it's often midnight before Dilly gets back from Ada Tucker's workshop. It's not Dilly's fault but, once disturbed, I find it hard to get back off to sleep.'

'You could always move out.'

'If only it was that easy. But, as an apprentice, I just don't earn enough to rent a place of my own. Why, I'd need to sell five bonnets a week at the market to even come close.'

'So move in with me.'

'Are you serious?'

'Yes. Since losing our parents to the flu epidemic it's just been my sister and me sharing our rented house. Then, a few weeks ago, my sister up and married and moved to Dunstable. So I'd be glad of the company.'

'I'm not sure ... I'd want to pay my way.'

'Look, why not come home with me after work and take a look at the place? I'm sure you'll like what you see. For one thing, you'd have your own bedroom and, as for paying your way, I'm sure we can sort something out. And anyways, I've a feeling you'll not be my apprentice for long. Mr Luke was right, you've got natural talent.'

The next morning Kate entered the kitchen to find Maude Proctor and tell her of her intention to move out. Maude was at the stone sink peeling potatoes.

'Good morning, Mrs Proctor, might I have a word?'

Maude turned and wiped her wash-red hands on her wrap around paisley patterned apron. She smiled at Kate. 'The kettle is on the boil, have you time for a brew?'

'I'll make time. In fact, if you sit yourself down then I'll fill the tea pot,' Kate offered.

'Thanks, ducks, I could do with a rest. Now what's this word you want?' Maude asked. She was never one for beating about the bush.

With the teapot filled, Kate set it on the table to steep a while and took a seat next to Maude.

'The thing is ... I've been offered a place to live.'

Maude nodded her head. 'I can't say I'm surprised. It's a bit crowded here, eh?'

Kate reached for Maude's hand. 'It's been fine, honestly. I really don't know what Annie and I would have done if you hadn't put us up. It's just ... I need a more permanent place to stay.'

'I understand, ducks. So where are you moving to? And more to the point, who with?'

'It's with Ruby Cooper, the girl I'm apprenticed to. Her sister got married a few weeks ago and moved in with her in-laws, they're well-to-do and have a big house Dunstable way. Anyway, Ruby said if I'd help share the rent, I could move into her small terraced house on Queen Street.'

'It makes sense, I suppose. It's much closer to where you work.'

'I hope you don't think me ungrateful but—'

'Don't be daft,' Maude interrupted. 'You and Annie bunking in with Dilly was only meant to be a stop-gap. With Annie settled up at Leagrove House, I understand your need to move on.'

'Ruby's house is small, but I'll have a big double bedroom and the use of a comfortable kitchen, a parlour and the usual outbuildings for the privy and wash house,' Kate enthused.

'So there'll be plenty of room for Annie, if she ever wants to visit?'

'Yes. As I said, I have a big double bed in my room. That's why I jumped at it.'

'When will you go?'

'I thought this coming Sunday if that's all right with you. As I've only needlework and a few belongings to move, I plan to be ready for when Liam comes to collect me. I'm sure he won't mind if I drop my stuff off at Ruby's, before we visit Annie – our last visit before Christmas.'

Maude looked pensive. 'I know how you'll miss not being at number 10 with your family, especially at this time of year, as will I. It was always a joy for us all to get together and share our Christmas fare.'

Kate gave a heavy sigh. 'I'm dreading my first Christmas without—'

'Well, while I understand Annie has her duties to fulfil up at Leagrove House, I see no reason why you, Liam, Daniel and your friend Ruby, if she's a mind, shouldn't come to us for Christmas Day.'

'Are you sure?'

'Of course I'm sure. The more the merrier.'

'Thank you so much. I can't wait to tell the others. You're such a good friend.' Kate threw her arms around Maude and gave her a big hug.

Maude gently brushed her hand on Kate's cheek. 'You've had a lot to cope with for the most part of this year. I bet you'll be glad to see the back of it. I just hope I've gone a small way in repaying the kindness your dear mother always showed to me and mine.' She gave a heavy sigh. 'I miss your ma so much.'

'Yes, we all do,' Kate said, choking back tears.

Maude nodded. 'Now come here and give this silly old woman another big hug.'

'First, a new job and now new lodgings, what's brought all this on?' Liam asked.

'Liam, I'm grateful to the Proctors' for taking me and Annie in, but now that Annie is settled, I feel the need to move on. Ruby's offer of lodgings couldn't have come at a better time.'

'Who exactly is this Ruby Cooper?'

'She's the one I'm apprenticed to at Stratton's. Liam, I really like her.'

'Well, if you like her, then I'm sure I will, too. Now come on. Let's get you moved before we head for Leagrove House, we don't want to be late for our Annie.'

Before leaving Plaiters Way, Kate took a long look at number 10 – the house that had once been a happy home to her and her family; now with its windows boarded up and fire blackened brickwork, it looked so sad. But then she remembered what her mother always said: 'The only thing you get from looking back is a crick in the neck'. She took a deep breath. It was time to move on.

'Are you ready, sis?'

'Yes. I'm ready.'

'Good.' Liam pulled on the reins and clicked his tongue twice to encourage his horse to move off.

'Now you remember what I said ... don't become strangers, do you hear?' Maude Proctor called out.

'We'll see you soon, I promise,' Kate answered.

As was to be expected at this time of year, the air felt cold and crisp and Kate was glad of the blanket Liam always carried in the cart. In the distance she could hear the peel of church bells, calling the townsfolk to attend the carol service.

As they made their way across George Street, just a few minutes' drive from Queen Street and their destination, there were no

hawkers or drays or heavy wagons today, the roads busy instead
with the splendid carriages, gigs and landaus of the well-to-do, all
dressed in their finery, expertly avoiding the many townsfolk on
foot milling to and fro. It was a day of rest, so men, women and
children, all dressed in their Sunday best, made their way to church
or the park. Kate had the urge to call out to each and every one,
'Make the most of your precious time together', but she stopped
herself. They'd probably think her mad.

'Ruby, this is my brother, Liam,' Kate proudly announced.

'So you're the lad I've been hearing so much about? I'm pleased
to meet you,' Ruby said, extending her hand to him.

Liam didn't move. His eyes were fixed on Ruby in amazement.

'You can shake my hand, I don't bite, you know,' Ruby
prompted.

'Liam, what's wrong with you? Don't stare so,' Kate admonished.

With eyes on Ruby's mass of curly auburn hair, he offered his
hand and gingerly shook hers.

'Sorry, you're just not what I expected and I hope for all our sake
that you're not as wild and scary as you look.'

'Liam! Don't be so cheeky. Ruby, I promise he's not usually this
rude,' Kate apologized.

Ruby chuckled. 'It's all right, Kate. I often have that effect on
folk, especially young men.'

Liam straightened his shoulders and stood tall. 'I'm not young.
I'll soon be sixteen.'

'Sixteen and still wet behind the ears, I'd say. Kate, I like this
brother of yours.' She moved closer to Liam and put her arm around
him. 'Liam, I like folk who speak their mind. I've a feeling we'll get
on well and might even become friends.'

Liam nodded his head and smiled. 'One thing's for sure, I'd
rather be your friend than enemy. What say you, sis?'

The two women caught around him, each placing a kiss on one
of his cheeks.

'I could get used to having two women fawning over me. Kate,
I think your choice of housemate is a good one – she's not scary

really. I can't wait to tell our Annie how you've landed on your feet.'

'I'm glad and, talking of Annie, it's time we were on our way,' Kate said.

Kate and Liam arrived at Leagrove House around 2.30 to find Annie waiting at the gate. She wasn't alone, Jasper the dog was sitting obediently at her feet and Simon Dobbs stood alongside her.

'Kate, Liam, you're here at last. We've been waiting in the freezing cold for ages, haven't we, Simon?'

The boy nodded and smiled at Kate. She smiled back at him. But as she lowered herself from the trap, she couldn't help but notice the way Simon kept looking at Annie. He was obviously fond of her.

'Mrs Montgomery said that if you've a mind, you can come to the kitchen for tea,' Annie told them.

'That'll be nice but first I want to hear how you've been getting on.'

'I'm fine, and with Christmas only a week away, we're all so excited. There's a party planned for Christmas Eve and a special dinner for Christmas Day!'

'That sounds wonderful. Although for my part, I shall miss seeing you on Christmas Day.' Kate saw the frown appear on Annie's face and checked herself. The last thing she wanted was to make her sister feel guilty. 'The good thing is that we have all afternoon together today and I think we should make it as special as we can, don't you?'

Annie beamed at her. 'Yes, I do! I thought we might go for a walk to the top of the hill over there. Kate, once at the top you can see for miles and miles. I remember when we lived in Plaiters Way, our only views were of the scullery, the backyard or the privy. It's so different here – we take the dog for a walk up the hill most days, don't we, Simon?'

Again the boy nodded and smiled.

Kate looked at her sister; her blonde hair gleamed, her blue eyes shone brighter than ever before, and her fair complexion was enhanced by a pair of rosy cheeks – a picture of health and a true beauty. And it wasn't only her looks that had changed. Her appreciation of her new surroundings was obvious. Oh yes, there could be no doubt that country living agreed with her.

'A walk up the hill sounds perfect. Are you coming, Liam?' Kate asked.

'Please come, Liam. Monty said if you tie the horse and trap to that post over there, they'll be quite safe,' Annie pleaded.

'Well then, that's what I'll do. I'll be ready to go as soon as I secure the horse and trap.'

Within minutes, they were on their way and heading for the hilltop. Annie held fast to Kate's hand and chased after Jasper, running excitedly ahead of them, his tongue lolling and ears flapping in the wind. Liam and Simon followed a few yards behind.

'Slow down, Annie, love. I thought you said we could go for a "walk". I'm not used to this,' Kate said, gasping for breath.

'The sooner we get to the top, the sooner you'll be able to see the view. You'll not be disappointed, I promise.'

At last they reached the top. As Kate caught her breath she took in the splendid view of the vast estate; a high fence marked the boundaries, field after field of fertile land surrounding the impressive large residence that was Leagrove House. Annie had not exaggerated. Kate could only imagine what it must have been like to have been brought up in such splendour. Luke Stratton certainly was a man of privilege.

And then as if she'd willed it, Luke Stratton was astride his mare and galloping towards her. As she watched him ride ever closer, she held her breath and she felt sure her heart missed a beat. Within minutes, the horse halted only feet away from her, and the handsome rider expertly dismounted and began to walk toward her.

'Miss Devlin, Liam, what a pleasant surprise.'

Kate tried to speak but no words would come. Thankfully her brother covered the silence.

'Good afternoon, Mr Stratton. My sister and I have just been admiring the wonderful view. We didn't mean to interrupt your ride out.'

'Nonsense, I'm pleased to see you both. Annie, I believe Mrs Montgomery has prepared tea for your visitors.'

'Yes, sir, I was just about to take them to see her.'

'That's good to hear. Annie, if you'd like to go ahead with Simon and your brother, I'll be happy to escort your sister.' He turned to Kate. 'Miss Devlin, though I don't wish to take up too much of your time … I would like a private word.'

Kate nodded.

While Annie, Simon and the energetic Jasper ran down the hill, Liam held back.

'I'll walk on slowly, sis, and wait for you at the bottom,' he said, with a look of brotherly concern.

'Good man, I'll not keep her long,' Luke Stratton assured him.

As Liam turned to make his way down the slope, Luke Stratton indicated that they should do the same and holding fast to his mare's reins, he walked alongside Kate, his wide smile and blue eyes far too close for comfort.

'Miss Devlin, how are you finding working at our factory? Does it meet with your expectations?'

She felt instantly deflated by his tone of voice, a tone often used by employer to employee. But what had she expected?

'Yes, sir, I'm really enjoying working with Ruby and learning the art of making straw boaters.'

'But is it enough of a challenge for you? I sensed when you first came to see me an ambition I rarely see in one so young.'

'You're right, sir. I do have ambition, but at present I enjoy what I do and consider myself lucky to be able to earn enough to provide for my family.'

'In the short term, perhaps, but I've this feeling that if I'm to keep you in my employ, I'll need to keep your interest. Still, enough of that, we're nearly at the bottom and I can see your brother waiting for you.' He took her hand in his. 'Thank you, Miss Devlin. I've enjoyed our little chat. Now you go and enjoy the rest of your day.' He raised her hand and brushed his lips on her skin. 'Hands as clever and lovely as these should be protected with velvet gloves … one day, eh?' The tender look he gave her left her confused.

'What was all that about and should he be kissing your hand like that?' Liam demanded.

'Don't worry, everything's fine. We just talked about work. The kiss on the hand was only a kind gesture.' As she spoke the words, she knew the kiss had meant a lot more to her.

For Kate, the rest of the afternoon added to her feeling of contentment. Mrs Montgomery had prepared a special tea of ham sandwiches, mince pies and ginger beer, and afterwards, with Monty at the piano, they all sang along to Christmas carols.

'I really enjoyed today, did you?' Kate asked Liam as they headed for Luton Town.

'Yes it was good ... especially the lovely spread that Mrs Montgomery put on.'

Kate laughed. 'You've always loved your food. I agree, though, it was very good. The Montgomerys are such a warm, genuine couple. You only have to look at Annie to see how happy and settled she is with them. It's taken such a weight off my mind.'

CHAPTER SIXTEEN

IT WAS MONDAY – less than a week before Christmas and the factory workers were in high spirits.

'While I understand your excitement in anticipation of your seasonal break, you still have to work until leaving on Saturday. No slacking, do you hear?' Mrs Hobson instructed.

'Yes, Mrs Hobson,' the workforce replied in unison.

'Just think, after Saturday comes Christmas Eve, then Christmas Day and Boxing Day – three whole days off work!' Ruby said.

A screech of excitement went around the factory floor.

'All right, you lot, that's enough. And just so you know … I'll expect every one of you here first thing Wednesday morning. No excuses, is that clear?'

The factory floor became eerily silent.

'Is that clear?' Mrs Hobson repeated loudly.

'Yes, Mrs Hobson!' the workers called out.

It was the end of day at the factory and everyone was preparing to leave, when Mrs Hobson approached Ruby and Kate.

'Girls, Mr Luke has asked to see the two of you in his office. So come with me, it won't do to keep him waiting,' Mrs Hobson advised, leading the way to the main office.

Minutes later, they were stood in Mr Luke's office. He was standing at the window, dressed in a black frock coat and dark grey trousers, looking down onto George Street.

'The weather has changed. I wouldn't be surprised if we had a fall of snow in time for Christmas. What do you think, Mrs Hobson?'

he asked, turning to face her, showing off a light grey waistcoat and a black stock knotted beneath a white wing collar.

'I think you could be right, sir, although I hope not. At my age the cold weather goes right to me bones.'

'I'm afraid we have no control over it,' he said as he walked to his desk. 'Ladies, please, take a seat.'

Mrs Hobson proceeded to pull two chairs together and beckoned Ruby and Kate to sit. She chose to stand.

Kate noticed Ruby's attempt to make eye contact with Luke Stratton, but he was having none of it. His eyes were firmly fixed on the forewoman.

'Mrs Hobson, I've called you here today to discuss one of our annual summer orders. Even though it's Christmas, I strongly believe we should plan ahead and, to this end, I want to focus on fulfilling the summer order for 200 police straw helmets – worn throughout the summer months by constabularies all over the country.'

'Beg your pardon, Mr Luke, but it's been normal to start this order the beginning of March.'

'I believe that's far too late. This year, I want to create a new department and to start work on the helmets after the Christmas break, and I want Ruby and Kate here assigned to it.'

Kate felt her colour rise; this was the first time he'd used her Christian name.

He looked at her and smiled. 'Kate, as expected, under Ruby's guidance, you have completed your apprenticeship and your commitment is to be applauded. Mrs Hobson has only good things to say about you. That's why I have chosen you to work with Ruby to fulfil this prestigious order.'

'But, sir, do you think it wise? We usually have a table of eight girls working on this particular order.' Mrs Hobson sounded concerned.

'Yes, eight girls with a lot of chatter to slow down production.'

'And may I ask what the rest of the department will be doing, while Ruby and Kate tackle this project?'

'The other girls will carry on making straw boaters to increase our stock. I need to stay ahead of my rivals.' He then turned to

Kate and Ruby. 'Now, what do you say, girls, are you up for the challenge?'

Kate and Ruby looked to one another and nodded. 'Yes, we are,' they said in unison.

'Kate, as Ruby already knows, the one thing I expect above all is your loyalty to this company. Isn't that right, Ruby?'

'Always, Mr Luke,' she said coyly, deliberately pouting her lips.

This caused Luke Stratton to clear his throat before continuing, 'Of course, both your wages will reflect your new position. Ruby, I expect you to take control of this particular order.'

'You mean be in charge?'

'Yes, although Mrs Hobson will need to inspect each helmet before being moved on for packing.'

Kate was mortified by the way Ruby blatantly flirted with her boss. Had Kate imagined his embarrassment or was that just wishful thinking on her part?

It was nearing ten o'clock and the girls were preparing to go to their beds.

'I doubt if I'll get a wink of sleep tonight,' Kate said. 'I'm so excited about our new project. I bet you are, too.'

'You do know making two hundred helmets means a lot of hard work, but you're right to be excited, as am I. It's a big feather in our cap,' she giggled. 'Mind you, there's to be no feathers on the police helmets.'

This made Kate laugh. 'Now that's something I'd like to see.'

Ruby touched Kate's hand and smiled. 'Kate, I'm really glad you're here. I hope we can be good friends.'

Kate hesitated. While part of her wanted to tell her new house-mate how much she welcomed her friendship, something niggled at her – a question she needed to ask so, taking a deep breath, she turned to Ruby.

'Ruby, can I ask you something?'

Ruby shrugged her shoulders. 'Depends what it is.'

'It's about the way the factory girls always make jokes about you and Mr Luke.'

'It don't bother me none, they're only jealous.'

Kate remembered the day she saw Luke Stratton and Ruby enter the Red Lion together. 'So it's true what they say then? You two are—'

'What, friends or ... maybe even lovers?' She gave an exaggerated laugh. 'I can't believe what you're asking.'

'I'm sorry. Please forget I asked.'

'Not likely. You've got me wondering on your reason for asking. Could it be that you've got *your* eye on him? If so, be warned, Luke Stratton is a wild one. I don't think there's any *one* girl who could tie him down, especially one with no experience of men's ways.'

'And you don't mind that?'

'No. I understand a man's needs. And yes, Luke Stratton and I have had some *fun*. No ties. No commitment. It's his way.'

Kate felt sick to her stomach at the thought of them having some *fun*, as Ruby called it, but she pressed on. 'So it's not love then?'

Ruby gave another loud laugh. 'My dear girl, if it's love you're looking for, then my advice is to stick with the Groves lad. Now don't look so surprised. I saw the two of you at the crossroads the other day. I thought him quite handsome in a rugged sort of way, and from what I hear, a man with prospects.'

'I think of Daniel as an older brother.' She gave a heavy sigh. 'My ma and pa really liked him and appreciated the way he took our Liam under his wing. He's a true friend.'

'He sounds a good man. It's not often a girl finds a true man friend. Most men want more than friendship, if you know what I mean.' She gave a knowing wink.

'Yes, he is,' Kate said. She didn't mention how Daniel had indeed wanted more. Was Ruby right? Did *all* men expect more? She banished that thought from her mind. She and Daniel had made up and were again the best of friends. 'And in answer to your question, Ruby Cooper, I *do not* have my eye on Mr Luke. I was just curious, that's all,' she lied.

Ruby yawned. 'Come on, I think that's enough home truths for one night.'

'I think I'll call and see Maude Proctor after work tomorrow and tell her our good news,' Kate said as they headed upstairs.

'Good idea. And please say a big thank you from me for the invitation on Christmas Day. I'd much rather spend it with you and yours than with my sister and her stuck-up new family.'

The next evening Kate left the factory and headed in the direction of Plaiters Way. And as she approached the crossroads, she was pleased to see Daniel standing alongside his hay-wagon.

'I've just dropped my workers off and I thought I'd wait to give you a lift back to Maude Proctor's, always assuming that's where you're heading.' He was frowning.

Kate thought he seemed in a strange mood and wondered if he'd heard about her move. She hoped not. She wanted to be the one to tell him.

'Yes, I'm just on my way to *visit* the Proctors. The thing is, Daniel, I don't live there anymore. I—'

Daniel's blue eyes stared into hers. 'So it's right what Liam tells me? You've actually moved in with Ruby Cooper?' He clipped his words.

'Yes, you sound as if you don't approve.' His reaction surprised her.

'I don't. In my mind, you could have made a much better choice of lodgings.'

'How can you say that? Do you even know Ruby?' Kate demanded.

'Let's just say I know of her – a bit free with her favours, some say.'

'And when did you start listening to gossip? I'll have you know that Ruby Cooper is a very hard-working, generous person and—'

'And from what I hear, a person of low morals,' he interrupted.

'That's so unfair. If you took the time to get to know her—'

'I have it on good authority that your precious Luke Stratton knows her *very* well.'

'As her employer, I'd think it strange if he didn't,' she said, in defence of both Ruby and Luke Stratton.

'Are you really that naïve? Take it from me, Ruby Cooper is

nothing but trouble.'

'Oh I am, am I?' Ruby's voice came from behind.

'Ruby, I'm sorry, this is my friend, Daniel Groves.' Kate's voice sounded every bit as embarrassed as she felt.

'I guessed as much. I saw you together the other evening, remember?' Ruby's eyes fixed themselves on Daniel.

'Daniel, this is Ruby Cooper, the person I lodge with. I had hoped you two could be friends—'

'He'd need to apologize first. I'd like to know what right you have to blacken my name,' Ruby demanded, her piercing green eyes staring defiantly into his.

Daniel appeared taken aback. 'I was simply looking out for Kate. I didn't mean—'

'What, didn't mean for me to hear? And there was I, telling Kate how lucky she was to have you as a friend. Well, I take it all back. A true friend doesn't question who the other may talk to or, for that matter, live with. It sounds to me as if you want to run her life.' She didn't wait for a reply. 'I'll see you back at the house, Kate.'

Kate watched her storm off.

'Daniel, how could you be so rude? Ruby is my friend.'

'I'm sorry. I—'

'You just can't help yourself, can you? When are you going to stop trying to live my life for me? Ruby's right ... a true friend just wouldn't do that.'

'Kate, I really don't want to quarrel with you – we've only just made up,' his voice pleaded with her.

'Neither do I, but this time, saying sorry to me isn't enough, you need to apologize to Ruby. Now, I'm off to see Mrs Proctor.' Kate made to walk away.

Daniel reached out and caught her arm. 'Kate, I'm sorry. I know you're right ... you're a grown woman and it's time I stopped looking out for you.'

The tender way he looked at her made her heart melt, reminding her of the closeness they shared. 'Daniel, I hope you never stop looking out for me. It's just ... sometimes you take things ... too far.' She leaned towards him and placed a soft kiss on his cheek.

He beamed a smile. 'Does this mean we're still friends?'

She shook her head and sighed. 'Yes, I suppose so. But I meant what I said about apologizing to Ruby.'

As Daniel headed slowly out of town with his hay-wagon, he reflected on his behaviour earlier. He came to the decision that both Kate and Ruby were right. He had been wrong to say what he had about Ruby. The truth was, when Liam told him about Kate's move to Queen Street, he'd felt aggrieved at not having heard the news from Kate. In his anger, perhaps he had been too eager to listen to the gossip amongst his employees. The question was, having done Kate's new friend an injustice, how could he rectify it? He smiled to himself. One thing was sure, it wouldn't be easy. Ruby Cooper was quite a girl; with long, dark-auburn hair allowed to hang loose, a face sun-kissed with freckles and large green eyes, she looked almost wild with a temper to match. The thing was, he doubted Ruby would readily accept his apology. But there was only one way to find out. He instantly pulled on the reins and clicked his tongue.

'Come on, Samson, we need to make a detour before heading to the farm.' Daniel expertly turned the wagon in the direction of Queen Street and Ruby's house.

Ruby had just arrived at her front door when she saw Daniel Groves's hay-wagon enter her street. With her front door key in hand, she watched him approach and halt the wagon outside her house.

'If you've come to see Kate, she's not here,' she called.

'I know. She told me she was going to see Maude Proctor.' He stepped down from the wagon. 'It's you I've come to see,' he said, walking towards her.

Ruby thought his voice sounded different, nowhere near as confident or abrupt as earlier. 'Is that so? And what business would you have with someone with such low morals?' She hoped her voice sounded as cutting as intended.

'I've come to apologize to you. I spoke out of turn earlier. I should never have listened to the gossips who work for me ... I'm truly sorry.'

'And that's it? You say sorry and that makes everything all right, does it?' She turned her back on him and proceeded to open her front door, glad he couldn't see the smile on her face – a smile that said she would accept his apology, but not yet.

'What more can I say? I knew you wouldn't make this easy but—' He stopped.

Ruby turned to face him, her smile even wider.

'Ruby Cooper, are you playing games with me?' He gave a low chuckle. 'I suppose it's what I deserve.'

'You're right there, but at the risk of fuelling the gossips and denting my reputation even more, I suppose you'd better come inside.'

'I'll risk the gossips if you will.' He laughed and made an exaggerated bow.

'The truth is, I really don't care what the gossips say. What I do is my own business, and they can all go to hell.'

He believed she meant what she said. He was quickly finding out how outspoken Ruby Cooper was.

Ruby went straight to the pantry and reached for a porter of ale and two pewter mugs. She sat at the kitchen table and beckoned for Daniel to join her.

'Now, regarding my morals,' she said, handing him a mug of ale. 'I admit to being able to recognize genuine attraction when I see it and in my mind, life's too short to stand on ceremony.' She raised her mug to his. 'For instance, let's take the way you look at *our* Kate and hang on her every word.'

'Is it that obvious?'

'Yes.' She stared into his lovely eyes and felt an instant bond with this caring man. 'So what do you intend to do about it?'

'Nothing.' He took a long sip of ale. 'Kate has made it blatantly clear that she only wants us to be friends.'

'You don't look to me like a man who'd give up so easily.' Ruby topped up their mugs with ale.

'Thank you,' he said. The ale tasted good. 'It was never my intention to give up, but a man can be turned down only so many times.' He wondered if it was the ale that was making him talk so openly with a girl he'd just met.

'Well, Daniel Groves, I've a plan that might change all that. It's time to make Kate Devlin sit up and take notice.'

'What, of me? I can't see that ever happening.'

She chuckled. 'Trust me, there's a first time for everything,'

Kate returned to the house to find Ruby in the kitchen reading the *Luton Weekly Journal;* the warm glow of the fire was a welcome sight. It was cold outside.

'So you're back then?' Ruby gently set the newspaper to one side.

'Ruby, I'm sorry for Daniel's behaviour earlier. I don't know what came over him.' And to Kate's surprise her friend flashed a wide smile. 'Ruby, why the smile? I thought you'd be furious.'

'I'll explain later, but first I want to hear how your visit to the Proctors' went. What did Maude have to say about our promotion?'

'I decided not to tell Maude about our new project. Her daughter, Dilly, is having a hard time of it working for Ada Tucker. It didn't feel right to tell her about our good fortune – it would have felt like rubbing salt in her wound. So I just stayed for a chat. She seemed in better spirits when I left.'

'I'm glad you cheered her up. Anyway Mr Luke did tell us not to mention our promotion to the other workers. He plans to announce it after Christmas.'

'I'd forgotten that. Maude's not the best at keeping secrets. Now what's for supper? I'm starving.'

'I thought we could warm the leftover stew from yesterday with bread and dripping and some ale.'

'Sounds good to me, and while we're eating, perhaps you'd like to tell me what happened while I was away.'

The hot stew hit the spot for Kate and warmed her. However, Ruby seemed to have lost her appetite.

'Come on, Ruby, you'd best tell me what's happened. It must have been something bad to turn you off your food,' Kate pressed her.

'It wasn't bad ... in fact, the opposite.'

'Well, I'm waiting.'

'Kate, while you were out, I had a visitor. It was Daniel Groves.'

'Daniel's been here, really? I hope he came to apologize?'

'Yes, he did. And I accepted. He did seem genuinely sorry. So I asked him in and we shared a porter of ale.'

'I'm glad. Did he stay long?'

'About an hour, the time went quickly … he's so easy to talk to.' Ruby's green eyes stared into Kate's. 'Kate, I really like him.'

For a moment, Kate was dumbstruck.

'I don't understand. When I left for the Proctors' you two were at loggerheads. So what changed?' Kate demanded.

'It changed the minute I looked into his sapphire-blue eyes. I couldn't believe that such a handsome man didn't have a love in his life. You have to admit he'd be a good catch for any woman.'

'Ruby Cooper, I hope you're not intending to play fast and loose with him. Daniel's very dear to me and I wouldn't want him hurt.'

'That's not my intention, but I would like to get to know him better.'

'Would you now?' Kate shook her head in disbelief.

'Kate, you sound annoyed. I thought you wanted us to be friends.'

'I do. It's just hard for me to—'

'To what, share him? Kate, I've heard you talk about Daniel enough to know he's not like other men. How many times have you told me what a caring and considerate man he is? Unlike the men who only want women for one thing – men like Luke Stratton.'

To hear Ruby speak of Luke Stratton this way cut Kate to the quick. 'I don't know why you feel the need to bring Luke Stratton into this.' Kate's voice was raised.

'Kate, I'm sorry.' Ruby reached out and gently squeezed Kate's hand. 'It's not my intention to hurt you, I know how much you like Luke Stratton, but you have to see that Daniel Groves is the much better man.'

Kate had little or no argument with that. After all, Ruby knew Luke Stratton better than she did. And that fact hurt her even more. 'I agree that Daniel *is* a special person but that doesn't give you the right to go around slandering others. Daniel's my friend and we've always been protective of each other.'

'I understand. For a moment there, I thought you sounded jealous. If so, may I remind you that you chose to turn him down.'

The smile on Ruby's face was broad and friendly, but there was something else about it that Kate couldn't quite fathom. 'I don't need reminding and believe me when I say I'm really not jealous. Now please, let's change the subject and have our supper.'

It was dusk and the light was fading as Daniel made his way back to the farm and although there was a distinct chill in the air, all he felt was a warm glow. He'd enjoyed his time with Ruby. She was a good listener, although the fact that she'd guessed his true feelings for Kate made him a little uncomfortable. And although he'd agreed to go along with her 'plan', he really didn't believe that Kate could ever be jealous. Ruby had said it was worth a try. Ruby Cooper was quite something and a true friend to Kate. He felt guilty for having wrongly judged her.

In bed later that night, Kate had time to reflect on what Ruby had told her about Daniel and it made her put into question her own feelings for him. Ruby had touched a nerve because Kate had indeed felt a tinge of jealousy. But what right did she have to feel jealous of Daniel with another girl? For months now the only man in her thoughts had been Luke Stratton. Ignoring everything Ruby had said about him, she lay in her bed and imagined what it would be like to have Luke Stratton next to her, kissing her, caressing her and ... She hid her head under the sheet, not wanting her thoughts to get out ... not wanting anyone to know that she was capable of such thoughts.

The next day at work, Kate decided to keep herself to herself, afraid she might give away to Ruby and the rest of the girls her secret thoughts of Luke Stratton. She scolded herself for the fanciful thoughts in her head. Added to this, she had whatever was going on between Daniel and Ruby playing on her mind.

'What's up with you today, cat got your tongue?' Ruby

whispered. 'I hope you're not dwelling on what I said about Daniel yesterday.'

'It's nothing to do with Daniel or you. I've a bit of a headache, that's all,' she lied.

'If you say so, but this is not like you. Do you think you could be sickening for something? We don't want you ill over Christmas.'

'I'm fine, Ruby. Now please can I get on with my work?'

Kate didn't want her friend asking any more questions. Oh yes, she was definitely sickening for something – something she knew was out of reach. She looked up to Luke Stratton's office. Mrs Hobson had told them that he was away on business and was due to return on Saturday – the last day before their Christmas break.

'Be careful, Kate,' Ruby whispered.

'What do you mean?' Kate blushed.

'I know the signs. You've gone and fallen for him, haven't you?'

Kate shook her head in denial.

'It's all right, Kate. Just be on your guard, you'd never hear the end of it if the other girls found out.'

The last thing Kate wanted was for anyone to guess how attracted she was to Luke Stratton. Unlike Ruby, Kate could not stand the embarrassment if she became the butt of the factory girls' jokes.

'There's nothing to find out. He's never ... it's just me being silly,' Kate whispered.

'I know. I doubt there's a girl here that hasn't felt the same, he's a very attractive man.'

Kate knew her friend was trying to help, but what she said about the other girls hurt. And how could Ruby know when she didn't really know herself?

CHAPTER SEVENTEEN

IT WAS SATURDAY evening and the girls were preparing to leave the factory. They were all excited. This was the start of their Christmas break. And after days of resisting looking up toward Mr Luke's 'ivory tower', Kate finally succumbed. He was staring down at her. She held his gaze and he was the first to look away.

As she made her way to the end of the line waiting to leave the factory, she heard his voice.

'Miss Devlin – Kate, might I have a word?' Luke Stratton asked.

Ruby and the other girls turned and one of the girls called out, 'What have you got that the rest of us haven't then, Kate?'

'Perhaps she's doing a bit of *overtime* with the boss, if you get my meaning ... How do you feel about someone else getting the *overtime*, Ruby?'

The other girls laughed.

'Isn't it sad that none of you have ever been offered overtime,' Ruby was quick to answer.

'Come on, girls. Get a move on and I suggest you put a stop to thisvulgar banter. There's always a chance that some of you might not have a job to come back to after Christmas,' Mrs Hobson advised.

This instantly silenced the girls and they quickly made their exit.

Kate was mortified by the girls' comments.

Luke Stratton approached her. 'I'm sorry, Kate. It was not my intention to embarrass you in front of the workforce.' He spoke quietly, his dark eyes intent on hers.

'It's all right. I don't mind,' she lied.

'I think you do. But I just wanted to see you to give you this gift.'
He handed her a long rectangular box.

'A gift? I ...'

'Please open it. I'd like to know the gift meets with your
approval.'

She slowly opened the box and lifted the white tissue paper that
covered a pair of midnight blue velvet gloves. She gasped at the sight
of them. 'They're beautiful, thank you.'

'Try them on. I guessed the size. I do hope they fit.'

She fumbled to remove them from the box.

'Let me help,' he said. Taking the box from her, he handed her
the right glove and then the left. All the time his eyes continued to
watch her.

The velvet gloves fitted perfectly and felt soft to the touch. 'I've
never had anything so lovely in my life. Thank you, Mr Luke, but
I'm not sure I should accept such a generous gift.'

'Please. The other day when you were up at Leagrove, I mentioned that your hands should have a pair of velvet gloves ... well,
now you do.'

'But—' she made to protest.

'There's no but. I understand your reluctance to accept a gift
from me, especially after what your co-workers suggested. Kate, rest
assured, I want nothing in return – no, that's not true.'

Kate held her breath, afraid of what he might say next.

'What I would like is for you to think of me as your friend.'

Kate was still hesitant. What was it Ruby had said about men-
friends always wanting more?

'Kate, I know how difficult this first Christmas without your
parents must be. These gloves, while obviously for you, are also a
thank you for the loyalty your family has shown this company over
the years.'

'My parents always thought highly of both you and your father.
Thank you for the gloves, I shall cherish them.'

'Good. May I ask what you're doing for Christmas?'

'With our Annie spending Christmas up at Leagrove House,
Liam, Daniel and I have been invited to spend Christmas Day at

the Proctors' – our old neighbours in Plaiter's Way.' As she said it she wondered why she hadn't mentioned that Ruby was also joining them. Had she secretly wanted him to think she and Daniel were...? 'I'm glad you'll have your brother and close friends around you.' He leaned forward, his face almost touching hers.

She held her breath, willing him to kiss her. Instead he took her hand. 'I'll not keep you any longer, I'm sure you have lots to do in preparation for the festivities.'

She felt deflated, she'd hoped for – for what exactly? Why couldn't she get it into her head that he was her employer and nothing more?

'Yes, I'd best be on my way. Thank you again for the gloves.' She made herself turn from him and head out the factory door.

For a while Luke Stratton didn't move, he just stared at the factory door. Kate Devlin had long gone and another opportunity missed. He longed to take her in his arms, to kiss her, to hold her, to bed her and have her willingly respond to his every wish. He shook his head. What was he thinking of? She was in his employ and hadn't his father warned him off? But where Kate Devlin was concerned he couldn't help himself. He ached for her, and the thought of her sharing Christmas with Daniel Groves made him angry. In truth, he knew he had no right to such feelings. His Christmas was already planned out for him....

'Don't forget that the Pendletons are due to arrive early Christmas Eve. I trust you'll be here to welcome them,' his father had said over breakfast.

'Yes, Father. I'm looking forward to their visit,' Luke said, in an attempt to humour his father.

'Good. And there's to be no sloping off into town while they are here. Luton is strictly off limits. Is that clear?'

'Yes, Father,' Luke answered through gritted teeth. He knew how important his betrothal to Caroline Pendleton was to both families. For his father, having a wealthy banker related to them would indeed be an asset. And for the Pendleton family securing a connection with the well-established Luton Hat Company would ensure growth.

Luke was in no way against the betrothal or subsequent marriage. Caroline Pendleton was an exquisitely beautiful young
woman and the fact that her father was hugely wealthy was an
added bonus. But Caroline was no Kate Devlin and in another life
… perhaps things could be different. The truth was, he wasn't about
to cross his father and risk being disinherited. After all, the girl *was*
in his employ and in his father's eyes, this made her totally unsuit-
able. One thing was for sure, Kate Devlin was an itch he needed to
scratch … betrothed or not.

When Kate returned to the house, Ruby couldn't wait to question
her.

'What was all that about? Why did Mr Luke want to see you?'

'He wanted to give me these.' Kate proudly held out her gloved
hands.

Ruby's eyes opened wide. 'Kate, they're lovely. But why would he
single you out?'

Kate couldn't fail to notice how peeved her friend looked. Did
she still hanker after their boss? And if so, what was her real interest in Daniel?

'It wouldn't do to let on to the girls in the factory that he gave
you a Christmas gift, they'd be up in arms,' Ruby quipped.

'I've no intention of telling them and I'll thank you not to
mention it, either. It's none of their business. I only told you because
you're my friend.'

'I'll not breathe a word, but I'm puzzled. Why you? Is there
something you're not telling me? Are you and he—'

'No, definitely not. He said they were in appreciation of my
parents' loyalty in providing straw-plait to the Stratton Company
for so many years. He also said he understood how difficult this
first Christmas without them must be.'

'Well, if that's the truth, then it was a nice gesture. But I'll repeat
what I said earlier, I've seen the way you look at him. Be careful,
Kate.' Ruby took Kate's hand in hers. 'I don't want to see you hurt.'

Kate was touched. 'I know and thank you, you're a true friend.'
Even if you've taken a shine to my Daniel, Kate thought but didn't

say out loud. 'And yes, you're right, I do like Luke Stratton, but only as my employer. Now can that be the end of it?'

'All right, you win.' Ruby smiled.

'Good. Now, with the four of us invited to the Proctors on Christmas Day, I thought I'd invite Liam and Daniel to drive over to us early Christmas morning. What do you think?'

Ruby beamed at her. 'I'm all for Daniel ... and Liam, calling early Christmas morning ... in fact the earlier the better!'

It was obvious to Kate that Ruby was eager to see Daniel again and she suddenly felt concerned for him.

CHAPTER EIGHTEEN

'COME AWAY FROM the window, Ruby. They'll not come any sooner by you watching the street.'

'I'm that excited, Kate. It feels good to be spending Christmas Day with friends. My sister didn't even ask what I was doing for Christmas.' She gave a deep sigh.

Kate looked at Ruby and felt a tug at her heart. Ruby Cooper was not as tough as she made out. 'Well, for my part I feel it's our gain and your sister's loss. Now smile. It's Christmas Day!'

Ruby gave an exaggerated smile. 'Will that do?'

Kate chuckled. 'Yes. That'll do.'

Ruby threw her arms around Kate and hugged her. 'Thank you,' she whispered. 'Now if it's all the same to you, I'm going back to watch for Liam and Daniel in the window.'

Kate shook her head. 'All right, if you insist.'

'Oh, Kate, I can see their trap. Come on, let's go and welcome them,' she said, as she headed down the hall.

Kate followed. She had never seen this side of Ruby before. It set her thinking that maybe she was right for Daniel after all. But it still made her uncomfortable.

Minutes later, Daniel and Liam stood at the front door, both dressed in their Sunday best.

'A merry Christmas to you both,' Ruby gushed. 'How lucky are we, Kate, to have two such handsome men to spend our day with?'

Kate noticed the way Ruby's eyes fixed on Daniel's. Kate thought Daniel looked embarrassed, but then it quickly changed and when he smiled at Ruby, there was a definite glint in his eye. Kate felt …

what exactly?

'Behave yourself, Ruby. Just remember, I've known these two a long time and with a compliment like that there'll be no living with them,' Kate said.

'Merry Christmas, ladies, and can I say how pretty you both look?' Daniel nudged Liam. 'What say you, Liam?'

'I suppose so. Now is there any chance of us going inside? It's freezing out here.' Liam gave an exaggerated shiver.

'Not before you and Daniel give me a big Christmas hug,' Kate demanded.

Liam and Daniel obliged, but Kate couldn't fail to notice Daniel's awkwardness toward her.

'Now can we go inside?' Liam pestered.

'Of course you can. Come on in, we've mulled wine warming on the hob,' Ruby said.

Once inside, Daniel went to his pockets and produced a few bags of dried lavender and a bottle of fragrant oil. 'Liam and I thought you girls might like to sample our products.'

'Thank you,' Ruby said, as she picked up one of the bags and read the name on the front. '*Heaven Scent,* I'm sure it is.'

'Thank you, we shall use them on our next bath night. Now who's for a mug of mulled wine?' Kate asked.

With the wine poured, Kate watched as Ruby edged closer to Daniel.

'I think you two making up is the best Christmas present I could have.' Kate smiled.

'I didn't even know they'd fallen out. When was this?' Liam asked.

'About a week ago, but then Daniel saw sense and called on Ruby to apologize. Isn't that right, Daniel?' Her eyes stared into his.

'Yes, on your strict instructions if I remember rightly.' He returned her stare.

'And for once you listened me,' Kate teased.

Daniel's eyes darted from Ruby to Kate and then back to Ruby.

'What did you fall out about?' Liam asked.

'Let's just say Daniel and I started off on the wrong foot and now we've decided to be friends.' Ruby looked pleased with herself.

Kate noticed how relieved Daniel looked. It was almost as if he hadn't wanted to be the one to answer.

'And that's it?' Liam looked puzzled.

Daniel and Ruby looked at each other and smiled. 'Yep!' they answered in unison.

'How do you feel about this, sis?'

'I'm really happy they're friends. Now come on, let's raise a toast to family, and friends.' Kate poured them each some mulled wine. She swallowed hers in one go. Liam, Daniel and Ruby followed suit.

'I think it's time we headed to the Proctors',' Kate prompted as she picked up the wicker basket. 'Ruby and I baked a ham with cloves and honey – our contribution to Maude's Christmas table.'

'And I have one of my mother's Christmas puddings and a bottle of port wine in the trap. So with Liam's flagon of ale, I'm sure we'll have a right feast.'

They were soon on their way and Kate, Ruby and Daniel huddled together on the front seat and Liam held onto the billboard in the back. Kate couldn't help but notice how Ruby's eyes followed Daniel's every move.

'This'll be the first Christmas without Ma and Pa, and it doesn't half feel strange not having Annie with us. I do hope she's all right.'

'Liam, you were there when she told us about the party and the special dinner organized for the workers. I'm sure she'll have a great time.'

Maude Proctor and her family welcomed them with open arms. They ate a hearty meal and later on played charades. Kate and Dilly teamed up to sing a few carols. Dilly seemed in good spirits, even though Ada Jackson had insisted her workforce returned on Boxing Day. As the girls caught up with news, it was almost like old times. Jake Proctor, Daniel and Liam played cards for matchsticks, while the children built with their wooden bricks on the floor.

Kate had the distinct impression that Daniel was avoiding Ruby. It was as if he didn't want the Proctors to know about their new friendship. She found this a bit strange, although that said, it did turn out to be an immensely enjoyable family day but all too soon it was time for them to go.

'It's been a lovely day and thanks for inviting us, but I think we should be on our way. I don't like travelling too late at night with the trap.' Daniel flashed a smile to Ruby and Kate. 'And as you know, Liam and I have precious cargo to drop off at Queen Street before we head back to the farm.'

'You're right there, lad. Today has been a grand day. It's been a pleasure having the four of you here with us. Isn't that right, Jake?'

'It has,' Jake Proctor agreed. 'Mind you, I'm not too happy at being white-washed at cards!'

They all laughed.

'Daniel, before we go, I just want to take a walk to number 10. Mrs Proctor, I hear our old house has been sold at auction, any idea who's bought it?'

Maude shook her head. 'No one seems to know. Does it upset you to think of someone else living there, child?'

'No. Not really. As much as I'd like to turn the clock back, I know it's out of the question. I just want to take a look at the old place.'

'I'll come with you,' Daniel said.

'Thanks. I'd like that.'

Ruby nodded and smiled. 'Yes, you two go along. Liam and I will go and wait by the trap.'

'Here, Ruby. Take this jar of my homemade preserve. I made so much we'll be eating it for a year!' Maude enthused.

'Thank you, you're too kind,' Ruby said, placing a soft kiss on Maude's face.

'Get away with you.' Maude blushed.

Daniel smiled. 'Ruby, we'll not be long. See you at the wagon.'

Minutes later, Kate and Daniel stood outside 10 Plaiters Way. Kate shivered and Daniel placed his arm around her shoulder.

Number 10 was no longer boarded up. A new front window and door windows had been installed and both painted glossy black. 'It's good to see our old home brought back to life. Oh, Daniel, we had such good times in this house and it's hard to believe that like

Ma and Pa, they're gone forever.'

'Kate, they may be gone but they're not forgotten. You, Liam and Annie have memories you can treasure for the rest of your lives ... and that's something no-one can ever take away from you.'

'You're right there. I suppose we're so lucky to have been blessed with such loving and caring parents. I strive to be a credit to them.'

'And you succeeded. Kate, you do know I'll always be here to help, don't you?'

She smiled and nodded. 'Daniel, what's going on between you and Ruby?'

Daniel removed his arm from around her. He fidgeted with his hands, he looked embarrassed. 'There's nothing going on. We're just friends ... I thought that's what you wanted?'

'I did – I do.' Although Kate meant what she said, part of her wanted to cry out and ask him to stop being Ruby's *friend* ... but she knew it would only confuse things.

'I know. And Kate, can you forgive the way I pushed myself on you, pestered you and even fell out with you. I—'

She raised her hand to his lips. 'Daniel, you just mistook our friendship for something else.'

'I didn't mistake my feelings for you, but I do understand why you didn't return them. You were happy to stay as we were but I wanted more.' He coughed, 'Sorry, I've said too much. Now, come on. It's time we went back.'

It was past ten o'clock when Daniel dropped Kate and Ruby back to Queen Street, where they bid each other goodnight with a peck on the cheek after a long, yet enjoyable day. It didn't go unnoticed to Kate how Daniel and Ruby's peck seemed to linger and then they were whispering.

'Ruby, I can't go on pretending like this. It's not fair to deceive her this way. We have to stop.'

'But it's working. Look, even now she can't take her eyes off us.' She gave a quiet chuckle.

'Lying to Kate or anyone else for that matter makes me feel

uncomfortable. This plan of yours has to stop now.'

'Is that why you've kept your distance while we were at the Proctors?'

'Yes.'

'All right, but you can't say I didn't try.'

'Daniel, what's the delay? I'd like to get back to the farm sometime tonight!' Liam shouted from the trap.

'Keep your hair on. I'm coming,' Daniel called out. 'Goodnight, girls, see you soon.'

'Kate, thank you for today, I had a lovely time,' Ruby said when they were indoors.

'Yes, it was good, wasn't it? But there's no need to thank me, it was Maude who invited us.' Kate slumped into the chair.

'I doubt I'd have been invited if I wasn't your friend.'

'Well, now you're Maude's friend, too. It's obvious she likes you.'

'I'm glad.' Ruby crossed the room and proceeded to rake the ashes. 'This grate is still warm, as is the mulled wine. What say we have a nightcap before we go to bed? There's something I need to tell you.'

'I'm intrigued.'

Ruby handed Kate a mug of mulled wine. 'I've decided not to take mine and Daniels' friendship any further. I—'

'What's changed?' Kate interrupted. 'I thought you said he was a good catch.'

'Kate, I really like him. After all, what's not to like? But it really wouldn't work. I tried to kiss him earlier and he was having none of it. I think I frightened him,' Ruby lied.

For a moment, Kate pondered this fact. She and Daniel had never had a proper kiss. Oh yes, there had been the odd peck on the cheek but nothing more. In fact, no man had ever kissed her. For some reason this saddened her.

'Was that what you two were whispering about before he left?'

Ruby nodded and, raising her cup took a big gulp of mulled wine. 'We're opposites. Daniel's too nice and dependable for me and I'm too flirty and unpredictable for him.'

'I don't know what to say.' Kate tried to look surprised. But in truth she was relieved and … and what?

It was Boxing Day. Kate looked out of her bedroom window to see the most beautiful winter scene. A carpet of snow lay on the ground, stretching as far out as possible and all the rooftops were glistening white. The sky was blue and the dawn sun was low in the sky. Kate felt a glow deep inside and longed to be outside.

Having quickly dressed for the weather: heavy skirt, jacket and a thick woollen shawl, she crept downstairs. It was very early and she didn't want to disturb Ruby. In the hall, she spotted a pair of sturdy boots; she was sure Ruby wouldn't mind her borrowing them. Once outside she began to walk through the virgin snow; untrodden, crisp and brilliant white. It felt so good she began to walk with purpose across town and in the direction of Daniel's lavender farm.

When she reached the edge of town she could see the country lanes thick with snow and soon realized how foolhardy it was to attempt to walk the four miles to Daniel's farm in such wintry conditions. But she so wanted to see him, to make sure he was all right. Unfortunately, she would have to wait until the snow melted and that could take days … damn the snow!

Kate entered the hallway and headed to the kitchen. Ruby had been busy in her absence, she had already lit the fire in the grate, the kettle was boiling on the hob and Ruby was sitting with the toasting-fork in hand, toasting a chunk of bread.

'Where have you been?' Ruby asked.

'I saw the snow and felt the urge to go for a walk. It looked so inviting from my bedroom window but in truth it's freezing out there.'

'Come and sit by the fire. I've made us some hot toast to eat with Maude's homemade preserve and with a fresh brew of tea, you'll be warmed up in no time.'

'I borrowed your boots. Is that all right?' Kate struggled to hold back tears that threatened.

'Of course it's all right. Kate, what's wrong?'

'I don't know. I'm happy and yet, at the same time sad.'

'It's understandable. The first Christmas without your parents must be very hard for you.'

Kate nodded. Was that it? It was true, she did miss her parents. But it was Daniel she longed to see.

'You'll feel better after some breakfast. Come on, tuck in. What say we go outside later and build a snowman ... we can pretend we're children again.'

This made Kate smile. Ruby did have such a warm heart.

By late afternoon, the snow had almost gone and the snowman they'd made was melting before their eyes. But it had been good fun making it.

Queen Street was unusually quiet except for a few children playing and a couple of landaus with the occupants no doubt off to spend the festivities with relatives. Most folk had spent the morning following the traditional Boxing Day hunt, and she wondered if Luke Stratton and his father had attended. Funny, this was the first time she'd thought about Luke Stratton since he'd presented her with the gloves before Christmas, but then she'd had more pressing things on her mind.

Kate looked down the street and in the distance, saw a cart heading toward her being pulled by the unmistakable Samson and, much to her delight, Daniel was at the reins.

'Kate, look. It's Daniel!' Ruby called out.

'What a reception committee.' Daniel beamed a smile, as he jumped down from the trap. His eyes went first to Kate and then to Ruby, his gaze questioned her.

'It's all right, Daniel, I no longer have designs on you ... you're far too nice and I need someone strong who'll take me in hand or I'll run rings around him.'

'Whatever man you end up with, he'll be lucky to have you.' He reached out and took Kate and Ruby's hands. 'Now that's firmly sorted, I hope the three of us can still be friends.'

'Always,' both girls said in unison.

'Grand. Now, any chance of a brew? The lanes give no protection from the wind and I need to thaw out.'

Ruby smiled at him. 'I'll go indoors to mash the tea and stoke the fire, you two follow when you're ready.'

Daniel sensed Ruby's motive was to give him and Kate a little time alone.

'Thank you, Ruby. I'll just tie Samson up and we'll be in,' Daniel called after her.

With Samson secured to the post he walked over to Kate and took her hand in his. 'I'm glad the thaw came when it did. I awoke this morning and had this overwhelming urge to see you.'

The tender way he looked at her melted her heart. 'I had the same urge,' Kate admitted. 'In fact, I started to walk to your farm but the heavy fall of snow in the lanes made me turn back.'

'I'm glad you did ... although it was a nice thought. Kate, there was never anything going on between me and Ruby. It'll take a strong man to tame her.' He flashed Kate a warm smile. 'Mind you, the same might be said about you.'

'Why, Mr Groves, I'm sure I don't know what you mean. Where men are concerned, you know I'm spoiled for choice,' she joked.

Daniel suddenly looked sad.

'Daniel, I'm sorry. That was insensitive of me. I promise there's no one. If and when I fall in love ... you'll be the first to know.'

He smiled. 'I should hope so, too.'

'Come on, let's go and have that brew.' She took his hand and led him into the house.

That night as she lay in her bed, Kate had time to reflect. The thought of Daniel and Ruby as a couple had certainly opened her eyes and made her think about her true feelings for him. She felt confused but she knew she couldn't mention anything to him; where she was concerned he'd been messed about enough. They were friends once again and for the time being that would have to suffice. Of course, there was also the matter of her attraction to Luke Stratton and the feelings he had aroused in her. She now questioned if those feelings had been misplaced.

CHAPTER NINETEEN

The week after Christmas, Ruby and Kate were set up with their own table leading off the hat-room, ready to begin work on the summer order of police helmets. The two girls worked well together. Kate's decision to move in with Ruby had proved a good one and she felt happy and settled.

It was getting dark when they arrived back at Ruby's house. On the doorstep was a package which Ruby quickly picked up before she unlocked the door and entered the passageway. Kate followed.

'Kate, I'm so happy you moved in with me. I used to hate coming home to an empty house. Here, take these and light the oil lamp,' Ruby said, handing her a box of lucifers.

The house was in darkness. Kate, with box of matches in hand, felt her way gingerly down the passageway and into the kitchen, where she knew she'd find the oil lamp on the kitchen table. Soon they had light.

'Well done. I'll get the fire started in no time. I just want to take a peek at this first.'

Kate watched as Ruby eagerly opened the package.

'You carry on, I'll do the fire,' Kate offered.

'Thanks. This is the highlight of my month. My cousin Lillian lives and works in London. She serves on the counter at Harrods – a fancy grocery shop in the heart of the city. Each month she buys this magazine and, after reading it, she sends it to me,' Ruby enthused, before holding the magazine up for Kate to see. 'It's called *The Ladies Cabinet* and it's full of interesting articles. Inside the cover it tells you *This issue contains short stories, special interest pieces, and reports on the latest in women's fashions from London, Paris and Rome*, all the places I hope to one day visit.' She gave a heavy sigh. 'Anyway, you're welcome to look at them any time you want. I keep all the back issues in the bottom of the kitchen cabinet over there.' She handed the magazine to Kate.

As Kate slowly turned each page, she stared in awe at the artist's sketches and hand-coloured picture plates and fashion pages, and she was certain her heart stopped. Page after page of sketches of elegant ladies, dressed in the latest fashion – clothes she could only dream of ever wearing and the hats; elegant fashionable hats, in such modern designs and vibrant colours. For her, the hats were the making of the outfits; complementing them and drawing the reader's eye to the face and neck of the wearer.

'Oh, Ruby, these are the hats *I* want to make ... hats with style and elegance that—'

'So why not do it?'

'I wouldn't want Mr Luke to think me ungrateful, not after he gave me the chance as an apprentice. I feel I owe him.'

'That's silly, you're a good worker and he's lucky to have you. Listen, there's a haberdashery in Dunstable that sells all the fancy materials you need. If you like, we could catch an omnibus after work on Saturday and spend some time there. It'll be market may, so all the shops stay open till late. I also think Dunstable market is the best place to sell any new style hats you make.'

'What's wrong with the market here in Luton?'

'I think it's a bit too close to home. I'm not sure Luke Stratton would approve – he'd not like the competition.'

'I hadn't thought of it like that. I wouldn't want him to think of me as being disloyal, it's just that—'

'It's just that you've got ambition. I always knew you were too good to work on a production line, churning out exactly the same hat day after day.'

'That's funny. Mr Luke said the very same thing the day I applied for the job.'

'Well, there you go then.'

'Oh, Ruby, I feel that excited. While I love working with straw I want to try other materials like felt, cotton, calico, flowers and colours and much, much more.'

'That sounds like a lot of work and commitment to me. I enjoy my work but all work and no play ... I frequent ale houses, I love being wooed by men and just ... have fun. What about you?'

'The truth is, Ruby, I've this yearning deep inside to make and sell beautiful hats, so any thoughts of having fun or finding romance have to be shelved.'

'If that's truly the case, then the sooner we get you to the haber-dasher's in Dunstable the better.'

'And may I ask how we get the money to buy the materials to make the new hats?'

'From selling *your* straw bonnets, like the ones you sold at Luton market. We could easily buy in a few scores of straw-plait. How many hats can you make in a week?'

'The most I ever managed was three.'

'I bet if I were to help you, you could almost double that.'

'And you'd be willing to do that for me? That would be wonderful. I'd happily give you a share of the profits.'

'Don't be daft. All the money will go to buy the materials for your new venture.'

'No Ruby ... *our* new venture. Partners ... what do you say?'

Later that night, Kate lay in bed and read *The Ladies Cabinet* by candlelight. She was totally mesmerized by the fashion stories and couldn't wait to read the special interest pieces about the well-to-do. She turned another page and was confronted by an artist's impression of Queen Victoria. She looked sombre; dressed completely in black, she still mourned the death of her beloved Prince Albert, even though he had departed this world four years ago. Kate gave a heavy sigh ... how very sad. She turned another page and was startled to see a likeness of Luke Stratton looking as handsome and debonair as always, with his arm wrapped around a beautiful blonde young woman. She sat bolt upright and stared at it. He looked happy – a wide grin from ear to ear, the girl looked entranced by him and serenely happy. It was then she read *The Honourable Joshua Pendleton and his charming wife, Rose are pleased to announce the engagement of their only daughter, Caroline Pendleton, to Luke Stratton Esquire, heir to the Stratton Hat Company of Luton. The date of the forthcoming wedding will be announced in due course.*

'It can't be!' Kate heard herself cry out.

Ruby rushed into her room. 'Kate, what's wrong? You look as if you've seen a ghost.'

Kate couldn't speak. She simply handed the open page to Ruby.

Ruby's eyes stared at the page. 'So he's gone and done it. Kate, I should have said something. It's common knowledge that he made regular train journeys to London. I always thought they were business trips ... obviously not.'

'And all the while he let me think—'

'That he was interested in you?'

Kate nodded. She couldn't speak. She felt angry, used and ... stupid.

'That's Luke Stratton for you. I did try to warn you.'

'Well, I'll show Mr Luke Stratton that I'm made of stronger stuff than he thinks. Ruby, the sooner we get to work on my hats the better.'

'That's my girl!'

Over the next week, the girls worked late into the night to create a stock of straw bonnets and by Sunday evening, they had five new straw bonnets to sell at the market.

'Ruby, I'm going to visit Maude Proctor. As you know, she has a weekly stall at the Monday plait market and I'm sure that if I took these bonnets to her, for a small commission, she'd add them to her stall tomorrow.'

'I think that's a clever idea. That way no one will know we've had a hand in making them.'

'Exactly. I'll tell Maude to keep it quiet. She's a crafty old one,' Kate said.

'As are you, by the sound of it. I think there may be more to you than I first thought.'

Kate arrived at the Proctors' house at around 5.30. Dilly was just leaving. She looked ill; pale-skinned, with dark rings around her eyes from lack of sleep, and her mouth covered in bleach sores.

'Hello, Kate, I can't stop long. I'm off back to Ada Tucker's to work another shift,' she said as they crossed on the doorstep.

'What, on Sunday?'

'Yes, Ada has a big order and woe betide us if we refuse the extra work. Truth is, I need the money.'

'So things are not good there?' Kate asked.

'I hate it. It's not like working for your ma. Ada's an old battle-axe, always finding fault and looking for ways to cheat us out of our wages. She even charges us to use the privy.'

'That's awful. It would serve her right if you left to find work elsewhere.'

'The truth is there isn't much work here about for the likes of me. I suppose I'm lucky to have a job ... any job.'

Kate felt saddened by Dilly's despondency – she'd always been so spirited and full of fun. Kate wished she was in a position to help her, but she wasn't, not yet, but if all went to plan then one day soon....

'Sorry, I've got to go. If I'm a minute late Ada will dock my pay. You go on through, Ma's in the kitchen. She'll be that glad to see you.' And pulling her shawl around her shoulders, she headed off.

Kate entered the Proctors' kitchen and breathed in the familiar smell of freshly-baked oatcakes, reminding her of her mother's home baking and the happy times they'd shared around the tea table. She missed her so much.

'Well now, here's a welcome sight. Kate, it's so nice to see you. Come on in and take a seat. You've just missed our Dilly.'

Maude's warm greeting managed to lift Kate's mood. 'No, I met Dilly on the doorstep.'

'I'm glad. She does miss you – we all do. There's hot tea in the pot and a fresh batch of oatcakes, if you've a fancy. I always try to make sure Dilly has something in her belly before she goes back to work. She'll not be home till well after midnight, that's a long time to go without a drink or a bite to eat. I so wish she didn't have to work for that slave driver, Ada Tucker. But with six of us to feed and clothe we need the extra money.'

'She looked tired and not her normal self. I wish there was something I could do to help her – and you.'

'Now, now, don't you go fretting 'bout us, sit yourself down and let me pour you a brew. It's not often you catch me on my own. My Jake has taken the little 'uns off to visit his sister. I didn't want to go. His sister never approved of me, she always felt that her brother could have done better and, truth be told, she was probably right.'

'I'll not believe that. I think you make a perfect pair.'

'Nice of you to say so, ducks. I must admit we do rub along well together. He's a good, hard-working husband and father.' She gave a deep sigh. 'That's enough 'bout me and mine, let's hear what you've been up to since you moved out. Now, are they bonnets I see in your basket?'

Kate smiled. Nothing got past Maude Proctor.

'So what do you think, Mrs Proctor, do you think you could sell my bonnets on your stall?'

'Well, child, now that you've told me of your plan, I'm more than happy to do what I can to get you on your way to the haberdasher in Dunstable.'

'Thank you. I knew you'd help … you always have. Are you sure you're happy with tuppence a bonnet?'

'Of course I am. In fact, let's shake on it and with a bit of luck I'll manage to make a few sales for you. Call around after work tomorrow and I'll tell you how I got on.'

'Thanks. But remember, if anyone asks, I made them when I was lodging with you. I need people to think they were made long before I started work in the hat factory. I'll be in trouble if Luke Stratton finds out what I'm up to.'

'I'm of the mind that as long as you do a good day's work for them, they have no right to tell you what you can and cannot do in your spare time. You leave it to me, girl.'

*

It was the end of the working day at the factory, and everyone was packing up to leave.

'Kate, you take yourself off to Maude Proctor's, I'll see you back at the house. I can't wait to find out how she got on at the market.' Ruby's voice was so quiet, Kate had to strain to hear.

'Neither can I. If the news is good, I'll pick us up some pie and mash for our supper, by way of celebration,' Kate whispered.

'What are you two whispering about? What's the big secret?' Peggy asked.

'There's no secret. Why would there be?' Ruby rebuffed.

'They're up to something and that's for sure,' Peggy assured onlookers. 'Since they've been working on the police helmets, they've been huddled together like sheep in a field.'

'Perhaps they're discussing how to share Mr Luke. Mind you, I can't see Ruby wanting to share *him* with anyone,' a younger girl said.

'Well, from what I've heard, he's more than man enough for the job,' another voice called out.

This caused fits of laughter from the onlookers.

Kate felt her colour rise and hoped no one noticed. The workforce obviously hadn't heard of Luke Stratton's recent engagement.

'That's enough!' Mrs Hobson's voice carried across the factory floor. 'Let's have you all on your way. If you're still this lively after a full day's work, then maybe I'm not working you hard enough. This can easily be remedied.'

The workforce meekly made their way to the exit in silence.

'Is that pie and mash I see in your basket?' Ruby asked.

'It is.'

'Well then, would I be right in thinking that your Mrs Proctor came up trumps?'

'She certainly did. She managed to sell four of the five bonnets I left with her. At one shilling a hat, that's four shillings! After her eight pence commission and the four pence spent on our supper and a bottle of ginger beer—'

'That means we still have three whole shillings to spend at the haberdasher's in Dunstable,' Ruby interrupted.

'Yes. Maude also suggested she take the bonnet she had left with her to the market next week, along with any others we might have. I think she's in need of the extra money now that Dilly has gone and lost her job.'

'That's awful. What happened?'

'Apparently, Dilly spoke up for one of her young friends. Unfortunately, Ada Tucker thought it a good enough reason to boot her out. I really like Dilly and I wish I was in a position to help her.'

'Well, if your hat-making goes to plan, we're going to need someone to sell them at the market for us. I see no reason why that someone couldn't be Dilly Proctor. What do you say?'

'I say yes! Ruby, I've got a busy couple of days ahead. Saturday, Dunstable market, Sunday, Leagrove House to visit Annie, then I think I'll have Liam drop me off to tell Dilly of our plan.'

'Just make sure she keeps it to herself. We don't want the Strattons to get wind of it. At least, not until we've finished the police helmet order.'

CHAPTER TWENTY

IT WAS SATURDAY evening and Kate and Ruby had already worked a full day at the factory, but they were excited as they boarded the horse-drawn omnibus to Dunstable. As the omnibus pulled away, they saw Daniel's wagon head into town. The girls raised their hand to wave to him, but he passed without seeing them.

'I wish we could have seen him and told him what we're up to. I'm sure he'll be pleased for us. Tomorrow when I see Liam, I'll ask if he and Daniel can call to see us.'

'Then we can tell them both,' Ruby agreed. 'Kate, do you think Mr Luke will be at Leagrove House tomorrow?'

'I hope not. There's been no sign of him at the factory all week. If you remember, Mrs Hobson told us he was on business in London, that's why she was in charge. Perhaps he'll stay there for the weekend as well in order to woo his newly betrothed.' Kate dreaded having to see him. She knew she couldn't trust herself not to tell him what she thought of him. In doing so she would definitely put her position at the factory at risk. She needed more time to think things through.

'Try not to think of him – think of our adventure in Dunstable instead.' She wrapped her arms around Kate and gave her a squeeze.

The journey took around twenty minutes, although for Kate, who was eager to get to her destination, it seemed a lot longer.

'I know it's a bit of a trek, but you'll not be disappointed when you see inside the haberdasher's,' Ruby said.

'I can't wait. I've brought a few of my drawings in the hope of finding what I need,' Kate enthused.

*

Daniel Groves was on his way to see Kate. Earlier today he'd picked up the *Luton Weekly Journal* and saw the announcement of Luke Stratton's engagement. His first thoughts had been for Kate and he wondered if she'd seen it. For all her denials he suspected she was indeed attracted to her employer. What troubled him greatly was the depth of that attraction. Luke Stratton, a handsome man of means, was known in the town as a philanderer who enjoyed women's company a little too much. He believed Kate to be vulnerable and could easily have had her head turned by such a man. If this was indeed the case, then how would she feel about his betrothal?

The charabanc came to a halt.

'Come on, we're here,' Ruby said, and made her way to the door of the charabanc.

Kate followed and as she stepped down onto the dirt road, she was amazed to see a very long street, lined either side by an array of splendid-looking shops and stores all displaying their wares to the best advantage in large, ornate glass-fronted windows.

'Kate, follow me. The haberdasher's is just across the road,' Ruby called out.

The street was busy and noisy. Kate hitched up her skirt to avoid the mud, a mix of straw and horse dung, and crossed the road, expertly dodging the various oncoming vehicles: carts, landaus and market trader wagons. She saw Ruby enter the haberdasher's. Kate quickened her pace, filled with anticipation of what she was about to see and was not disappointed.

The shop was as big, long and more colourful than any she had ever seen before; the walls draped from floor to ceiling with lengths of brightly coloured materials: calico, velvets, silks and the like. Down the middle of the shop were trestle-tables laden with wooden boxes, each filled with what Kate could only describe as a milliner's dream come true: bows, feathers, buttons, dried flowers, cottons, twine, felt, mouldings and much, much more. She felt like a child in a sweet shop.

An hour later, Kate's basket was filled with an assortment of hat accessories, sewing needles and various coloured cottons. She could have bought a lot more but had limited herself to spending two shillings and sixpence of the three shillings earned. She knew that their charabanc wasn't due to arrive for another hour, so they had plenty of time to walk around the busy street market. The proprietor of the haberdashery was more than happy for them to collect their purchases later.

Dunstable street market was packed with shoppers, street urchins, hawkers, and no doubt villains. Kate clutched her purse, she was not about to let some thief grab the money she had left. As they made their way through the crowded street, she estimated there had to be a hundred or more stalls selling an array of items, from pots and pans to home-made preserves. It was much busier than the market held in Luton. Yet the only hats they found on sale were plain straw bonnets and nowhere near the standard of the ones Maude had sold on Kate's behalf.

'I can't wait to get started on my new designs. I really feel there's a market for them. I—' She stopped in her tracks and felt the colour drain from her face.

'Kate, what is it? What's wrong? You look as if you've if you've seen the devil himself.'

'I think I just did. I'm sure I just saw my Uncle Joseph.'

'How can that be? He's locked up in prison.'

'He is.'

'Then how—'

'I don't know. I saw him walking among the crowds over there. He was wearing a black long coat and a bowler hat – and now he's disappeared.'

'It was probably someone who looked like him. Your eyes must have been playing tricks.'

'But I was so sure. He was of the same build, with the same lank dark hair. It gave me such a fright.'

'I can see that. Come on, let's go and pick up our parcels from the haberdasher's, then treat ourselves to a port and lemon at the inn over there before getting the charabanc back to Luton. You look as if you really need a drink.'

Kate closed her eyes. 'Ruby, I wish I could shake off the feeling that my family is not yet rid of Joseph Devlin.'

In bed that night, Kate tossed and turned and although tired, found that sleep wouldn't come. Every time she closed her eyes she saw Joseph Devlin walking towards her, getting closer and closer, his misshapen nose larger than ever, his beady eyes full of vengeance and hate ... and then he was laughing at her – a sinister laugh that made her blood run cold.

She was relieved when morning came and she could see things differently. She had had a bad dream, nothing more than that. She scolded herself for letting Joseph Devlin back into her head. For months she had not given him a thought. The man she saw at the market yesterday had spooked her but that man was *not* her uncle.

With that thought firmly fixed in her mind she could now focus on seeing Annie.

'Ruby, what are your plans for today?' Kate asked.

'I thought I'd walk into town and call at the inn. It's been an age since I shared a porter of ale with my old pals. And if we're to be busy making hats, this might be the only chance I get, at least for a while.'

'Are you all right with that? If you're having second thoughts, I—'

'I'm not. Like you, I can't wait to get started. You enjoy your day with Annie.'

Liam arrived in good time for the trip to Leagrove House. Kate thought how grown up he looked. He had filled out. With his weathered complexion and dark, wild curly hair, he looked quite handsome and older than his years.

'Good day, Ruby, sis, how are you both?'

'We're fine, aren't we, Kate?'

'Yes. How are things up at the farm? How's Daniel? We've seen nothing of him since Boxing Day.'

'We're still very busy. Daniel called to see you yesterday evening but you were both out. He thought you may have been in the town.'

'A Saturday night in the town, it's been a while since I did that. If

I'm not careful I shall be losing my reputation as a good-time girl,' Ruby chuckled.

'Liam, don't listen to her. Yesterday evening Ruby and I took a charabanc to Dunstable Market, we had business there.'

'What business?'

'Why don't you and Daniel call around tomorrow night and we'll explain all?'

It was a cold, crisp January day but the winter sun shone bright, lighting up the wispy clouds in the sky. Liam steered the trap in the direction of Leagrove House. As soon as they left the grime of the town, Kate, having dressed for the weather and with a warm blanket around her legs, looked forward to the ride into the country.

'It feels so good to breathe clean air, even if it is cold. I'm so used to breathing in the smoke from the chimney pots in town, it's easy to forget that just a few miles away there's this.' She looked around her and marvelled at the open farmland.

'Yes, working the land is a privilege I never take for granted, I don't think I could go back to living in town. Now what's this business you and Ruby—'

'We'll tell you tomorrow. Today is all about Annie.'

Annie was so pleased to see them, as was Simon Dobbs. It appeared he and Annie were inseparable. In the beginning Kate had reservations about the friendship, but not anymore. She watched the lad help Liam secure the horse and thought how pronounced the boy's limp was today. His whole demeanour tugged at her heart. She was so grateful to have two such healthy siblings.

'So come on, tell me. How was Christmas?' Kate asked.

'It was lovely. In the morning we all went to church; Mr Stratton insisted all staff attended and to be honest, I quite enjoyed it.'

Kate thought how proud her mother would have been to hear that. But she didn't tell Annie, she didn't want to dampen her sister's cheerful mood.

'When we got back,' Annie continued, 'Mrs Montgomery cooked loads of delicious food and all the staff sat around the table for

Christmas dinner. Simon and I ate so much I thought we'd burst. Isn't that right, Simon?'

The lad nodded, his eyes fixed on Annie and taking in her every word.

'In the afternoon we tended the animals and in the evening, Monty played the piano and we sang carols.'

'So you didn't miss us at all, is that what you're saying?' Liam asked.

Annie frowned. 'I did a bit. But—'

'Liam, don't be so mean. Annie, he's only joking. The truth is we're glad you had such a good time. It sounds as if you had quite a party.'

Annie was smiling once again. 'Yes, we did. And there's to be another one soon. An engagement party for young Mr Stratton and his bride to be ... I can't wait!'

For a moment Kate couldn't speak. She was afraid if she did, that she'd give away the hurt and embarrassment she felt inside. Eventually she decided to change the subject completely.

'What say we walk up the hill and take a look at the splendid view?'

'Yes, please. I'll just call the dog. Jasper, Jasper, come on, boy. We're going up the hill.'

Within seconds, the dog was running across the courtyard, eager to get to Annie's side.

'Are you coming, Liam?' Kate asked.

'No, thanks. I walk more than enough every day at the farm. I'll just rest here. Simon, what say you keep me company?'

The lad smiled. 'I-I'd like t-that, Mr Liam.'

Kate nodded in appreciation. It was obvious her brother had asked the lad to stay in order to give Kate and Annie time alone.

CHAPTER TWENTY-ONE

'D o you think Daniel and Liam will come this evening?' Ruby asked, as she helped Kate clear away the bread and cheese they'd eaten after work.

'I hope so. Ruby, I'm so glad you agree we should tell them our secret.'

'Kate, it's your venture ... your secret. It's up to you who you tell. Like I said when you asked me not to mention about last Saturday in Dunstable when you thought you'd seen your uncle, your secret is safe with me.'

'Thanks for that. With Joseph Devlin safely locked up, the lads would think me mad. But sewing hats is different.' Kate placed her sketch pad and pen onto the table. 'I've so many ideas going on in my head. I can't wait to get started.' Right then there was a knock on the door.

'If that's Daniel and Liam then you may have to wait just a little longer to get started,' Ruby called out as she headed down the hall to the front door, quickly followed by her warm greeting. 'Daniel, Liam, how nice to see you. Come on through, Kate's in the kitchen.'

Kate covered her sketchbook. 'Hello, you two,' she gushed. 'Daniel, I'm sorry we missed you on Saturday. Ruby and I went to Dunstable market.'

'So I hear.' He took her hand and gently pulled her to one side. 'Kate, I came yesterday to show you this.' He opened the *Luton Weekly Journal* that he was holding and showed her the announcement of Luke Stratton's betrothal.

Kate managed to force a smile. 'Oh, that. Why, that's old news.

I saw it last week in the London magazine Ruby's cousin sends her. And when I saw our Annie yesterday she told me about the engagement party planned up at Leagrove House.' Kate knew she was babbling on but couldn't stop herself. The fact that Daniel felt the need to show her the announcement meant he suspected her attraction to Luke Stratton and this mortified her.

'That's all right then. As long as you know,' he said, his voice tender and full of concern.

She squeezed his hand. 'Daniel, I'm fine, honestly.'

'What are you two plotting over there?' Ruby demanded. 'Kate, I hope you haven't told him about our new venture.'

'No, but he is very inquisitive, so I think it's time to reveal all.'

'You clever pair, finding something to do of an evening that you really enjoy is to be commended, but why all the secrecy?' Daniel asked.

'Ruby seems to think that if Luke Stratton found out about what we're doing, he'd say we were being disloyal and may even sack us,' Kate replied.

'That's daft. Surely what you do in your own time is your business,' Liam said.

Kate and Ruby exchanged glances. They both knew it was time to tell all.

'The thing is …' Ruby hesitated and waited for Kate to continue.

'The thing is, we're not just making hats for ourselves. We've asked Dilly Proctor to sell them at the market for us. She already holds some of our straw bonnets and plans to take them to sell at Dunstable market on Saturday.'

Daniel frowned. 'I see. Now that puts a different light on it. And if asked, who will Dilly say made the hats?'

'Dilly will say she works for a small cottage industry in Luton called Heavenly Hats. That's the name Ruby has embroidered under each crown,' Kate offered.

'Heavenly Hats, you say. A catchy name, but I think you're treading dangerous waters. My advice is to tell Luke Stratton before he finds out. He's no fool,' Daniel advised.

195

'And we will, but just not just yet.' They needed more time. 'In a couple of weeks we'll have completed the order for police helmets and by then, depending on how the hats sell, we should know if it's worth giving up our jobs for.'

'Daniel, Liam, please say you'll support us. Kate's got her heart set on this,' Ruby pleaded.

'And if Dilly's going to do this, she'll need help with the transport and to set up a table, especially if she's to do more than one market,' Kate elaborated.

'And you thought that our hay-wagon could do the job?' Liam piped up.

'How many markets a week?' Daniel asked.

'At the moment only the one, but if we give up our jobs and maybe take on a couple of girls, we could make enough stock to do three or four.' Kate tried to sound businesslike. If they were to succeed they would need Daniel and Liam on their side.

Daniel rubbed his chin. 'What if, until you create more stock, Dilly fills her table with produce from Heaven Scent, thereby killing two birds with one stone?'

'What a good idea? Heavenly Hats and Heaven Scent, a partnership literally made in *heaven*,' Kate enthused.

'Liam, could you sort out some stock from our store on Saturday, then collect Dilly and help her to set up her stall at Dunstable market?'

Liam nodded. 'I'll be happy to. In fact, I'll call to see her after I drop our workers off on Friday to arrange a pick up time.'

'Good lad.'

Kate looked to Daniel. 'Thank you, it means so much to me to have your support.'

For a while he held her gaze and the look he gave her warmed her heart.

Kate felt her colour rise and looked away, hoping no one noticed.

In the days that followed, Kate sketched for hours, to come up with her own new designs while Ruby tried different threads and stitches to complement them. When the very first hat was completed, they

196

were overjoyed with the result.

'Kate, I just love it,' Ruby enthused. 'The way you've shaped the felt crown to sit close to the wearer's head and the intertwined feathers work so well. You're so clever.'

'I couldn't have done it without your help. You stitch faster than I do and yet still manage even stitches.'

'I'm glad you think so. This certainly beats working the factory production line. I feel I've wasted so many years.'

'You're wrong there because, like my years spent at plait school, they were not wasted. Without them we might never have learned a trade or how to hone our talents. This hat, I hope the first of many, is proof of what we can achieve when we work as a team.'

'With your flair for design and construction and my stitching, I can't wait to make more. Remember our aim. To make six hats a week.'

'I think that may be a bit too ambitious, but we'll see.'

They worked through the night and by 4 a.m., they had their second hat shaped and ready to decorate the following night. After just a couple of hours' sleep, they were up and dressed and on their way to work.

An hour into their shift, Kate and Ruby were busy sewing at their workstation and well on target to meet their hourly quota of police helmets.

As Kate worked she couldn't help but smile. The funny thing was that, despite having had little sleep, she didn't feel at all tired. In fact, quite the opposite; she felt excited at the thought of Dilly taking her new designs to sell at the market. Dilly was overjoyed to be given the chance to have her own stall at Dunstable market, showing off Heavenly Hats and Heaven Scent products.

She turned to Ruby. 'I can't stop thinking about the market on Saturday. If Dilly was to sell just two hats, it would yield enough profit to pay her and buy some additional materials.' She spoke quietly.

'Kate, a word of warning,' Ruby whispered. 'I really don't think it wise to talk about our new venture while we're in the factory.'

'You're probably right,' Kate whispered back.

A few minutes later, she felt the urge to look up and as she did, she saw Luke Stratton's eyes boring down on her.

She felt betrayed. He'd made her think he liked ... she stopped in mid-thought, when the realization hit her. Could what she and Ruby were doing in secret also be seen as a betrayal? She stared up at him. His eyes were still fixed on her and she hoped he couldn't read her mind.

Luke Stratton looked down from his viewing platform. Earlier he'd seen Ruby and Kate with their heads together, obviously sharing a secret. Normally the girls' voices, especially Ruby's, echoed around the factory floor. Now, all of a sudden, she and Kate talked in whispers. He suspected they were up to something ... but what? Had Ruby set Kate up with a young lad? The thought galled him. He knew he had no right to feel galled, not with him being an engaged man, but he couldn't stop himself.

Daniel and Liam arrived late evening to help Dilly dismantle her stall at the end of the day at Dunstable market. Dilly couldn't wait to tell them about her eventful day. Unfortunately, the news they heard was not all good. Daniel had promised Kate and Ruby that they would stop off at the house on their way back. He hoped the news from Dilly wouldn't upset them.

They travelled slowly along the country lanes. Dilly, with her head resting on Liam's shoulders, fell asleep. Daniel and Liam stayed quiet so as not to disturb her. She had obviously had a long day.

'We've only a mile to go. How do you think we should handle this?' Liam whispered.

'I'm not sure. The girls need to hear exactly what happened at the market today. I can't help but feel they – we – should have thought things through a lot better.'

Kate and Ruby were standing on the doorstep, eager to find out how Dilly had got on. And when the wagon eventually arrived even before it came to a stop, Ruby, unable to contain herself, ran alongside. 'Well, Dilly, how did it go?'

'It went well, I think,' a sleepy Dilly answered.

As Kate watched her brother bring Samson to a halt, she saw him flash a questioning look at Daniel and immediately sensed something was not quite right.

Daniel dismounted and put his arm around Kate. 'Kate, I think we should all go inside, we don't want the neighbours knowing our business.'

They were standing in the kitchen and for a while no one spoke, until a frustrated Kate broke the silence.

'Well? What happened? Will someone say something, you're making me tense.'

Daniel took a deep breath. 'The good news is … Dilly did well. She sold all five hats and most of the Heaven Scent stock.'

'That's fantastic! Kate, that's better news than we could ever have wished for,' Ruby squealed with delight.

'Yes, it is, but there's something they're not telling us. Daniel, what happened, why the look of concern? Is there bad news?'

'Dilly, I think you should be the one to tell her,' Daniel prompted.

'Kate, young Mr Stratton came to Dunstable today and—'

'And he took more than a passing interest in Dilly's stall,' Liam interrupted.

Kate took a sharp intake of breath. 'Did he ask about the hats?'

'Yes. But I stuck to your story. I told him they were from a small cottage industry called Heavenly Hats.' Dilly looked pleased with herself.

'And did that satisfy the nosey bugger?' Ruby quipped.

Liam shook his head. 'Hardly, he then wanted to know the connection between Heavenly Hats and Heaven Scent. Dilly lied and said none, but she wasn't sure if he believed her.'

'Oh dear, I'm sorry, Dilly. I never intended to put you in such an awkward position.'

'I did say I thought you were playing a dangerous game,' Daniel reminded her. 'I suggest you and Ruby ask to see Luke Stratton first thing Monday morning and come clean.'

Kate looked to Ruby. 'Daniel's right. We have to tell him … no more lies.'

'Liam and I are off to see Annie tomorrow. I do hope I don't run into him at Leagrove House. I'd rather explain things at the factory.'

Liam picked Kate up promptly at twelve o'clock. During the trip to Leagrove House, Kate thought how different things were. A few months ago she'd have been hoping to cross paths with Luke Stratton; to hear the warmth in his voice and see the tenderness in his eyes when he looked at her, but things had changed since then. Not least the fact that he was now engaged to be married. What a fool she'd been. The fact that he'd been playing with her emotions angered her. At Christmas he said he wanted her to think of him as her friend – he was no friend of hers. And tomorrow when she and Ruby told him about their new venture, she hoped it would show him how independent she was.

As usual, Annie was eagerly waiting at the gate for their arrival with Simon Dobbs at her side. The lad limped over to help Liam tie Samson to the post while Annie ran to embrace her sister. She was wearing a new duck-egg blue, long-sleeved dress with a white calico pinafore over the top.

'Now don't you look pretty, where did you get the new dress?' Kate asked.

'Mrs Montgomery made it for me. She said I'm to keep it for best.'

Kate thought that very kind and made a mental note to thank her later.

'Sis, I've got so much to tell you. I actually helped Monty deliver a foal this week. I was frightened at first but Monty said I was to sit by the mother's head and stroke her. Oh, Kate, she looked at me with her big brown eyes. I really think my stroking helped because not long after the foal was born and I felt such a warm glow inside, I cried with joy,' Annie chatted on, hardly stopping for a breath.

'My goodness, fancy you helping to birth a foal. You clever thing.'

'I'll take you to see the foal in a bit, it's a colt – a boy – and

Monty wants *me* to name him.'

Annie's enthusiasm proved to Kate how happy her sister was at Leagrove House. She had thought that if – no, when – her new venture got off the ground, she wanted Annie to join them. Now she wasn't at all sure her sister would want to.

Thankfully, Luke Stratton didn't make an appearance. According to Mrs Montgomery he'd left early that morning for London. Kate felt relieved.

It was mid-morning at the factory and Kate was busy putting the finishing touches to another police helmet – it was a tedious job and one she didn't really enjoy. She was bored with having to do hour after hour of such repetitive work. She looked over to Ruby who seemed happy in her work. For the first time, Kate wondered if encouraging Ruby to join forces in what was after all ... Kate's dream, was too big a risk for her.

Luke Stratton paced the floor of his office. He was seething. He had trusted Kate and Ruby and they had let him down. He felt betrayed. Did they really think him that gullible to believe Dilly Proctor's blatant lies? As soon as he'd seen the well-made hats sitting next to Daniel Groves' Heaven Scent products on her stall, he knew the hats were Kate's. The flair shown in the design had Kate Devlin's name written all over them. His trip to London yesterday to see Caroline had been a mere diversion – he didn't want to confront her at Leagrove House. The rules had been broken – this was factory business and as such must be dealt with in the workplace. As it turned out, he'd had a splendid time. The lovely Caroline had been thrilled to see him. She was such an exquisite little creature, obviously naïve to affairs of the heart ... or the bedroom. He was sure she'd make the perfect wife and looked forward to his marital night. The very thought caused an immediate arousal, but he knew such feelings where Caroline Pendleton was concerned would have to wait until after the wedding or risk the displeasure of his father and future father-in-law. A risk he was not prepared to take.

*

'Ruby, Kate, Mr Luke wants to see you in his office, and I'll warn you he's not in a good mood,' Mrs Hobson informed them.

Ruby raised her eyebrows. 'Do you think he knows?' she whispered, as they followed the forewoman to the office.

'I think we're about to find out,' Kate whispered back.

Minutes later Mrs Hobson tapped on the office door.

'Enter,' Luke Stratton called out.

Kate tried to judge his mood but his business-like 'enter' gave her no clue.

Luke Stratton sat at his desk writing. He didn't look up when they entered.

'Mr Luke, I've brought Ruby and Kate to see you.'

'Thank you, Mrs Hobson. You may now return to the factory floor.' He still didn't look up.

As the forewoman turned to leave she looked at them and shook her head.

When Kate had heard that Luke Stratton wanted to see them, she hoped it was a coincidence and not connected to Heavenly Hats. But the warning look from the forewoman and the way their employer was purposely ignoring them could only mean one thing. The girls stood in front of his desk for what seemed like an age.

Eventually he stopped writing and slowly replaced his pen into the ornate, heavy glass inkwell in front of him and looked up. He looked first at Ruby and then Kate – he held Kate's gaze for a while, and she could tell how angry he was.

'What a fool I was to trust the pair of you. I truly believed in you and you repay me by being disloyal. Kate, Heavenly Hats, surely you'll not deny they're your handiwork?'

'No. But—' Kate began, desperate to explain.

'There can be no buts! You went behind my back and started up on your own while still working for me. That's the truth of it.'

'Mr Luke, it wasn't like that. We were all set to tell you about it this morning, I promise. We—' Ruby attempted to explain.

As with Kate, he didn't let her finish her sentence. 'And you expect me to believe that? It's just another lie to go with the ones you groomed Dilly Proctor to tell me.' He looked to Kate. 'How could you use her so? I thought she was your friend.'

'She is! I never meant it to turn out like this. We just wanted to—'

'Enough! I'd have thought better of you both if you'd given your notice before starting a new venture.' He shook his head.

'We didn't want to leave until we'd finished the police helmet order,' Ruby assured him.

'That was very considerate of you,' he said with more than a hint of sarcasm in his voice. 'I think it had more to do with having your cake and eating it.'

Kate had to bite her tongue not to blurt out that he'd know all about that. But she knew she mustn't. Now was not the time.

'I feel betrayed and I want both of you off the premises. I've instructed Mrs Hobson to pay you what you're owed, thus ending your employ in this company.'

Ruby turned to leave, but Kate stood her ground.

'Mr Stratton, while I admit it was wrong to have Dilly lie for us, I fail to see what it is we've done that's so wrong. In our own time, we made a few hats to sell at the market – where's the harm in that? Or is the problem that we teamed up with Daniel Groves and you don't like the competition?'

'If you believe that, then you're suffering from delusions of grandeur! My business has nothing to fear from a couple of inexperienced market traders.' He clipped his words.

Kate shook with rage and struggled to keep her composure. 'I may be a lowly market trader, but one with a dream to one day become the best hat-maker in Luton. Now, thanks to you, I'm free to explore my true potential.' And, although her knees felt like jelly, she had one more thing to add. 'Oh and by the way, congratulations on your recent engagement!' And with that, she turned and followed Ruby out of the office.

'I can't believe you had the nerve to speak to him like that. What possessed you?' Ruby's shock was obvious.

'He had it coming. I couldn't let him get away with just dismissing us out of hand.'

'You left him in no doubt of how angry you are. I'm proud of you.'

The way he had treated her proved to Kate how great the divide was between them. 'Ruby, I'm glad we no longer work for him. We now have the chance to show him, and everyone else, our true worth.'

Luke watched her go. To say he was a little taken aback by her offer of congratulations was an understatement. She was so angry ... surely the girl hadn't really thought...? He stopped himself. Of course she had, and for a while there so had he. He'd been besotted by her ... the one that got away. But he had secretly admired the way she had stood up to him and had to admit her argument was sound. What difference did a few hats make? If he was truly honest he really hadn't had a problem with that. He'd always known a girl with such flair and ambition was wasted on the factory floor. It was only a matter of time before she moved on to bigger and better things, but what had hurt and angered him most was the fact that she'd teamed up with Daniel Groves. She almost guessed the truth. He also suspected that she and Daniel Groves were not *just* business partners and that hurt and angered him more than he cared to admit. Oh yes, Kate Devlin was definitely ... the one that got away.

CHAPTER TWENTY-TWO

SINCE LEAVING THE factory Kate and Ruby had worked from the house. Dilly, when not at market, joined the workforce. It was hard work and sometimes, in order to achieve their fifteen hats a week target, they sometimes worked a twelve hour day. This meant that with Liam's help, Dilly now did two markets a week.

It was Friday evening. Kate, Ruby and Dilly were setting up their sewing table with the intention of working late. Daniel and Liam were there, they had called in for their tea after dropping off their workers.

'Come on, Liam. It's time we made a move. I don't want to be accused of holding up production,' Daniel teased.

'Daniel, surely you don't need to go yet. I was hoping Liam could walk Dilly home before you left.' Kate winked at Daniel.

'Liam, if you don't want to do it, I'd happily walk Dilly home,' Daniel said.

Liam was blushing. 'No! I'll do it.' He grabbed his coat and Dilly's shawl, then taking Dilly's hand, quickly led her from the room and toward the front door.

Kate, Daniel, and Ruby burst out laughing. Ever since Liam had been taking Dilly to the market, they had become inseparable.

'Young love ... how sweet is that?' Ruby said, with a hint of sarcasm.

Just then there was a loud knock on the door.

Liam opened the door to find Luke Stratton standing on the doorstep.

'Who's at the door?' Kate asked, as she entered the hallway.

'It's Mr Stratton,' Dilly informed her.

Luke Stratton was standing on the doorstep dressed in a dark, ankle-length coat, his collar turned up against the cold.

Kate was startled. 'Liam, take Dilly home and then come straight back. Dilly has to be at the market early in the morning,' she said, shooing them out of the door.

'All right, sis, we're going.' Liam and Dilly eased past Luke Stratton and proceeded down the street.

Luke Stratton coughed awkwardly. 'Kate, I'm sorry to call at this hour but I need to speak with you.'

They had parted on such bad terms, but the look he now gave her told her he was no longer angry with her and she was glad. Whatever might or might not have gone between them had now passed.

'Mr Stratton, what is it?' Then it dawned on her. 'Has something happened to Annie?'

By this time Daniel and Ruby had entered the hall.

Luke's eyes momentarily went to them, then back to Kate. 'I'm not sure. It might be something or nothing but ... may I come in?'

Kate beckoned him in and led the way down the hall. As he passed Daniel and Ruby, he gave a polite nod, they did the same.

He entered the living room, closely followed by Ruby and Daniel. Luke's eyes immediately went to the brightly coloured sewing materials and unfinished hats on the table. He walked over and picked up one of the hats in progress.

'I've seen young Dilly at market. I have to compliment you, your hats show flair.'

'I'm sure you didn't come here to talk about hats.' Kate spoke urgently.

'No, I didn't.'

'So why *have* you come?' Daniel demanded. 'If something has happened to Kate's sister, then you must tell her.'

'Kate, I came as fast as I could to tell you.'

'Tell me what?'

'That Annie has disappeared.' He looked worried.

Daniel went to Kate's side and placed his arm around her.

'What do you mean, disappeared? How can that be?' She stared at Luke Stratton in disbelief.

'The truth is, we don't know.'

'But I left her in Mrs Montgomery's care and she promised—'

'Mrs Montgomery's not to blame. She believed Annie had gone to the stables to work with Monty. The truth is, no one has seen your sister since she left the kitchen early this afternoon.'

'This afternoon, but that was ages ago.' Kate's voice was filled with dread.

'There was no reason to think anything was amiss until Monty came to the kitchen around three thirty, wanting to know why they hadn't turned up to tend the horses.'

'*They*? I don't understand,' Daniel said.

'Young Simon walked her to the stables and Mrs Montgomery believes that, wherever Annie is, the lad will be close by.'

'That doesn't make sense. Annie would never wander off of her own accord. Do you think Simon might have ...' Kate put her hand to her mouth.

'No, I don't. Simon wouldn't harm a fly. He's the kindest, most caring person I—'

'But,' she interrupted, 'where could she be?'

At that moment Liam entered the room. 'What's going on?'

'Oh, Liam, it's our Annie. She's missing.'

'How can that be?' Liam demanded.

'Daniel, Liam, we must go and look for her,' Kate urged.

'Kate, we've already organized a search party who, as we speak, will be diligently scouring the grounds in and around Leagrove House. I'm sure she'll be found soon,' Luke Stratton assured her.

'Then we must join them now!' Liam said forcibly.

'I agree, the more people looking for her the sooner she'll be found. Let's go,' Daniel urged.

'I agree, too.' Luke looked relieved.

'I'm coming to help,' Kate insisted.

'Kate, I'm not sure it will be practical for you to join the search party, but I will take you to see Mrs Montgomery at the house. I'd be happy to take you in the gig.'

Kate was suddenly reminded of how kind the Strattons had always been to her family and took his offer in the way she believed it was intended. However, her dear parents would never have let her travel alone with a betrothed man.

'No, thank you,' she said politely but firmly. 'If it's all the same to you, I shall ride with Daniel and Liam.'

'As you wish,' Luke Stratton replied.

'I want to come, too.' Ruby was not about to be left behind.

'I suggest you all dress in warm clothes. It's cold outside.'

'Did Annie have a coat?'

'Mrs Montgomery assured me that she was well dressed for the weather.'

Kate gave a sigh of relief. 'Thank God. That's some comfort. But I know she'd never wander off on her own.'

'Kate, here is your coat, shawl and gloves.' Ruby flashed a look of disapproval at Luke Stratton. 'I'm sure your Annie will be found soon enough,' she added, her voice full of hope.

Once outside, Luke pulled Daniel and Liam to one side. 'There's some information you both need to know. It may or may not have anything to do with Annie's disappearance but this afternoon I had a visit from our local constabulary. They came to inform me that Joseph Devlin has absconded from prison.'

'Oh my God, why wasn't I told?' Liam cried.

'They only found out themselves this morning. They came to me because I was the one who brought the case against him. And they think he may be out to seek revenge. They asked where they could find you and Kate. I told them I'd relay the message.'

Liam nodded.

'I think you were right not to mention this to Kate, she'd only have jumped to the worst conclusions,' Daniel said.

'And would that be the same conclusion we're all making?' Liam asked quietly. 'If he—'

'If he what?' Kate challenged from the doorway.

'I–if Simon and Annie are playing some sort of prank, then woe betide them, eh, Liam?' Daniel lied.

'Yes, yes, that's right.' Liam forced a smile.

Luke Stratton was soon leading the way in his gig, and Kate was sitting next to Daniel in the cart with Ruby and Liam in the back. Daniel clicked his tongue and tugged the reins.

'Move on,' he called to Samson.

It was getting dark as the convoy headed out of town. At night, it was not the best time to travel on country roads, but thankfully for them it was a dry night and there was a full moon helping to light their way. They had gone about a mile when Daniel became aware that Luke Stratton was slowing down, so he did the same. It was then Daniel spotted a figure ahead and had to squint to make out the shape. It was definitely a young lad – a young lad with an awkward slow gait. Luke Stratton's gig had now stopped.

Daniel pulled on the reins. 'Whoa,' he instructed Samson.

'Why have we stopped?' Kate asked.

'There's someone up ahead. I think we should go and take a look.'

They all left the cart and walked towards Luke's gig.

'Simon, is that you?' They heard Luke call out. Then, 'Simon, don't be afraid. It's me, Mr Luke.'

Kate took a sharp intake of breath. 'Oh my God, if that's Simon then where's Annie?'

Daniel took her gloved hand in his, 'Now don't go thinking the worst. I'm sure Simon will tell us soon enough.'

The touch of his hand on hers gave Kate the reassurance she needed. Together they moved to the front of Luke Stratton's gig; Liam and Ruby followed.

'Luke, is the lad all right?' Daniel asked, the concern in his voice obvious. 'Does he know where Annie is?'

Simon turned to face Luke Stratton, his eyes full of fear, like a rabbit caught in a lamp-light. 'Mr Luke, Mr Luke, we have to help her! I – didn't –want – to – leave – her – with – *him*,' he sobbed.

'Try to calm down, lad.' Luke Stratton spoke quietly.

Kate had to struggle to hear what he said.

'Simon, it's me, Liam. You know me, I'm your friend.' His voice was warm and reassuring.

The lad nodded.

Liam handed him a handkerchief. 'Now wipe your face. It's all right. You're not in trouble. Is it Annie we have to help?'

'Y-yes,' the lad stammered.

Kate let out a muffled cry. Daniel pulled her to him and kissed her forehead.

'Simon, we need to know where Annie is and who's holding her,' Liam prompted. 'Can you help us?'

'I'll t-try,' the boy stuttered, looking around him, 'I w-was on my w-way to find M-Monty.'

'Well, we're here to help you now, if you can take us to where she is, we'll do the rest,' Luke assured him.

Simon's eyes went to Daniel. 'Y-your f-farm.'

Kate took the lad's hand. 'Simon, are you saying Annie's at Daniel's farm?'

Simon nodded his head vigorously.

'I don't understand. Why would she leave Leagrove to go there?' It was then she saw Luke, Daniel and Liam exchange a look.

'What is it? What are you keeping from me?'

They stayed silent.

'Tell me! I need to know,' Kate commanded, her voice rising.

'Sis, we think it might be our Uncle Joe who's holding her. He's escaped from prison.' Liam dropped his head. 'I'm sorry. We didn't tell you because we didn't want to worry you.'

All colour drained from Kate's face. 'When did he escape?' she demanded.

'A few days ago but—'

'I knew it! Ruby, didn't I tell you I thought I'd seen him at Dunstable market?'

'Y-yes, but I said your eyes were playing tricks. I'm sorry,' Ruby apologized.

'Daniel, why on earth would he take her to your farm?' Luke Stratton shook his head. 'It doesn't make sense. I'd have thought he'd come looking for me.'

'Miss K-Kate. Annie t-told him that's w-where you w-were,' Simon stuttered.

'How very clever of her,' Luke said. 'Daniel, she led him to you,

210

looking for help.'

'And we were in Luton, damn it,' Liam snapped.

'How could we have known?' Daniel asked.

'Come on! Hurry! We've wasted enough time. We need to get to the lavender farm before he ... Oh God, what if he's harmed her?' Kate cried out.

Daniel nodded. It was time to take charge. 'You're right. Luke, you take Simon and head back to Luton and alert the constabulary of Joe Devlin's whereabouts.' He turned to Kate. 'Kate, love, I think you should go with them.'

The tenderness in his voice and the fact that he'd called her 'love' didn't go unnoticed.

'No, Daniel, I'm staying with you. I have to find Annie.'

'I feel I should also stay. After all, I'm the one he has a score to settle with,' Luke pointed out.

'Mr Luke,' Ruby said quickly, 'if Simon and I can take the gig to Luton and notify the police, then you could ride in the back of the cart with Liam.'

'That's a splendid suggestion, Ruby. And don't you worry, Monty has trained my horse so well, he almost drives himself.'

When Daniel and Kate were seated in front and Luke and Liam were standing directly behind them in the back, holding onto the buck board for grim death, they headed as fast as conditions would allow for the lavender farm. Meanwhile in the gig, Ruby and Simon made their way back to town.

The night was bitterly cold and an eerie silence hung over the worried group in the cart.

'I'm sorry, Kate. We should have told you sooner,' Daniel apologized.

'It was partly my fault. I didn't for one moment think he'd go after your Annie,' Luke Stratton explained.

'We knew he'd seek revenge,' she spoke quietly.

'Yes. But I honestly believed he'd go for me first, after all it *was* I who brought the initial case for fraud against him.'

'But I was the one who told you about the short lengths and I'll never forget the look of hatred he gave me when the police arrested him. He said then he'd get back at me and what better way than to hurt Annie!' She fought to hold back a sob.

Daniel moved closer, his arm pressed to hers. 'Kate, try to stay strong. Joe Devlin wouldn't be so daft as to hurt her in any way.'

'Daniel's right, your uncle's in enough trouble without adding to it,' Luke agreed.

'Kate, Uncle Joe always made a special fuss of Annie, why would he hurt her?'

Kate shook her head. 'None of you know the half of it. The man is evil. Why else would he have threatened a woman as kind and lovely as my mother, the very same woman who gave him another chance and welcomed him back into the fold? He made her—' She stopped, not knowing if she should tell them.

'Made her what, Kate? I'm your brother, I have a right to know,' Liam demanded.

She turned her head to face her brother. 'Liam, Uncle Joe black-mailed Ma. He threatened to rape Annie, if Ma didn't give herself willingly to him. To protect Annie, she did what he asked.' She turned her face away from him and stared bleakly into the blackness around her.

Liam raised his fist in the air. 'What an evil bastard. I swear if he harms our Annie, then I'll swing for him!'

'That's enough, Liam. Kate has enough to worry about. You making rash threats is not helping now, is it?' Daniel scolded.

Liam didn't answer.

For a while, no one said a word and only the sound of the cart's wheels as they rattled over the stones filled the silence.

Eventually Luke spoke. 'Kate, I'm curious. Is that why you gave him up and told me of your suspicions regarding short lengths?'

'Yes. I knew I had to rid our family of such a vile man – a black-guard, a rapist, a drunkard and a fraud. When he was put away my ma and I breathed a sigh of relief. She'd turn in her grave if she knew he was holding Annie.'

'Look, we're almost there.' Daniel steered the cart around the next bend. 'I think it best if we stop at the bottom of the lane. The sound of Samson's hooves and the cart's wheels might warn him.

We can walk the rest of the way.'

'What's the plan?' Liam asked.

'There isn't one,' Daniel answered honestly.

CHAPTER TWENTY-THREE

D ANIEL PULLED SAMSON to a halt and they all dismounted. Daniel took Kate's hand and helped her to the ground and looked lovingly into her eyes, then his arms went around her and he hugged her and she didn't pull away.

With the moon shining above and the aromatic scent of lavender filling the cold air, she wished with all her heart that she could turn the clock back. But there could be no hiding from the reality of where they were and what she had to face. She feared for Annie, her little sister had been missing all day. Kate looked up to heaven and prayed to God to keep Annie safe.

'Daniel, I can see a light in the store room,' Liam whispered.

Daniel kissed Kate's forehead and released her. 'I see it. Luke, if you take Kate and sneak round to the back door, Liam and I will slip in the front. I've just got to get this.' Daniel reached under his seat and pulled out a hunting rifle.

Kate took a sharp intake of breath.

'Don't be alarmed. It's only a precaution. Desperate men do desperate things and your uncle may have found one of my other hunting rifles at the farm. Luke, you take this,' he spoke softly and handed over his rifle. 'If we come face to face with Joe Devlin, then I don't want to provoke him.'

Luke shouldered the gun and nodded. 'I think that's wise. Kate and I will head around back. Thank goodness for the full moon, otherwise we'd struggle to find our way,' he said, taking Kate's hand.

Daniel and Liam tiptoed up to the double fronted barn door and gingerly pushed the left side. It creaked open with just enough space for them to slip quietly in.

'Welcome,' a surly voice called out through the darkness.

At first they couldn't see where the voice was coming from, so they edged closer to the light, it was then they saw the oil lamp, strategically placed on a table in the loft at the far end of the barn. The barn was spacious and in need of repair. It had a dirt floor, one high window with no window-pane, a straw roof and an open loft at the far end where the previous owner stored straw bales, remnants of which were still there. Daniel and Liam only ever used a small sheltered area away from the window to store boxes of dried lavender, which they usually kept covered with a tarpaulin. Yet they still called it their 'store-room'.

'I wondered how long it would take that stupid lad to find help. He thought he had me fooled, but I was always aware of him limping behind and following us.'

Daniel looked up to see Joseph Devlin standing high above in the loft area at the back of the barn. The man looked dirty and dishevelled; his face unwashed, his long coat in need of a stiff brush and his bowler hat almost in ribbons. But then he was a man on the run. Daniel's eyes darted around the loft area but he couldn't see Annie.

'Uncle Joe, where's Annie? If you've hurt her I'll—'

'Well now, Liam, me lad, is that a threat?'

'Yes! And I'm not your lad. Now where is she?'

From the shadows among some straw bales, somewhere behind Joseph, they heard a muffled cry.

'Annie, love, is that you? This is Daniel speaking. Liam's with me. Try to stay strong, you'll be safe soon, I promise.' Daniel tried to sound confident and in control in an effort to reassure her.

'It's very brave of you to make promises.' Joseph raised his right arm and they could plainly see the shotgun in his hand. 'If you can see this—' he vigorously shook the shotgun, '—then you'll understand that I'm the one in charge here.'

Daniel caught hold of Liam's arm and steered him behind the pile of wooden boxes filled with dried lavender. He knew how vulnerable they both were. If he had a mind to, Joseph Devlin could take a pot-shot at them any time he wanted.

'Glad to see that you're taking me seriously. Now where's the bitch that shopped me? I've spent many a day dreaming of my revenge. Where is she? Where's bloody Kate?'

'You're out of luck. She's not with us. She's in Luton,' Daniel called.

'Don't fucking lie to me.' Joseph reached down and dragged Annie from behind a bale and pulled her to her feet. Her arms and feet were tied up with twine and she was gagged with a dirty cloth.

'You've gone very quiet. Now, if you're speaking the truth and Kate's in Luton, then I'm afraid I'm going to have to continue taking my revenge out on sweet Annie here. Perhaps you'd like to watch.'

It took all Daniel's strength to hold Liam back, his natural reaction had been to go to the aid of his sister, but the man was armed and Daniel was in no doubt that he would use it. His eyes were now fixed on the back door and he held his breath as he watched it open....

Luke and Kate crept into the barn and stood at the far end under the loft. Kate was immediately overcome by the heady floral scent of lavender that lingered in the cold night air. Under normal circumstances she might have been calmed by it – but not tonight. Especially after overhearing her uncle's foul language and the immediate threat he posed to Annie. Through the darkness she strained her eyes, hoping to see Daniel or Liam at the other end of the barn. They were nowhere to be seen. She looked to Luke. He put his fingers to his lips, telling her to stay silent and motioned to the ground in front of her. It was then she saw Daniel crawling on his belly toward her. The relief she felt was immense. As he reached them he stood up and pointed above to indicate where Joe Devlin was. He then motioned for Kate to hold on to the wooden ladder strategically placed under the opening to the loft. She nodded. Daniel reached over to Luke and reclaimed his rifle before gingerly making his way step by step up the ladder. Kate's heart was in her mouth. Then from above she heard her uncle speak.

'What are you lads scheming?' he demanded. 'Whatever it is I'd have a care. I meant what I said, I'm not afraid to use this shotgun. Oh well, I can wait no longer. Annie, my sweet, let me untie your legs.' Kate heard her uncle's sinister chuckle and she froze to the spot. 'Come on, Annie, you were a good girl earlier. I only had to slap you once, admittedly it knocked you out. But it didn't spoil my fun.' He gave another sinister chuckle. 'Don't wriggle, girl! Liam, Daniel, I hope you two are watching. You might learn a thing or two on how to take a wench!'

Kate heard Annie's muffled cry and had to put her hand to her mouth to smother her urge to scream out. She looked up and saw that Daniel had reached the loft.

'I wouldn't do that if I were you. Get your hands off her this minute or I swear—' Daniel voice sounded fearless.

'What the hell?' Kate heard the surprise in Joe Devlin's voice.

Just then a loud gunshot reverberated around the barn. Kate heard someone grunt and fall to the ground. She raced up the ladder, quickly followed by Luke. The scene that greeted her wrenched a scream from her, as she saw the blood pumping from Daniel's chest. Kate knew she had to move fast. She picked up the rifle beside Daniel and stood to face her Uncle Joe. The sight of him made her cringe; with his small beady eyes, his dark hair matted and unkempt clothes, he looked every bit the brute of a man he truly was and the thought of him touching her sister, made her sick at heart.

'You evil bastard, how could you do this to us? Well, I'll not let you hurt those I love anymore. It stops here!'

'Now there's fighting talk if ever I heard it. I always said that you were the spirited one.'

By this time both Luke and Liam were at her side.

'Kate, give me the rifle,' Luke pleaded.

'Yes, sis, please hand it over. I don't want you hurt,' Liam urged.

'Step away from my sister or ...' Kate hesitated, she so wanted to shoot the man, but could she really do it?

'Look, why don't I put you out of your misery? After all, it was you I came for and the one shot left in this gun has your name on it.' Joe Devlin aimed the gun at her.

Kate heard a shot fired and thought she was about to feel the pain hit her. She looked across at her uncle and watched him fall to the floor with a bullet wound seeping a scarlet trail at the centre of his forehead. Joseph Devlin had been shot dead.

'Kate, are you all right?' Liam called out.

'Yes,' she answered, as she rushed to be with Daniel.

'Liam, please check on Annie. Luke, we need to get help!'

'My dear, dear Kate, thank goodness you're all right. That was a very brave thing you did. Your uncle might have killed you.' Ruby's voice was full of concern.

They were outside the barn. 'He certainly wanted to. Was it you who brought the police?'

Ruby nodded. 'Yes, I left Simon being cared for in Luton and travelled back with the constabulary and the hospital wagon. I dread to think what might have happened if the policeman hadn't been such an accurate shot.'

'My uncle is dead. Our Annie is in shock and Daniel was so badly hurt.... Oh, Ruby, I tried to stem the blood ... there was so much blood. I helped Liam and Luke carry him from the loft into the waiting hospital wagon. Daniel was unconscious and then they drove him away. For all I know he could be—' She couldn't bring herself to say the word. Her heart ached for him.

'You mustn't think the worst. He's in good hands.'

'I do hope so. Ruby, where's Annie? I must go to her.'

'As we speak, the kindly constables are driving Liam and Annie to the hospital. They just want her checked out. And yes, like you, she is in shock. She wanted to stay and wait for you, but I said I'd stay and look after you. Kate, Mr Luke is waiting in his gig down the lane to take you to the hospital.'

Kate headed down the lane with Ruby. It was dark and they were thankful for the full moon to light their way.

'Kate. Are you all right?' Luke asked, as she and Ruby boarded the gig. It was a tight squeeze but with Ruby sat in the middle they managed.

'I think so,' Kate answered. 'And thank you for waiting for us.'

218

'You're welcome. It's good to see you up and about. If it hadn't been for the timely intervention of a senior member of Luton's constabulary, Joseph could well have harmed you.'

'I thought he was going to. I wanted to shoot him but I just froze.'

'The policeman didn't hesitate. He shot your uncle right between the eyes and—'

'And I say good riddance!' Ruby interjected.

'I didn't see the policeman,' Kate admitted.

'You were and still are in shock,' Luke said.

Kate shivered. How many times had she prayed for her family to be free of Joseph Devlin ... and now they were. He was gone and with God's help, she, Annie and Liam could now get on with their lives.

Luke handed Kate a thick rug to place over her and Ruby's legs. And as Luke pulled on the reins to set off, Kate looked up to the sky at the full moon and the stars twinkling above and as the cold air brushed her face, she felt happy to be alive.

They travelled in silence for a while. It was Kate who spoke first.

'Mr Stratton, thank you so much for your help tonight. My family are in your debt,' Kate said.

'Not necessary. Your family have always been loyal to me, I just returned the favour. If anything, it's I who owes you, Kate, especially an apology.'

'P-please—'

'No. It has to be said. And I know Ruby here will be only too pleased to stand witness to it.'

'If you say so.' Ruby sounded unsure.

'Kate, I hope you don't think too badly of me. When I first offered you employment, I genuinely wanted to help with your hat-making. I saw the potential you had.'

'I know you did. And for that I thank you.' Kate meant every word.

'The thing is, as my father would no doubt tell you, I've always been a pushover for a pretty face.'

'And isn't that the truth? But you met your match when you tried to play fast and loose with our Kate here,' Ruby quipped.

'Kate, I'm sorry. I should never have used my position to lead you on the way I did. I'm a cad and I should be horsewhipped.'

Both girls struggled to muffle their giggles.

'I'm glad you both think it's funny. I'm baring my soul here.' He turned to Kate and flashed a wide grin. 'Am I forgiven?'

Kate smiled. 'Of course you are. If tonight has proved one thing, it's that life's too short to hold grudges.'

'Thank you. And if there's anything I can do to help you in your new venture then please don't hesitate to ask.'

'We may take him up on that, eh, Ruby.'

They travelled the rest of the journey in silence, left to ponder their own thoughts of what the future might bring.

Over the weeks that followed, Kate visited Daniel's hospital bed, situated in a small side room whose white-washed walls and white cotton bedding felt cold and unwelcoming. For a while Daniel's condition was a cause for concern. During most of her visits she held his hand, occasionally she stroked his pale face – his weather-beaten, healthy complexion now gone. He had remained unconscious for days and his doctor told her it was in the lap of the gods. Thankfully, once the shot had been removed from his chest, he began to recover. And as each day passed he got stronger and stronger.

'Thank God you're on the mend. You've given us all such worry. For a moment, I thought you were going to—'

'Die? Don't be daft. I could never leave you to fend for yourself – who knows what trouble you'd get yourself into?'

Kate laughed. 'You might be right there. Thankfully there are not many men hereabouts as evil as Joseph Devlin.' She stretched across his hospital bed and laid her head on his pillow. Daniel stroked her hair and she felt comforted.

'Kate, love, that's all behind you now. You can now look to the future. Our future....'

Kate's heart missed a beat. Was this it? Was he about to ask her to marry him? She waited with baited breath for him to finish the sentence, all set to scream out, 'Yes!' It was what she wanted more than anything else.

'... And the success I know we're going to achieve with Heavenly Hats and Heaven Scent,' Daniel added.

Kate felt deflated. Had she lost her chance of happiness with Daniel? If she had, she only had herself to blame.

'Why the sad face? I thought you'd be excited at the prospect of moving forward to bigger and better things.'

'I am – I truly am.' She tried to sound enthusiastic. 'If I'm to expand I need space to make a lot more hats. Ruby's house is all right in the short term, but if we're using the table to make hats then there's nowhere to eat our meals and vice versa.'

'I can see your dilemma. But you have to be patient. Believe me, everything comes to those who wait.'

'I know and I'm sorry. Right now the only thing that matters is for you to get back to full health.'

Daniel laid his head on his pillow and sighed. He had come so close to asking Kate for her hand in marriage ... but backed off from it. He loved her so much. He thought back to the night of the barn and how close he had come to losing her forever. Liam had told him how Joseph Devlin had saved his second shot for Kate. Daniel would willingly have taken it for her. Thankfully the police officer saved the day.

'Mr Groves, Daniel, may I come in?' Luke Stratton asked.

'Please,' Daniel politely replied.

Luke entered and stood at the side of the bed looking down on Daniel. He had the look of a man with something on his mind. Daniel was more than prepared to listen; Daniel had seen a different side to Luke Stratton that night in the barn.

'I saw Liam earlier today and he tells me you're on the mend. Good to hear it.'

'No one's happier than I am,' Daniel joked.

Luke gave an awkward smile. 'Quite ... Daniel, I'm here to apologize. I think we got off on the wrong foot. I'm about to be married and I want to be honest with you. I did have designs on Kate, but you must believe me when I tell you they came to nothing.'

'You turned her head,' Daniel snapped.

'Perhaps, but only for a short while, she soon saw me for the man I am – was. I saw how close you both were on that dreadful night. You took a shot to protect her and I know she would have done the same for you. It's you she truly loves.'

'I wish I could be as sure. Mr Stratton—'

'Please call me Luke.'

'All right, Luke. Thank you for taking the trouble to come see me. I hold no grudge, life's too short.'

'I'm glad you think like that, too. Now, regarding Heavenly Hats and Heaven Scent, I have some very good contacts in London whom you might want to do business with. Just give me the nod and I'll be happy to introduce you to them. Kate has a rare talent. I'm sure with your encouragement, the world can be her oyster.'

'Thank you. I'll discuss it with Kate and come back to you about it.'

Luke offered his hand. Daniel extended his and they shook hands.

The next day when Kate visited the hospital she found Daniel lying fully clothed but lifeless on the bed.

'Daniel! Daniel! Please wake up! Daniel Groves, don't you dare die on me. I so want to be your wife!'

Daniel opened his eyes. 'Is that so?'

Kate blushed. 'Daniel Groves, were you pretending? I can't believe you'd do such a thing.'

'It's a sad thing when a man has to use his wits to get to the truth. Now let me get this right. After all this time of my following you around like a lovesick puppy, you actually want to marry me?'

'Yes, yes, yes.'

His gaze was steady as he stood up, pulled her to him and kissed her – a gentle kiss at first but then full of passion. Kate responded eagerly, never wanting it to end.

Back at Leagrove House, things were almost back to normal. It was good to see Simon Dobbs fully recovered from the trauma he had endured and now returned to the happy, gentle and lovable lad he'd always been. Annie surprised everyone. She appeared to have made a remarkable recovery and was back working at the stables with Monty within a week. She had obviously been shaken by her ordeal, but Kate believed that the love shown by all around her gave her the strength to recover. Mrs Montgomery said she believed it was the resilience of her youth that got the girl through. And when Annie named the young colt Lucky, they believed it was how she truly felt.

Daniel and Kate were married in the spring. They honeymooned in London where Luke had arranged a meeting with his couturier contacts before travelling to Paris for his own honeymoon. Daniel's wedding present to Kate was the deeds to the house he'd bought at an auction a few months previously. He'd bought it with a view to turning it into a workshop for Heavenly Hats. The house was 10 Plaiters Way.

ACKNOWLEDGEMENTS

I wish to thank the following people for their assistance in my research.

Veronica Main – Curator Wardown Park Museum – Luton Hat Trail

Luton Museum & Art Gallery – traditional crafts of Bedfordshire notably hat-making

Luton Museum Education Service

View from the Alley by Aubrey Darby

Many thanks to the team at my publisher Robert Hale Ltd for their continued support and to Brixham Writers for their encouragement. Most of all thanks to my husband Barrie for his patience and love.